THE KAURAVA EMPIRE
EMPIRE
VOL.2

THE VENGEANCE OF ASHWATTHAMA

CAMPFIRE®

KALYANI NAVYUG MEDIA PVT LTD

THE KAURAVA EMPIRE
VOL. 2
THE VENGEANCE OF ASHWATTHAMA

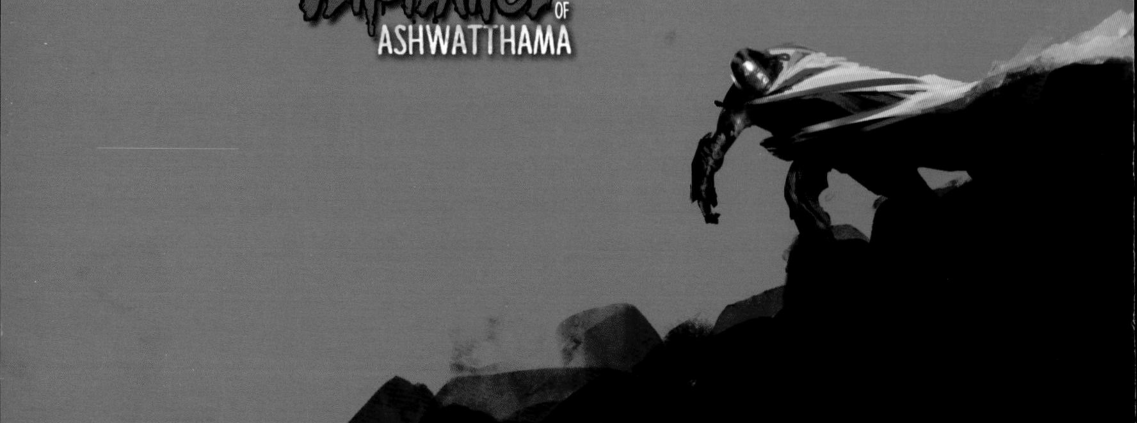

WRITTEN BY: JASON QUINN
ILLUSTRATED BY: SACHIN NAGAR
COLORIST: SACHIN NAGAR
EDITORS: JASON QUINN, SOURAV DUTTA
DESIGN: VIJAY SHARMA
LETTERING: BHAVNATH CHAUDHARY

CAMPFIRE®

www.campfire.co.in

Published by Kalyani Navyug Media Pvt Ltd
101 C, Shiv House, Hari Nagar Ashram,
New Delhi 110014, India

ISBN: 978-93-81182-00-0

Printed in India

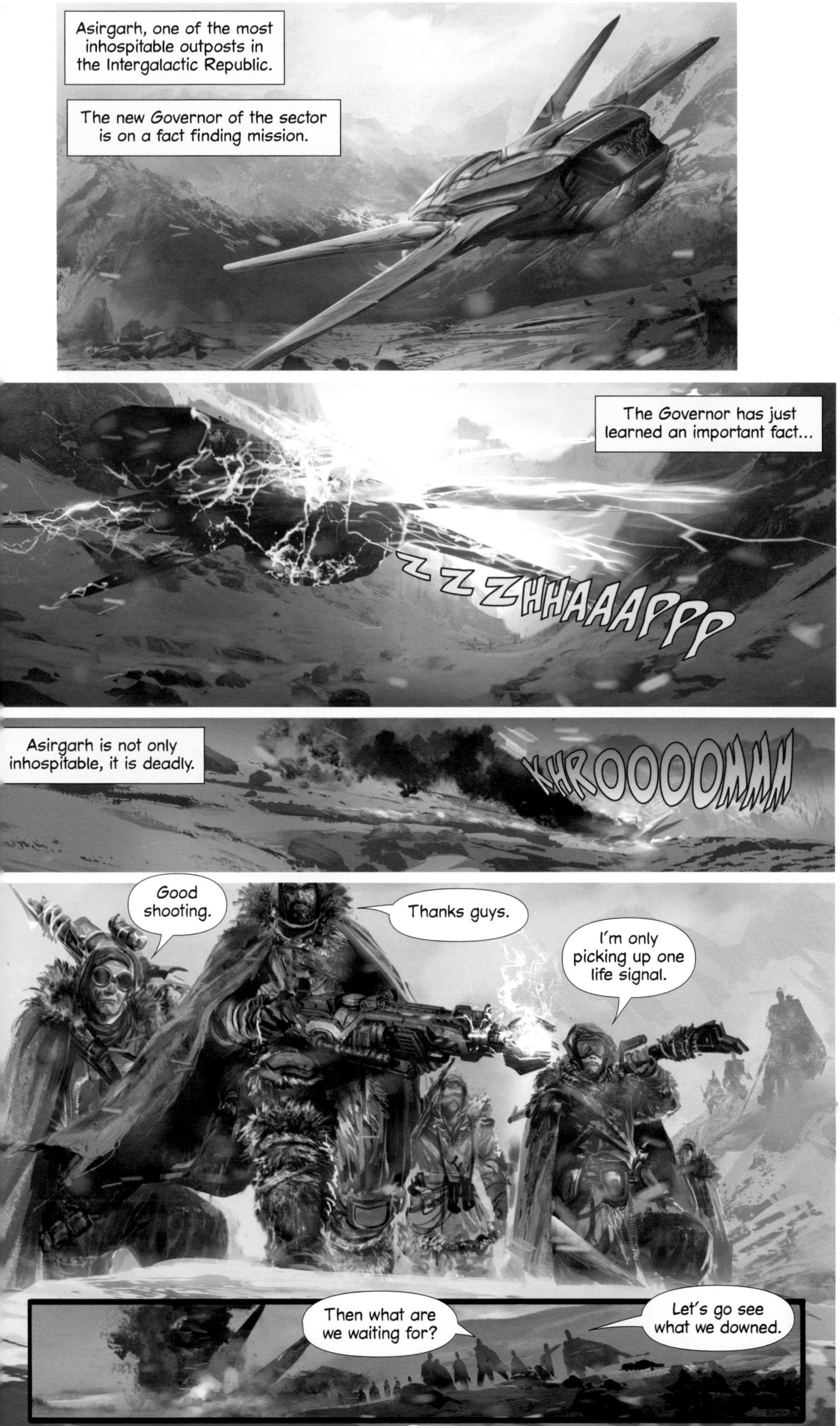

Asirgarh, one of the most inhospitable outposts in the Intergalactic Republic.
The new Governor of the sector is on a fact finding mission.
The Governor has just learned an important fact...
ZZZHHAAAPPP
Asirgarh is not only inhospitable, it is deadly.
KHROOOOOMMH
Good shooting.
Thanks guys.
I'm only picking up one life signal.
Then what are we waiting for?
Let's go see what we downed.

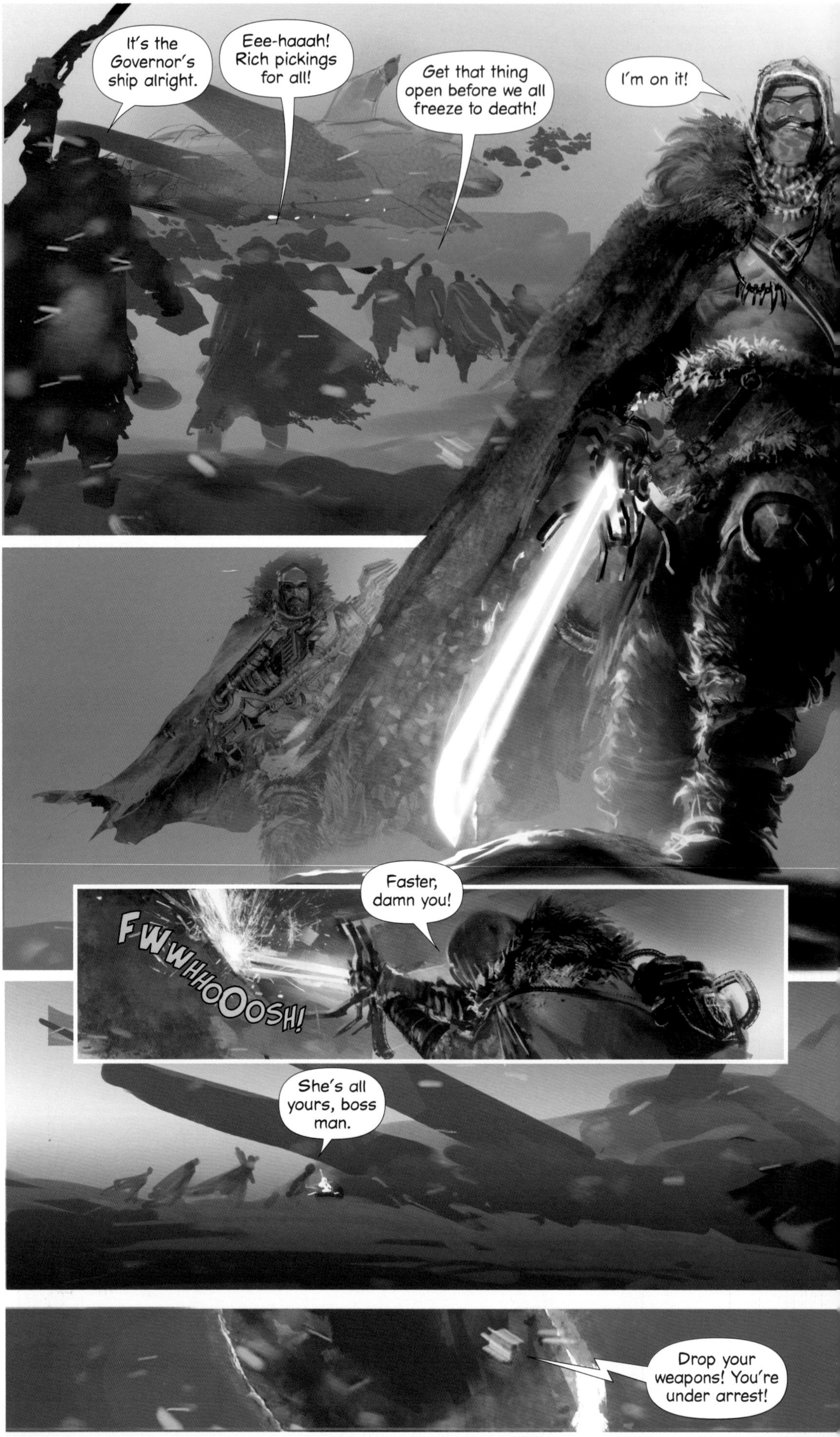
It's the Governor's ship alright.
Eee-haaah! Rich pickings for all!
Get that thing open before we all freeze to death!
I'm on it!
FWWHHOOOOSH!
Faster, damn you!
She's all yours, boss man.
Drop your weapons! You're under arrest!

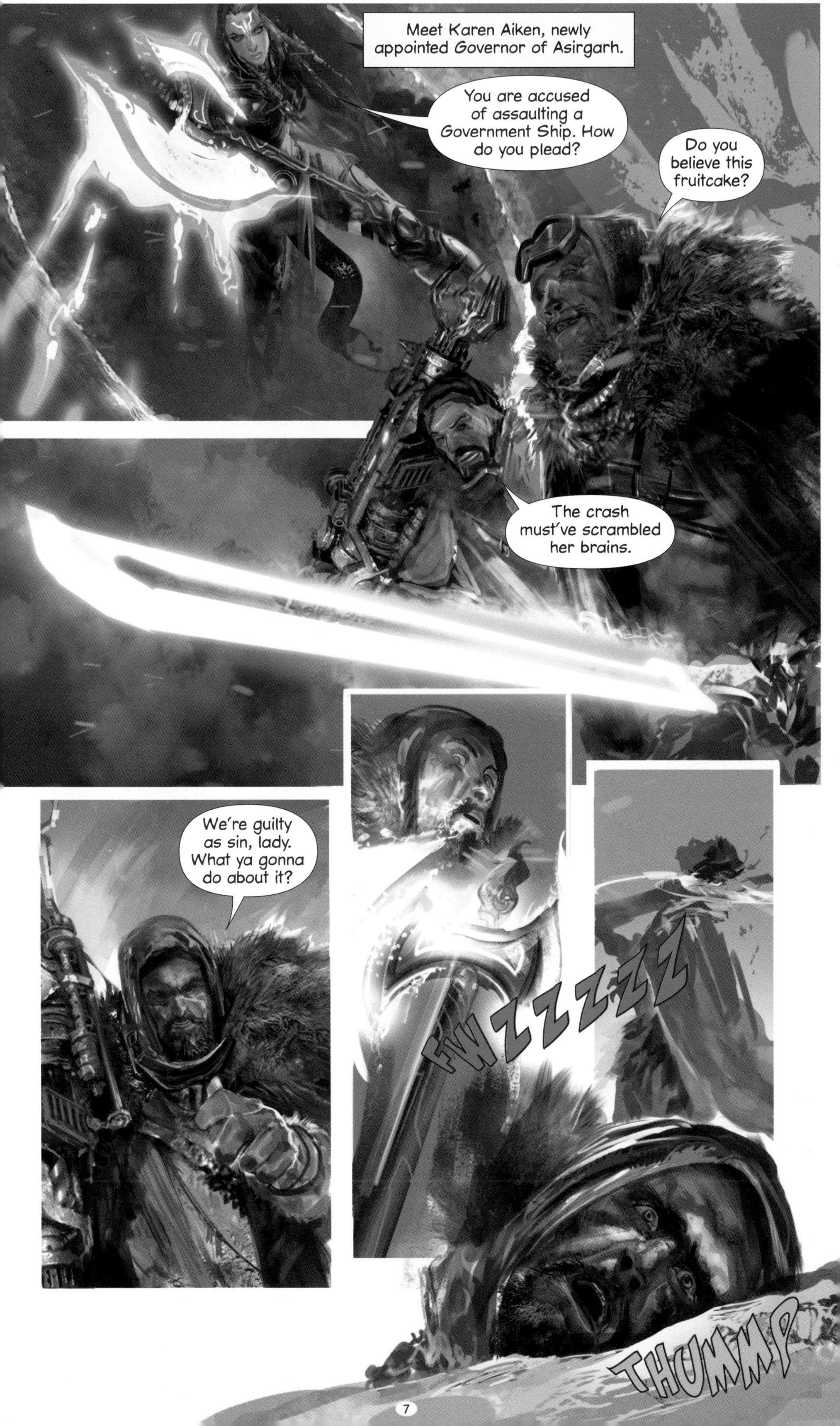

Meet Karen Aiken, newly appointed Governor of Asirgarh.
You are accused of assaulting a Government Ship. How do you plead?
Do you believe this fruitcake?
The crash must've scrambled her brains.
We're guilty as sin, lady. What ya gonna do about it?
FWZZZZZ
THUMMP

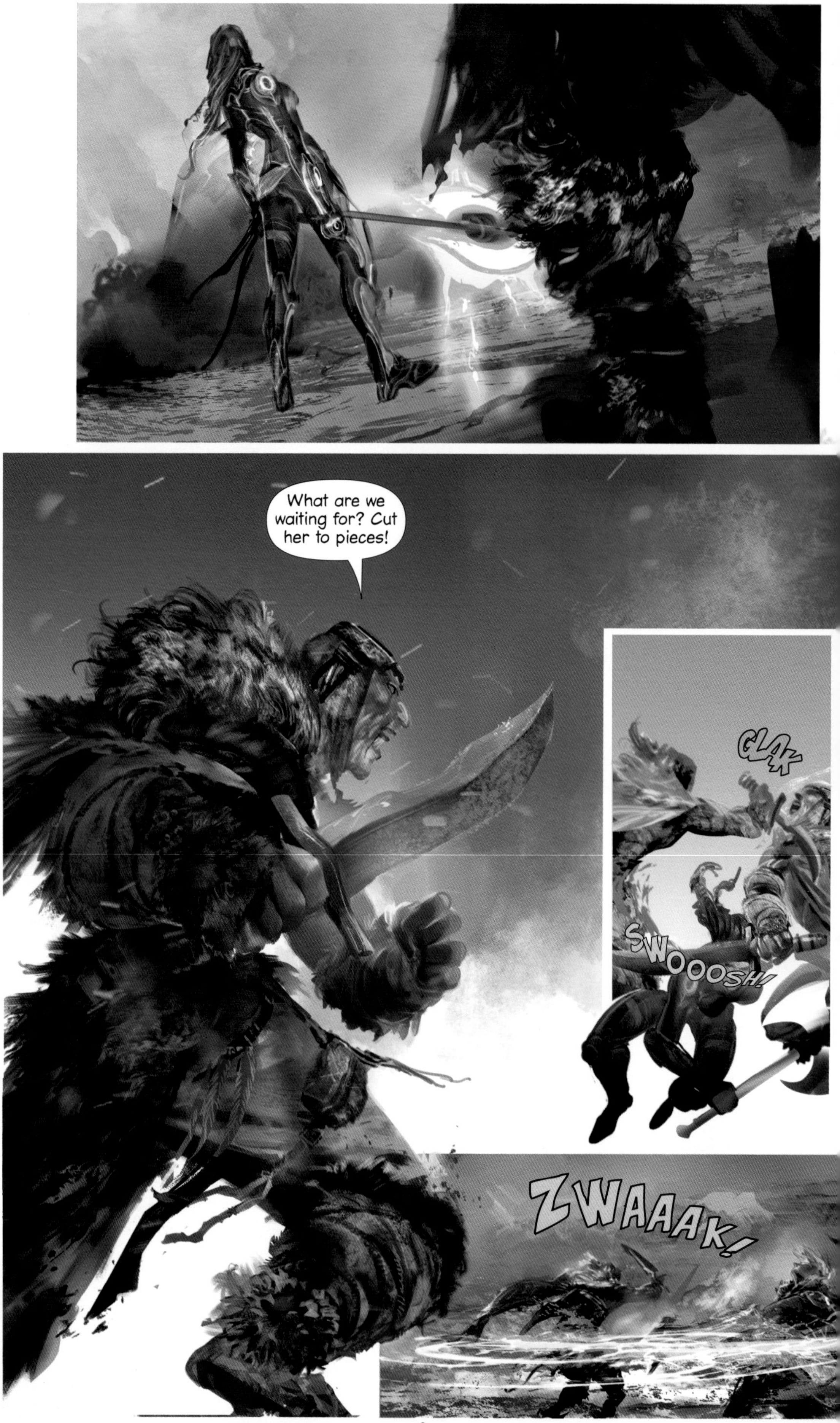
What are we waiting for? Cut her to pieces!
GLAK
SWOOOOSH!
ZWAAAK!

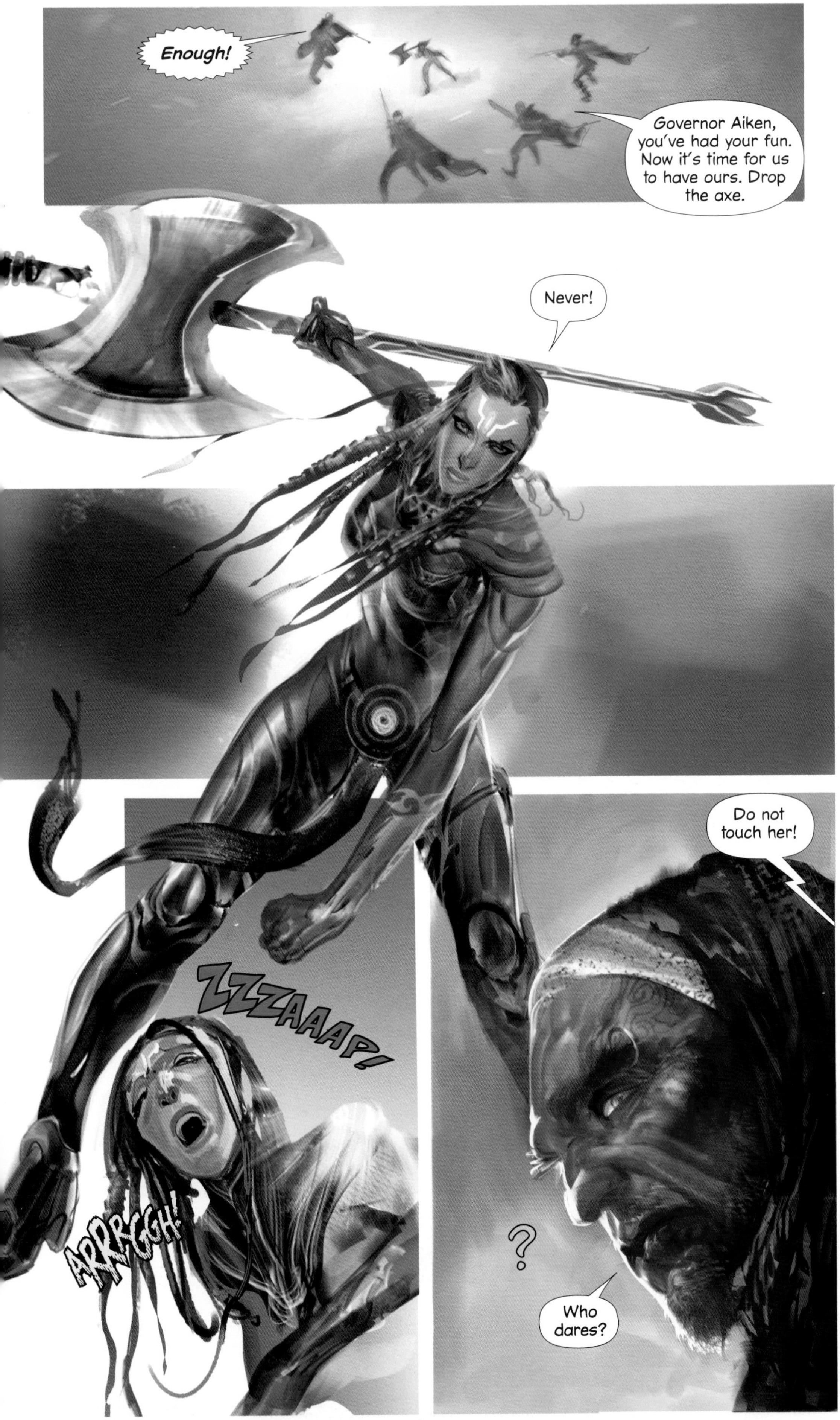
Enough!
Governor Aiken, you've had your fun. Now it's time for us to have ours. Drop the axe.
Never!
ZZZAAAAP!
ARRRGGH!
Do not touch her!
?
Who dares?

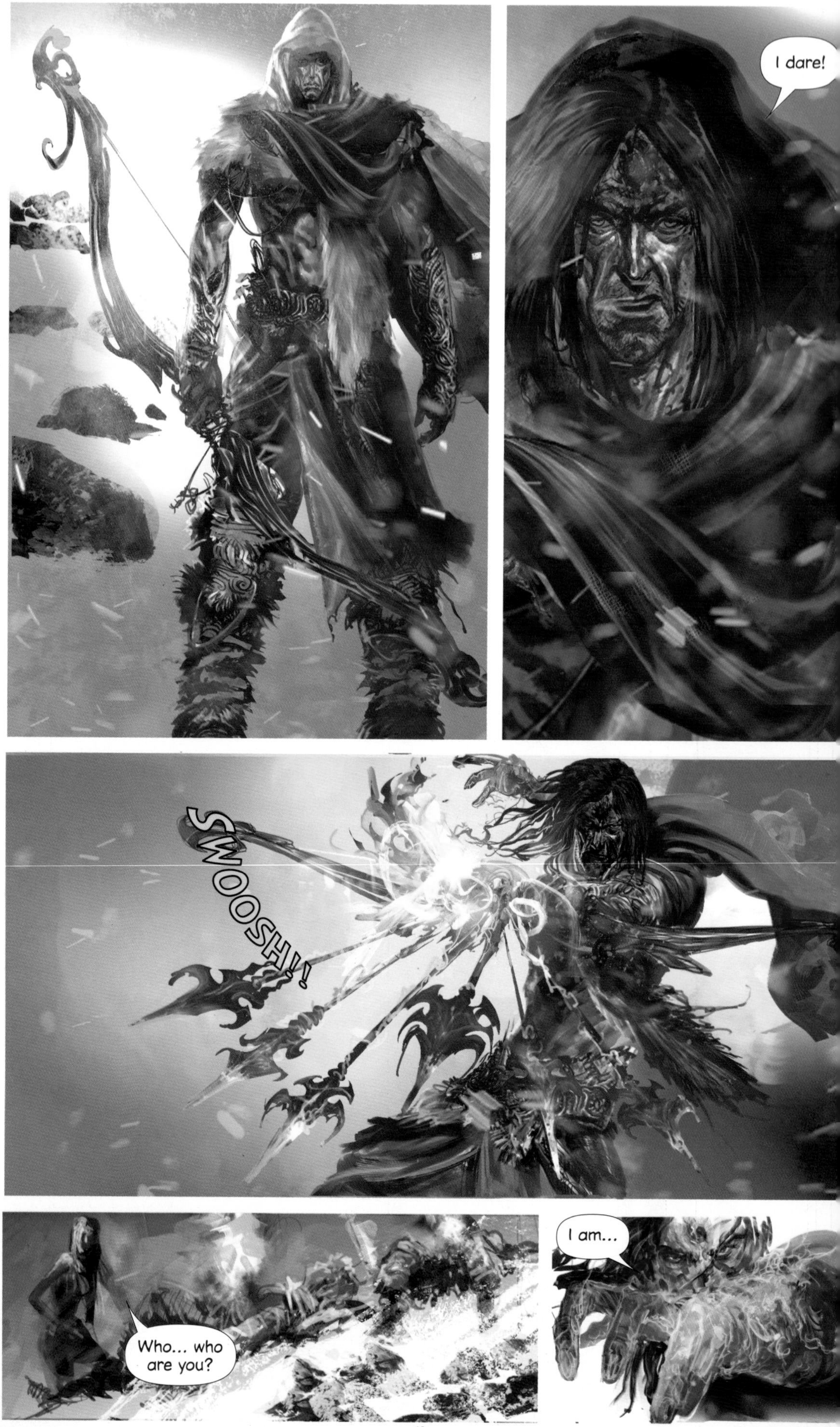
I dare!
SWOOSH!!
Who... who are you?
I am...

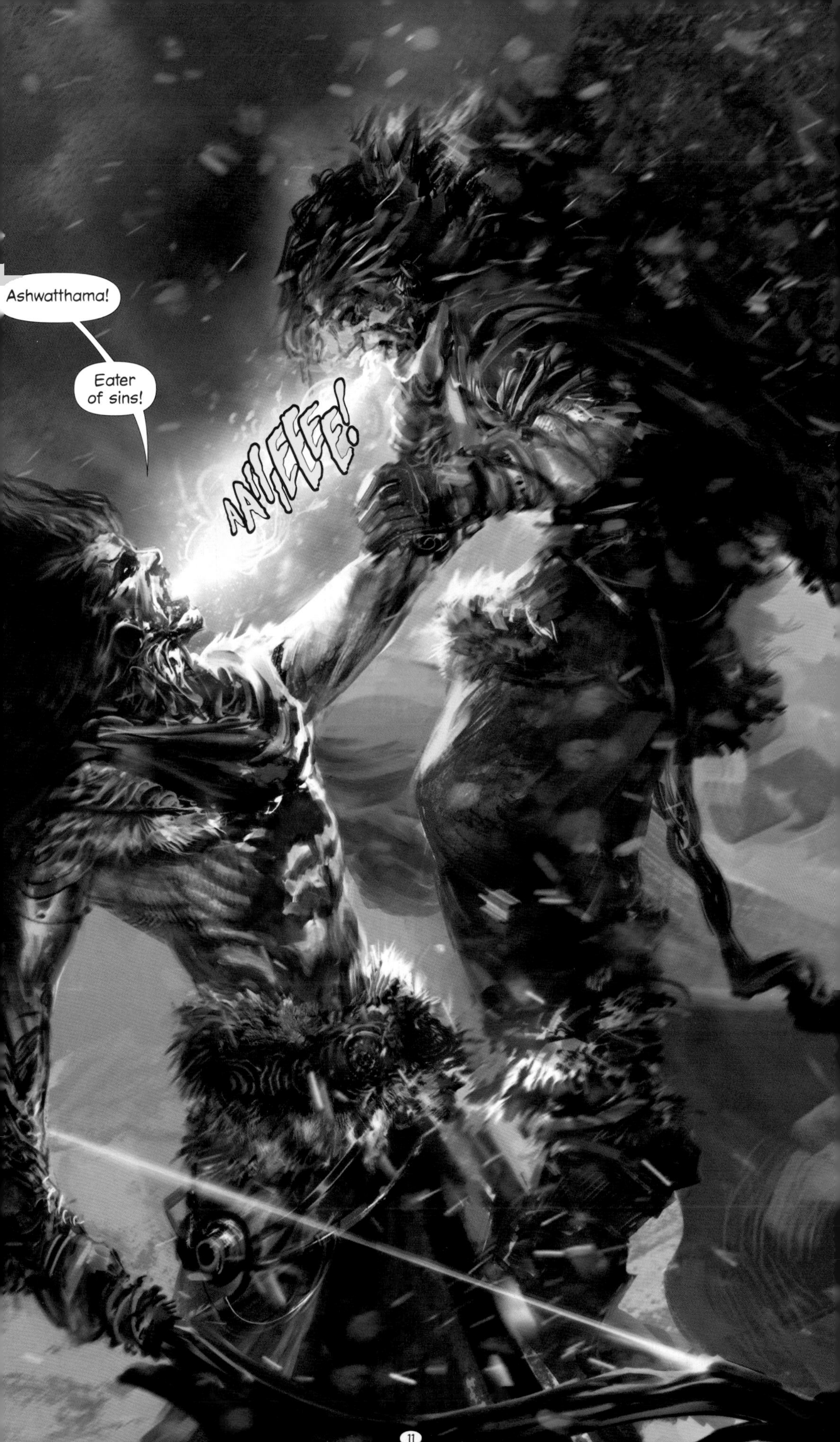
Ashwatthama!
Eater of sins!
AAIIEEEE!

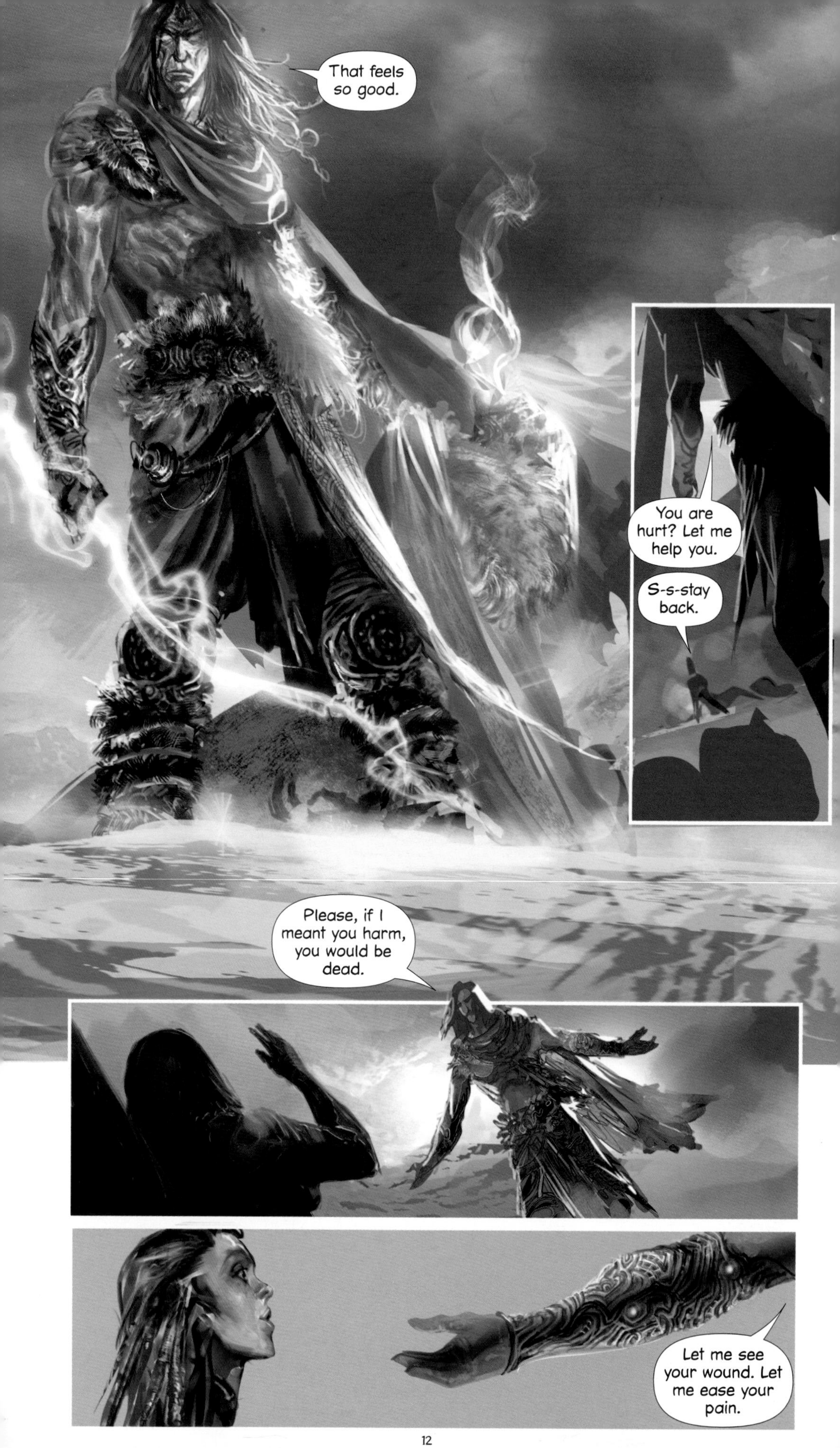
That feels so good.
You are hurt? Let me help you.
S-s-stay back.
Please, if I meant you harm, you would be dead.
Let me see your wound. Let me ease your pain.

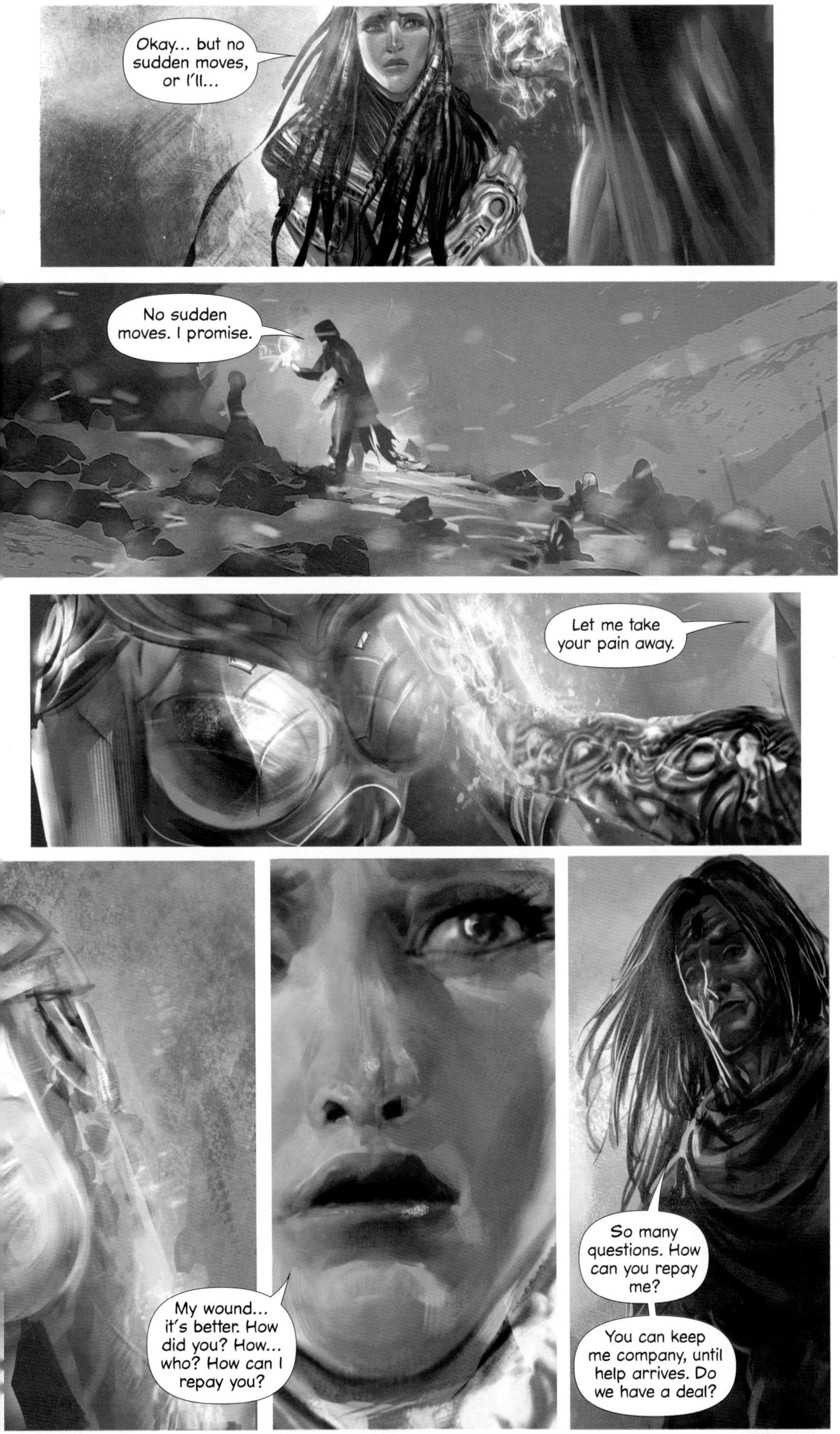
Okay... but no sudden moves, or I'll...
No sudden moves. I promise.
Let me take your pain away.
My wound... it's better. How did you? How... who? How can I repay you?
So many questions. How can you repay me?
You can keep me company, until help arrives. Do we have a deal?

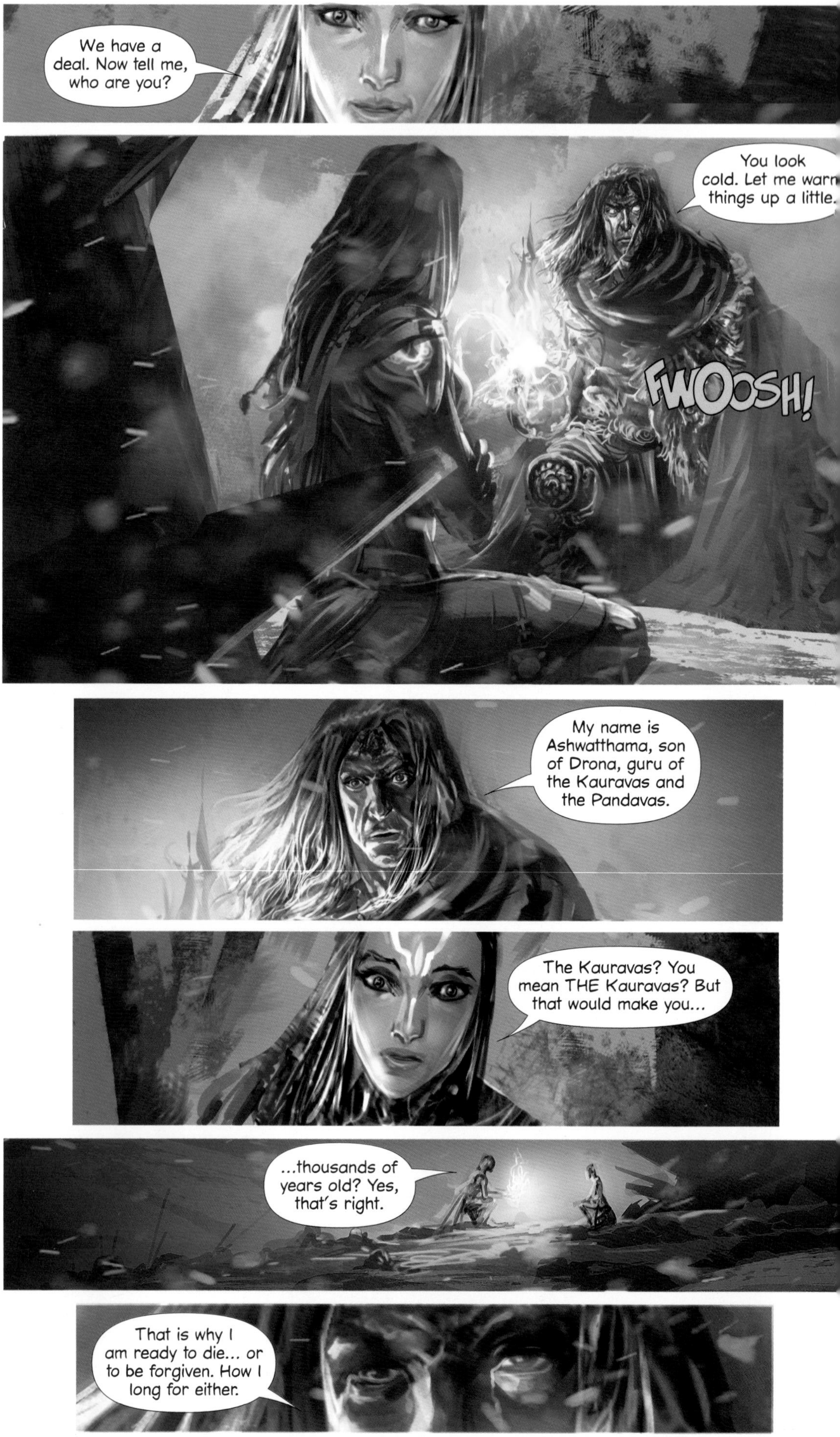
We have a deal. Now tell me, who are you?
You look cold. Let me warm things up a little.
FWOOSH!
My name is Ashwatthama, son of Drona, guru of the Kauravas and the Pandavas.
The Kauravas? You mean THE Kauravas? But that would make you...
...thousands of years old? Yes, that's right.
That is why I am ready to die... or to be forgiven. How I long for either.

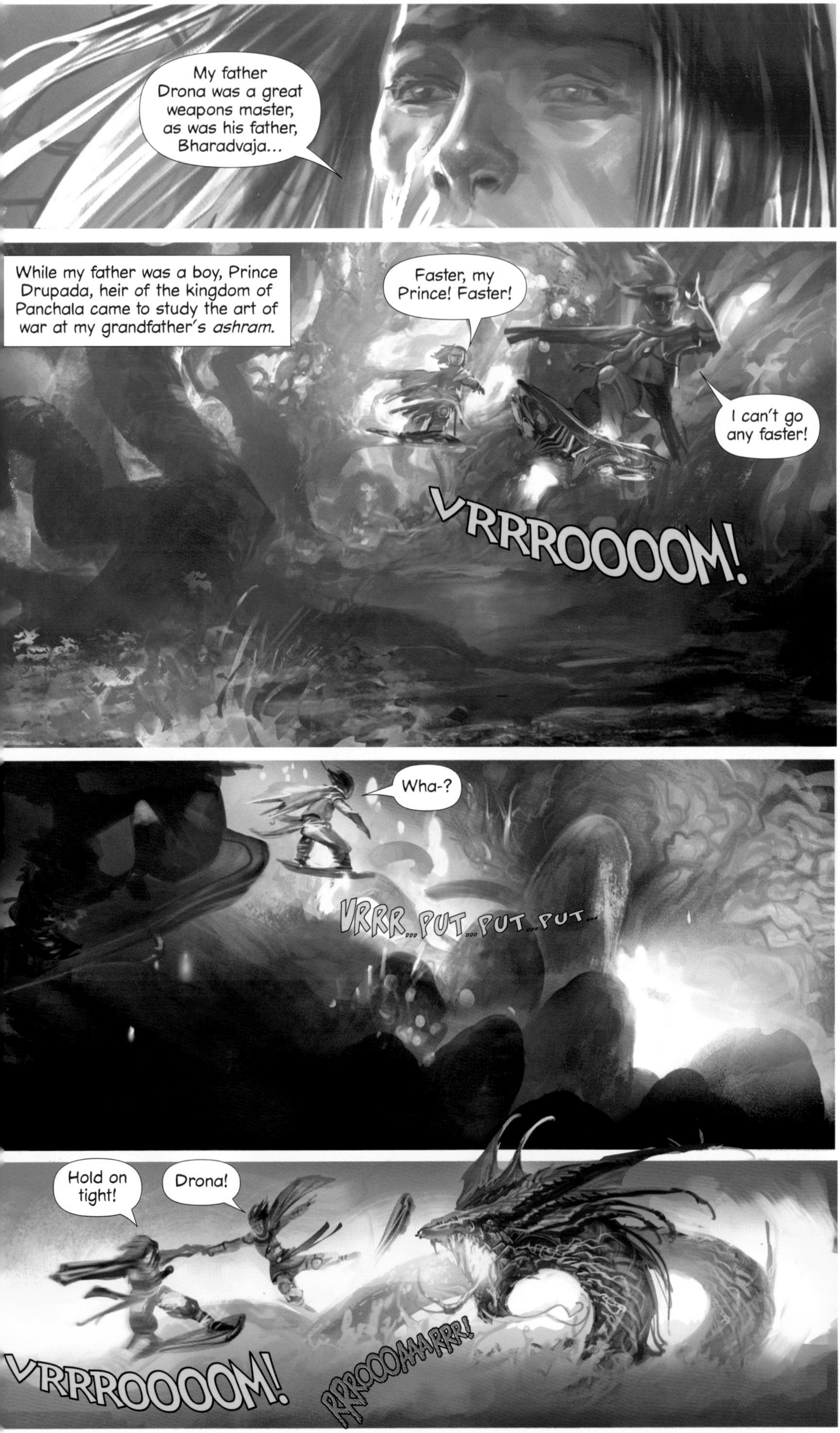
My father Drona was a great weapons master, as was his father, Bharadvaja...
While my father was a boy, Prince Drupada, heir of the kingdom of Panchala came to study the art of war at my grandfather's *ashram*.
Faster, my Prince! Faster!
I can't go any faster!
VRRROOOOM!
Wha-?
VRRR... PUT... PUT... PUT...
Hold on tight!
Drona!
VRRROOOOM!
RRROOOAAARRR!

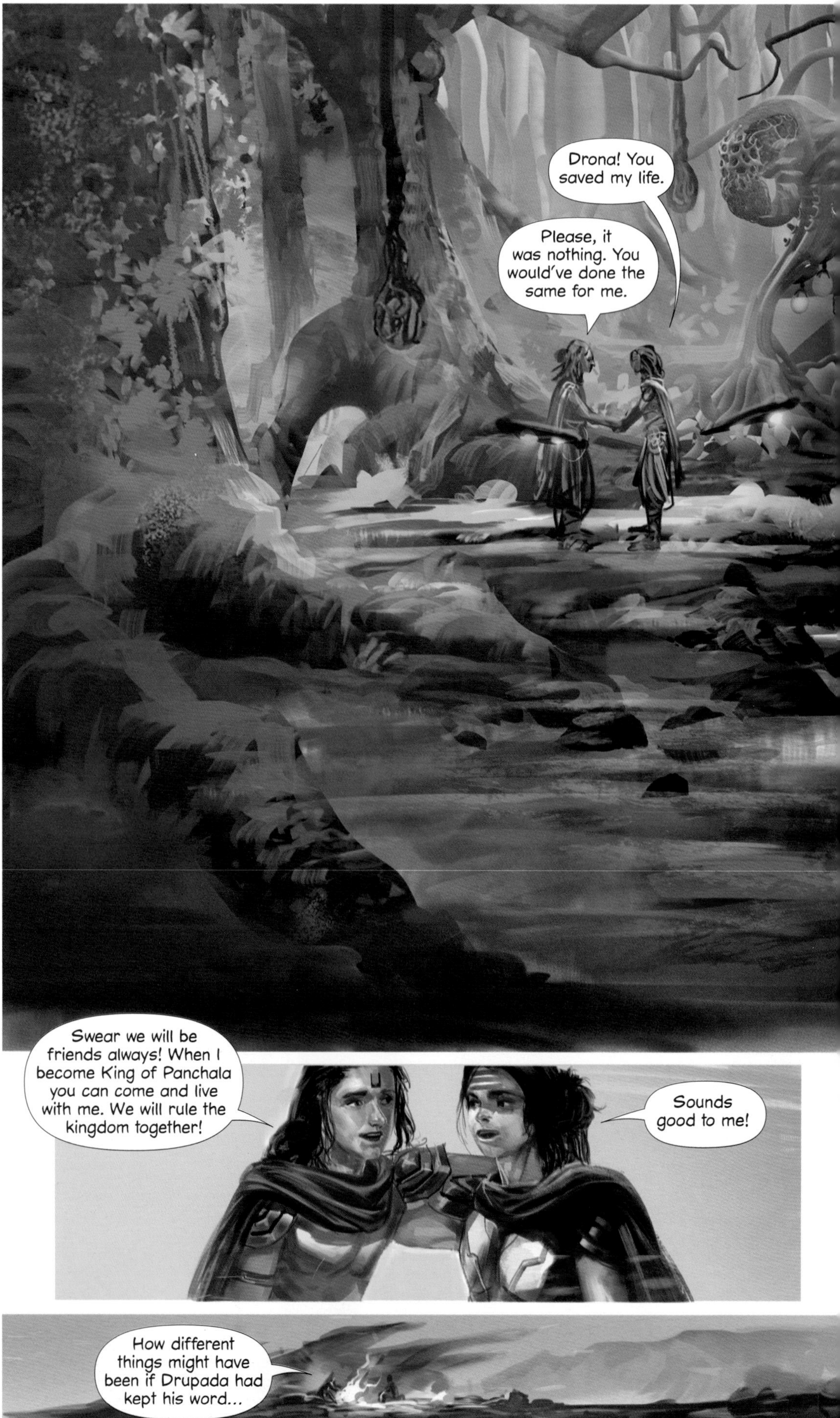
Drona! You saved my life.
Please, it was nothing. You would've done the same for me.
Swear we will be friends always! When I become King of Panchala you can come and live with me. We will rule the kingdom together!
Sounds good to me!
How different things might have been if Drupada had kept his word...

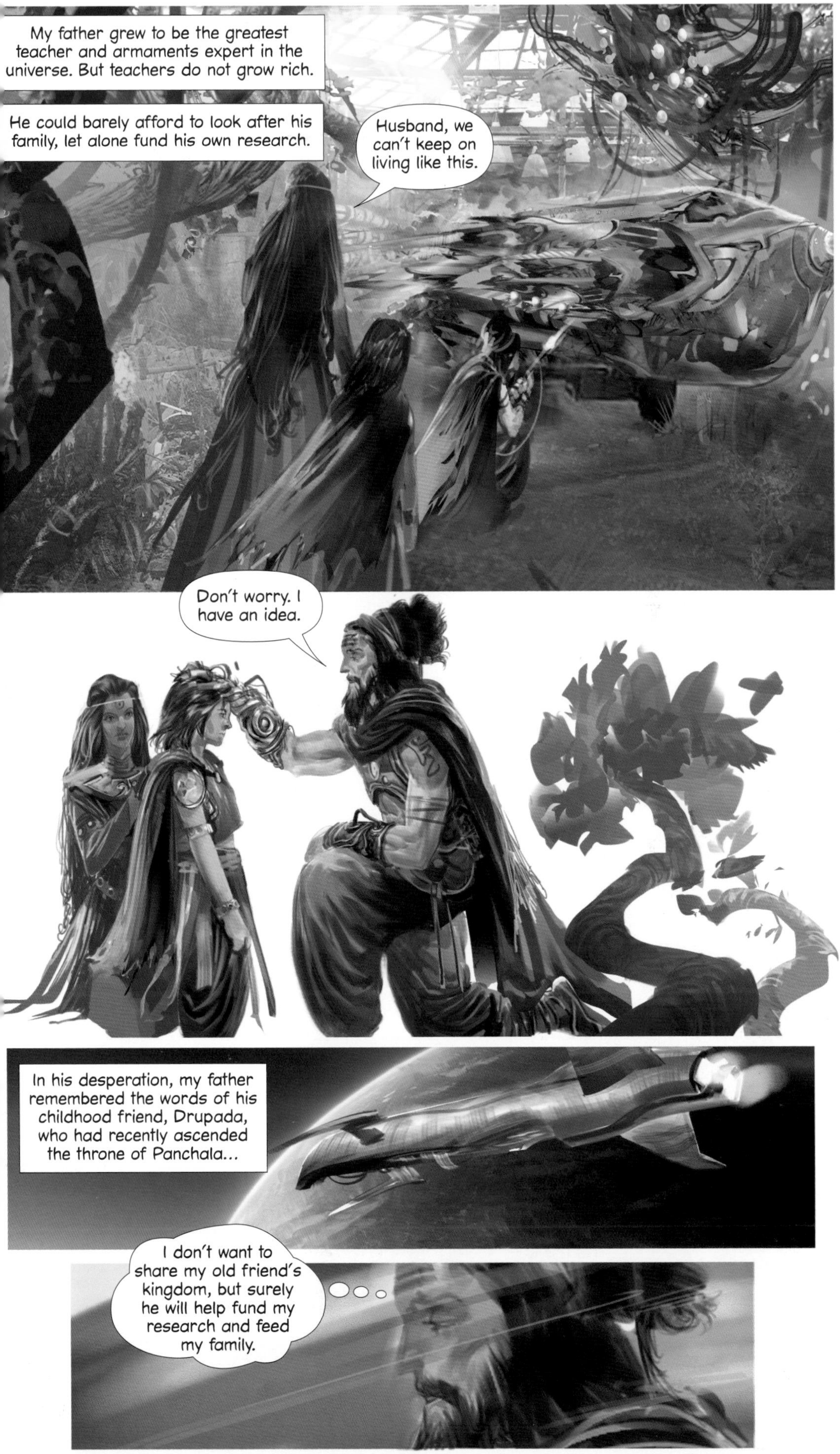
My father grew to be the greatest teacher and armaments expert in the universe. But teachers do not grow rich.
He could barely afford to look after his family, let alone fund his own research.
Husband, we can't keep on living like this.
Don't worry. I have an idea.
In his desperation, my father remembered the words of his childhood friend, Drupada, who had recently ascended the throne of Panchala...
I don't want to share my old friend's kingdom, but surely he will help fund my research and feed my family.

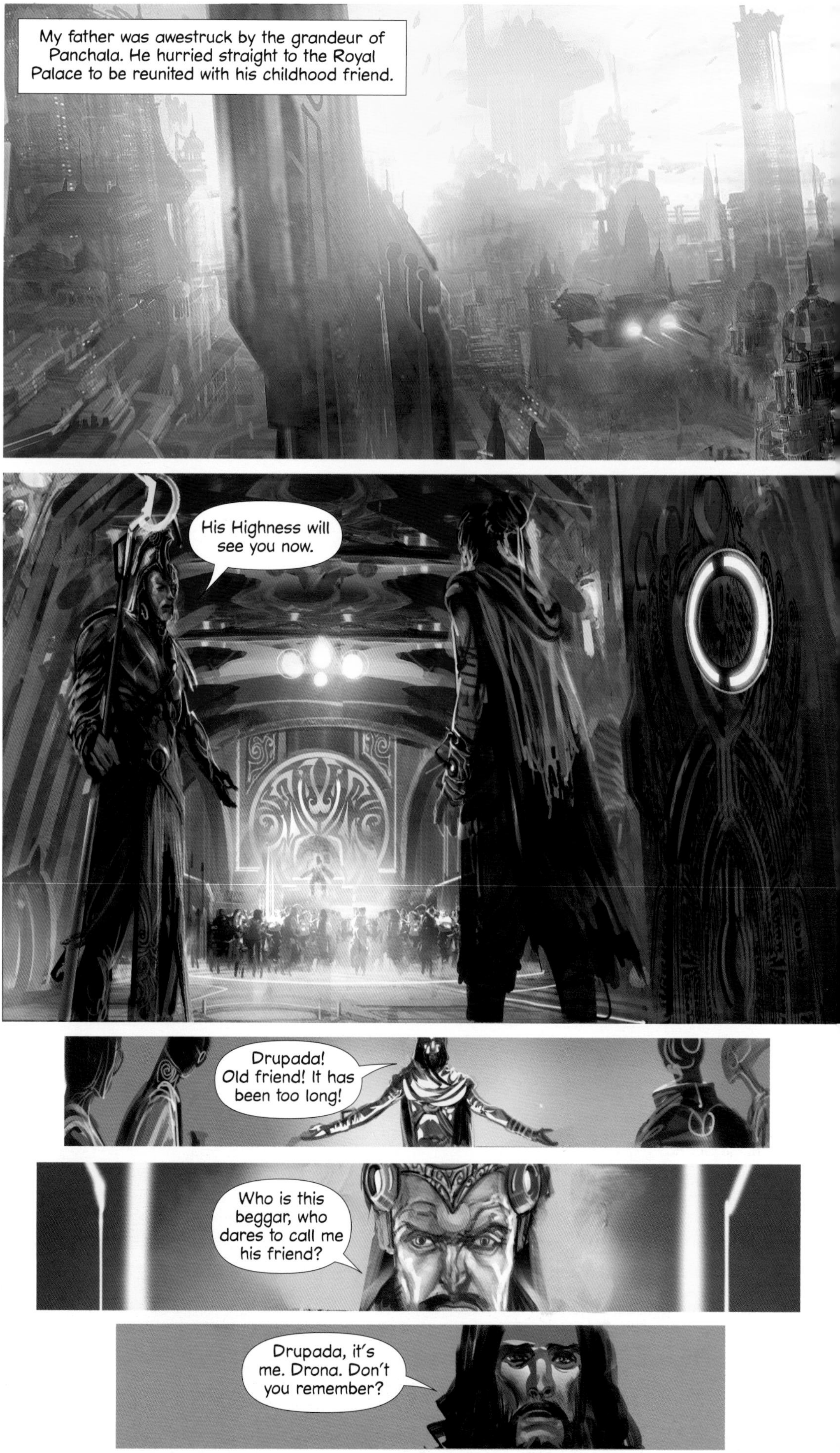
My father was awestruck by the grandeur of Panchala. He hurried straight to the Royal Palace to be reunited with his childhood friend.
His Highness will see you now.
Drupada! Old friend! It has been too long!
Who is this beggar, who dares to call me his friend?
Drupada, it's me. Drona. Don't you remember?

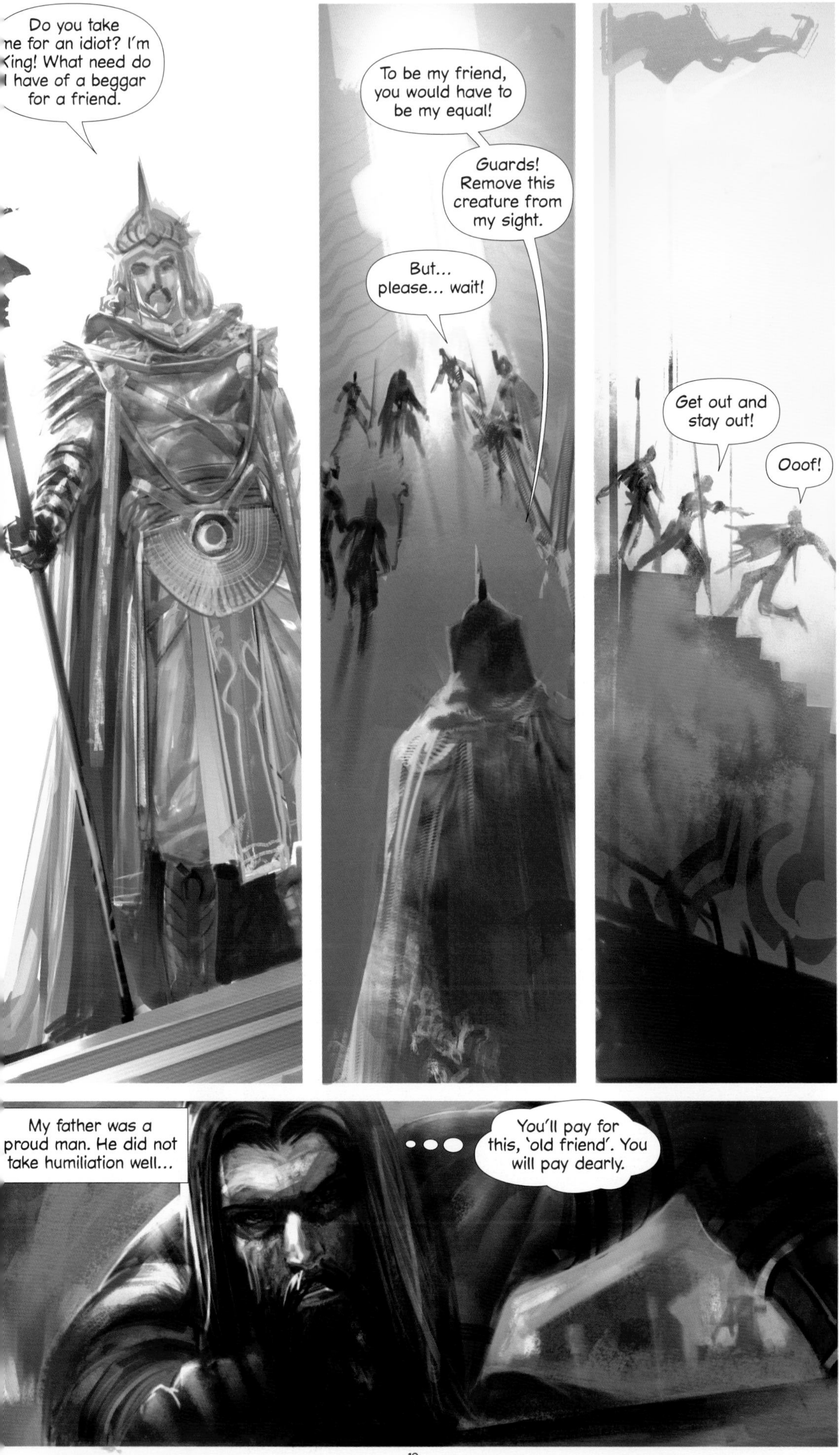
Do you take ne for an idiot? I'm King! What need do I have of a beggar for a friend.
To be my friend, you would have to be my equal!
Guards! Remove this creature from my sight.
But... please... wait!
Get out and stay out!
Ooof!
My father was a proud man. He did not take humiliation well...
...
You'll pay for this, 'old friend'. You will pay dearly.

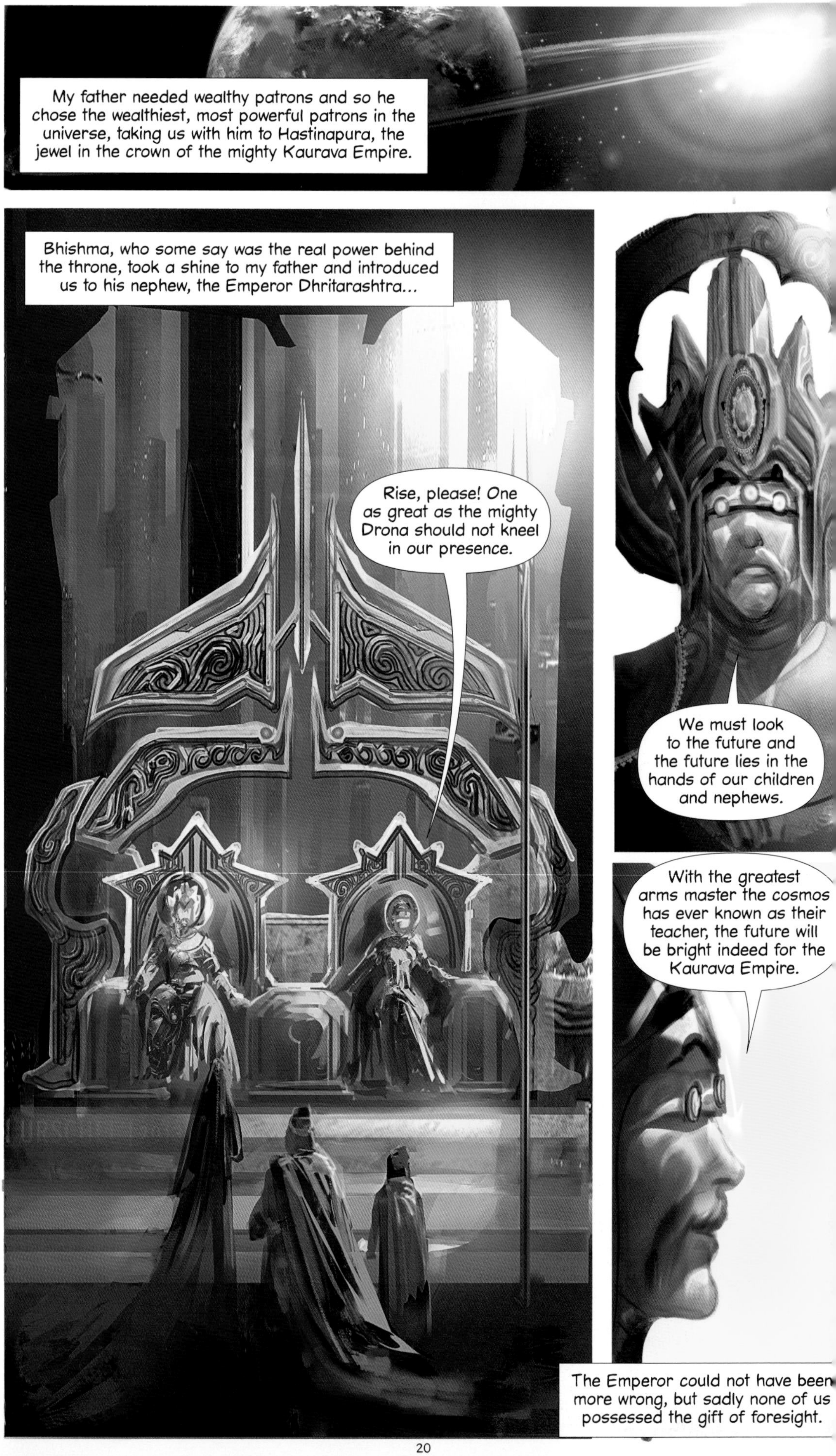
My father needed wealthy patrons and so he chose the wealthiest, most powerful patrons in the universe, taking us with him to Hastinapura, the jewel in the crown of the mighty Kaurava Empire.
Bhishma, who some say was the real power behind the throne, took a shine to my father and introduced us to his nephew, the Emperor Dhritarashtra...
Rise, please! One as great as the mighty Drona should not kneel in our presence.
We must look to the future and the future lies in the hands of our children and nephews.
With the greatest arms master the cosmos has ever known as their teacher, the future will be bright indeed for the Kaurava Empire.
The Emperor could not have been more wrong, but sadly none of us possessed the gift of foresight.

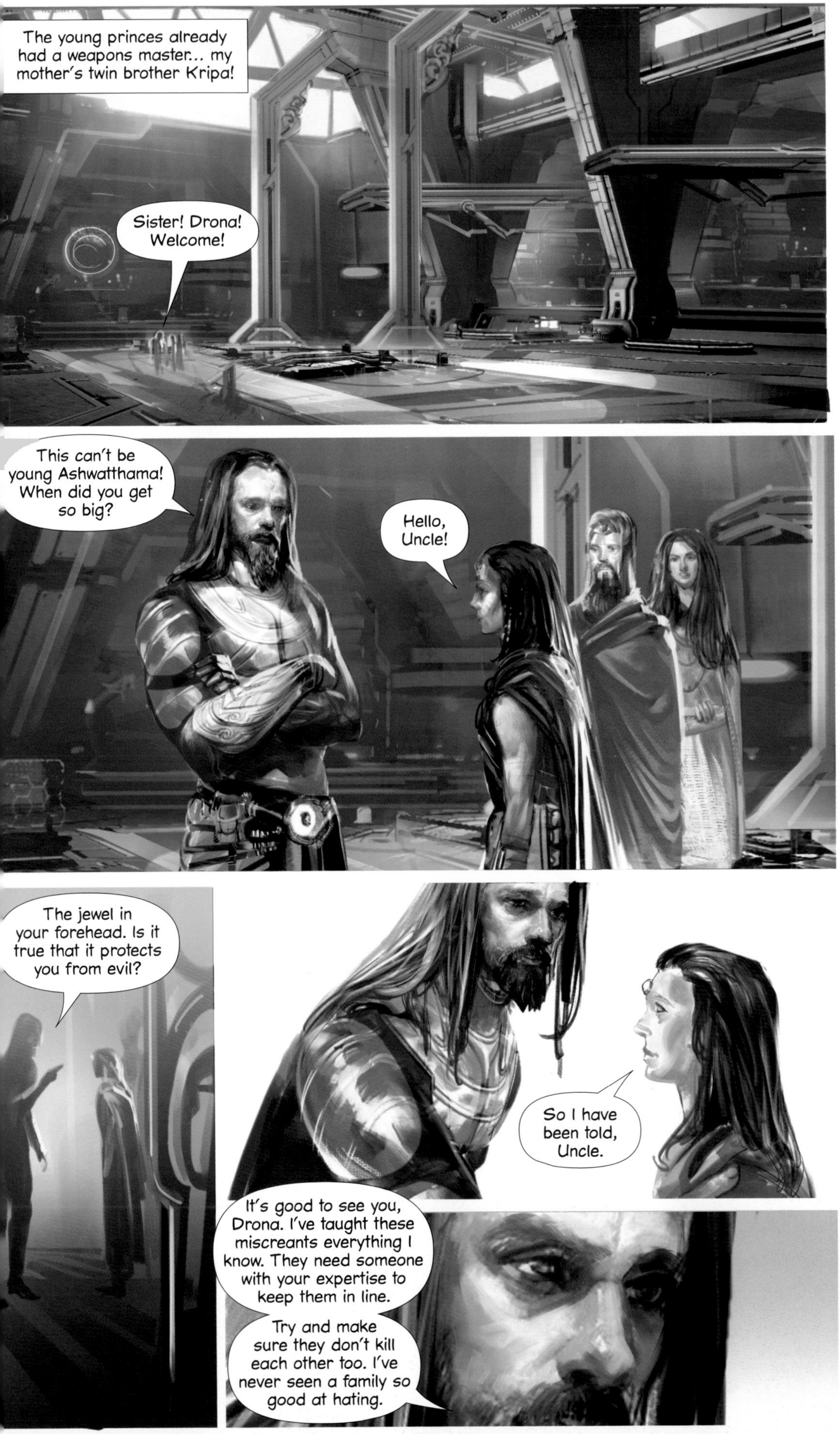
The young princes already had a weapons master... my mother's twin brother Kripa!
Sister! Drona! Welcome!
This can't be young Ashwatthama! When did you get so big?
Hello, Uncle!
The jewel in your forehead. Is it true that it protects you from evil?
So I have been told, Uncle.
It's good to see you, Drona. I've taught these miscreants everything I know. They need someone with your expertise to keep them in line.
Try and make sure they don't kill each other too. I've never seen a family so good at hating.

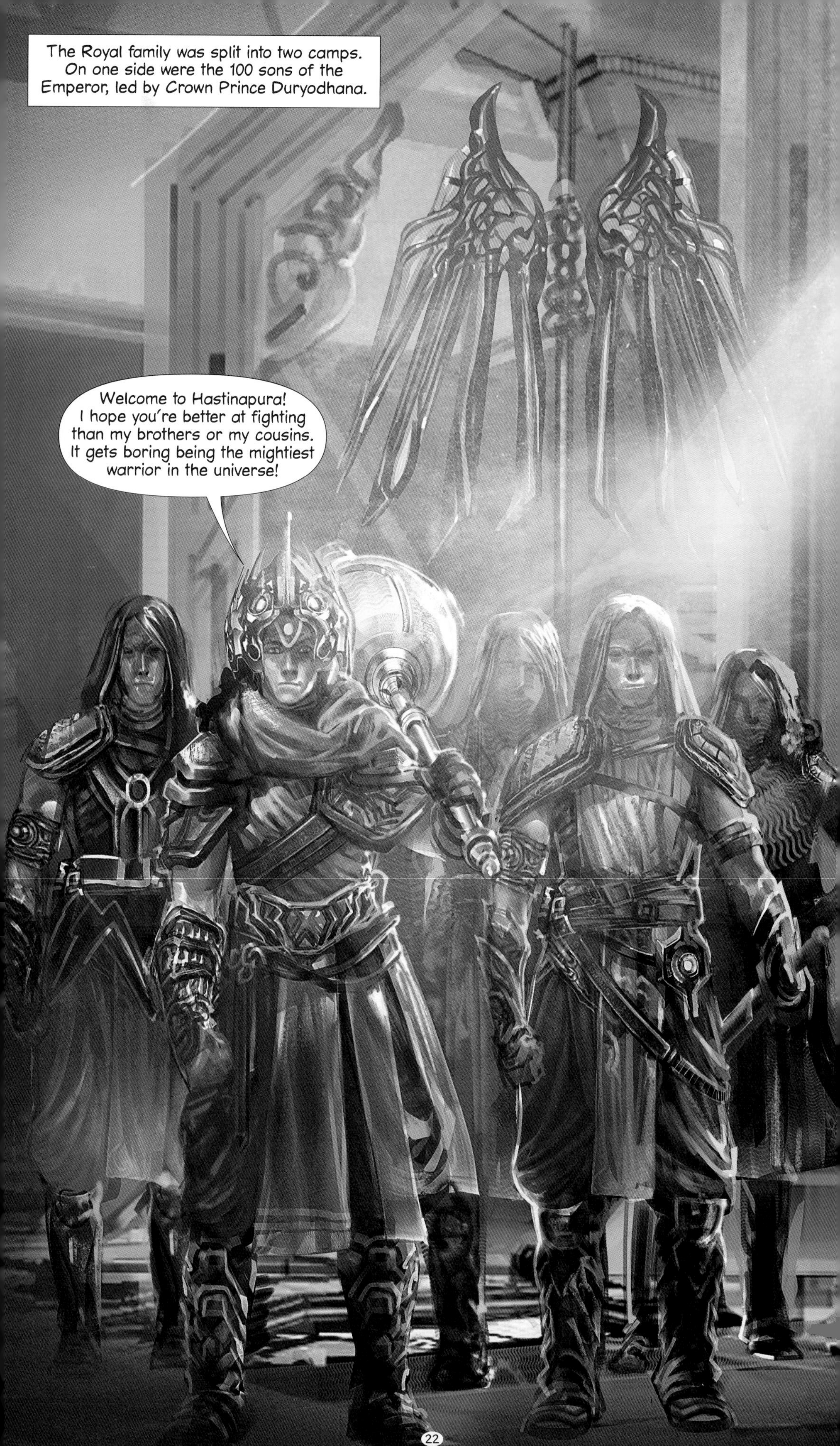
The Royal family was split into two camps. On one side were the 100 sons of the Emperor, led by Crown Prince Duryodhana.
Welcome to Hastinapura! I hope you're better at fighting than my brothers or my cousins. It gets boring being the mightiest warrior in the universe!

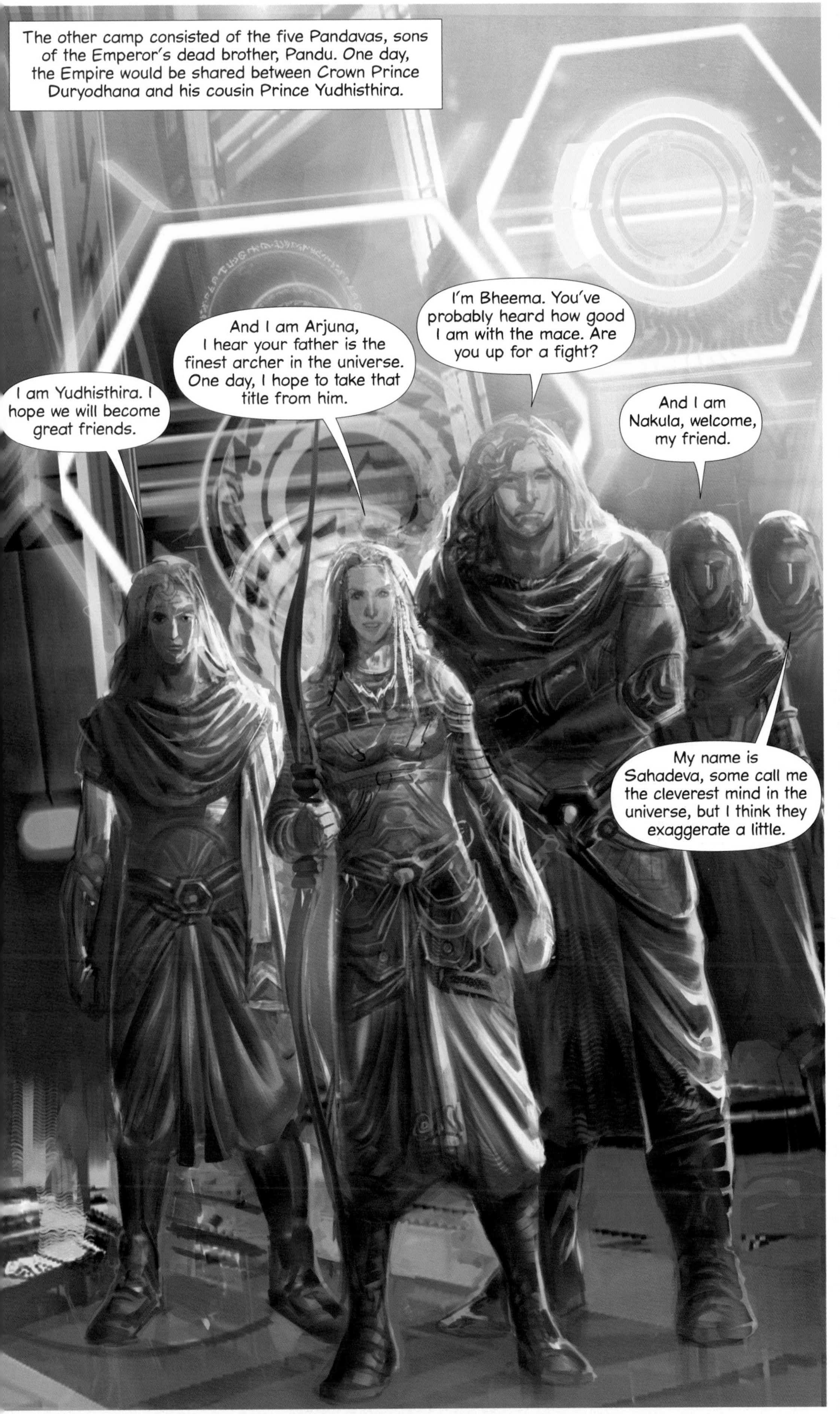
The other camp consisted of the five Pandavas, sons of the Emperor's dead brother, Pandu. One day, the Empire would be shared between Crown Prince Duryodhana and his cousin Prince Yudhisthira.
I am Yudhisthira. I hope we will become great friends.
And I am Arjuna, I hear your father is the finest archer in the universe. One day, I hope to take that title from him.
I'm Bheema. You've probably heard how good I am with the mace. Are you up for a fight?
And I am Nakula, welcome, my friend.
My name is Sahadeva, some call me the cleverest mind in the universe, but I think they exaggerate a little.

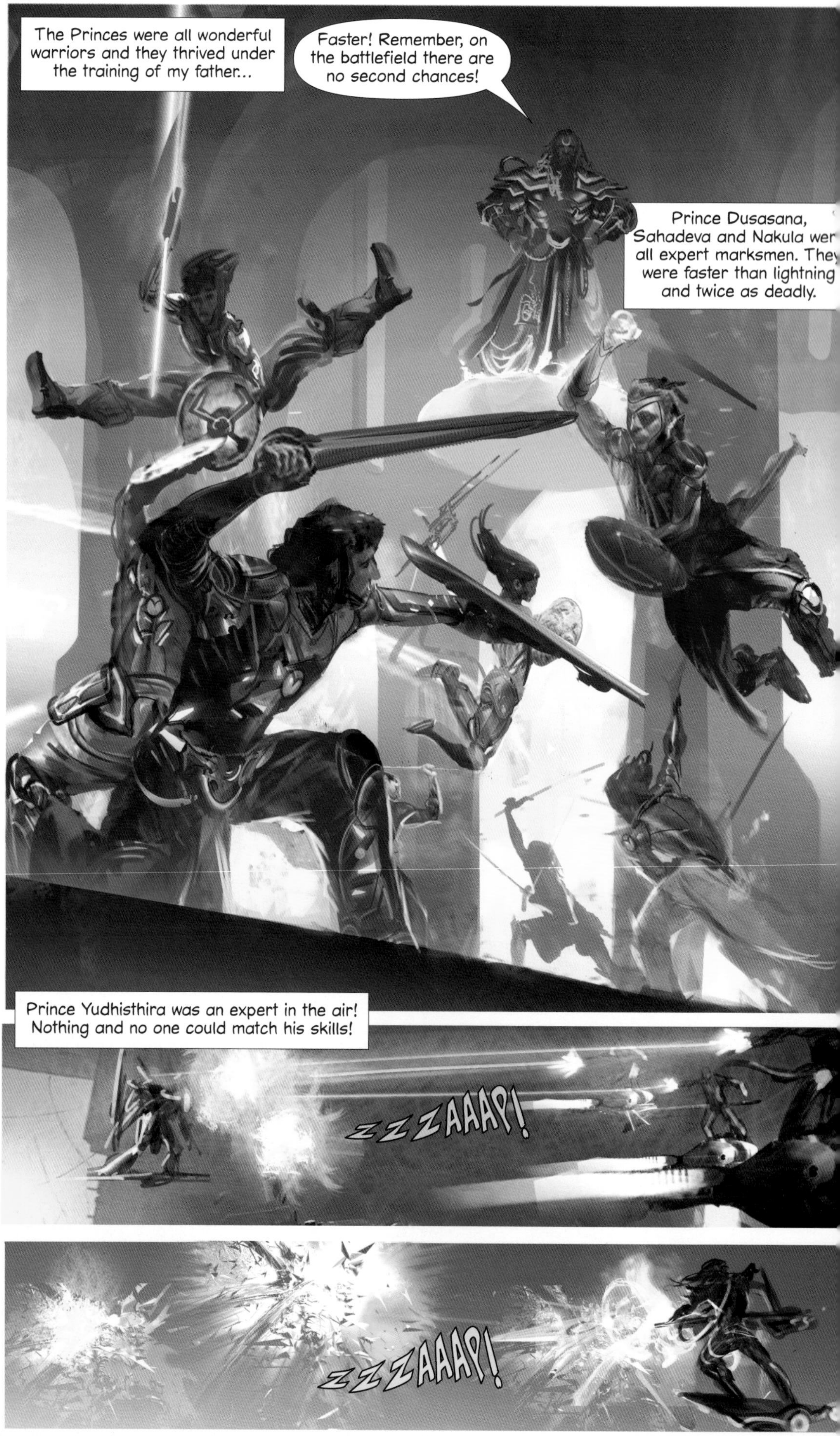
The Princes were all wonderful warriors and they thrived under the training of my father...
Faster! Remember, on the battlefield there are no second chances!
Prince Dusasana, Sahadeva and Nakula wer all expert marksmen. The were faster than lightning and twice as deadly.
Prince Yudhisthira was an expert in the air! Nothing and no one could match his skills!
ZZZAAAP!
ZZZAAAP!

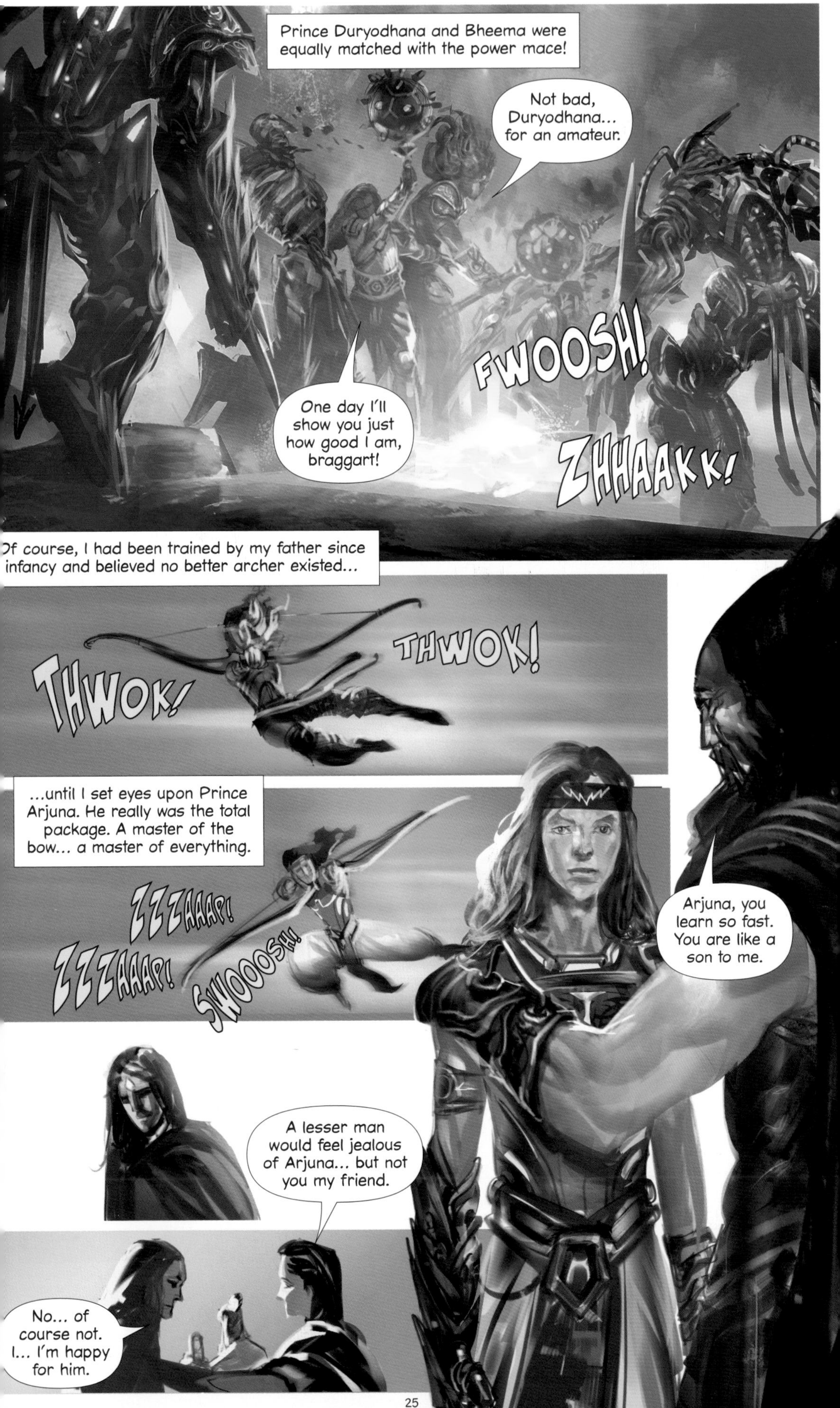
Prince Duryodhana and Bheema were equally matched with the power mace!
Not bad, Duryodhana... for an amateur.
One day I'll show you just how good I am, braggart!
FWOOSH!
ZHHAAKK!
Of course, I had been trained by my father since infancy and believed no better archer existed...
THWOK!
THWOK!
...until I set eyes upon Prince Arjuna. He really was the total package. A master of the bow... a master of everything.
ZZZAAAP!
ZZZAAAP!
SWOOOSH!!
Arjuna, you learn so fast. You are like a son to me.
A lesser man would feel jealous of Arjuna... but not you my friend.
No... of course not. I... I'm happy for him.

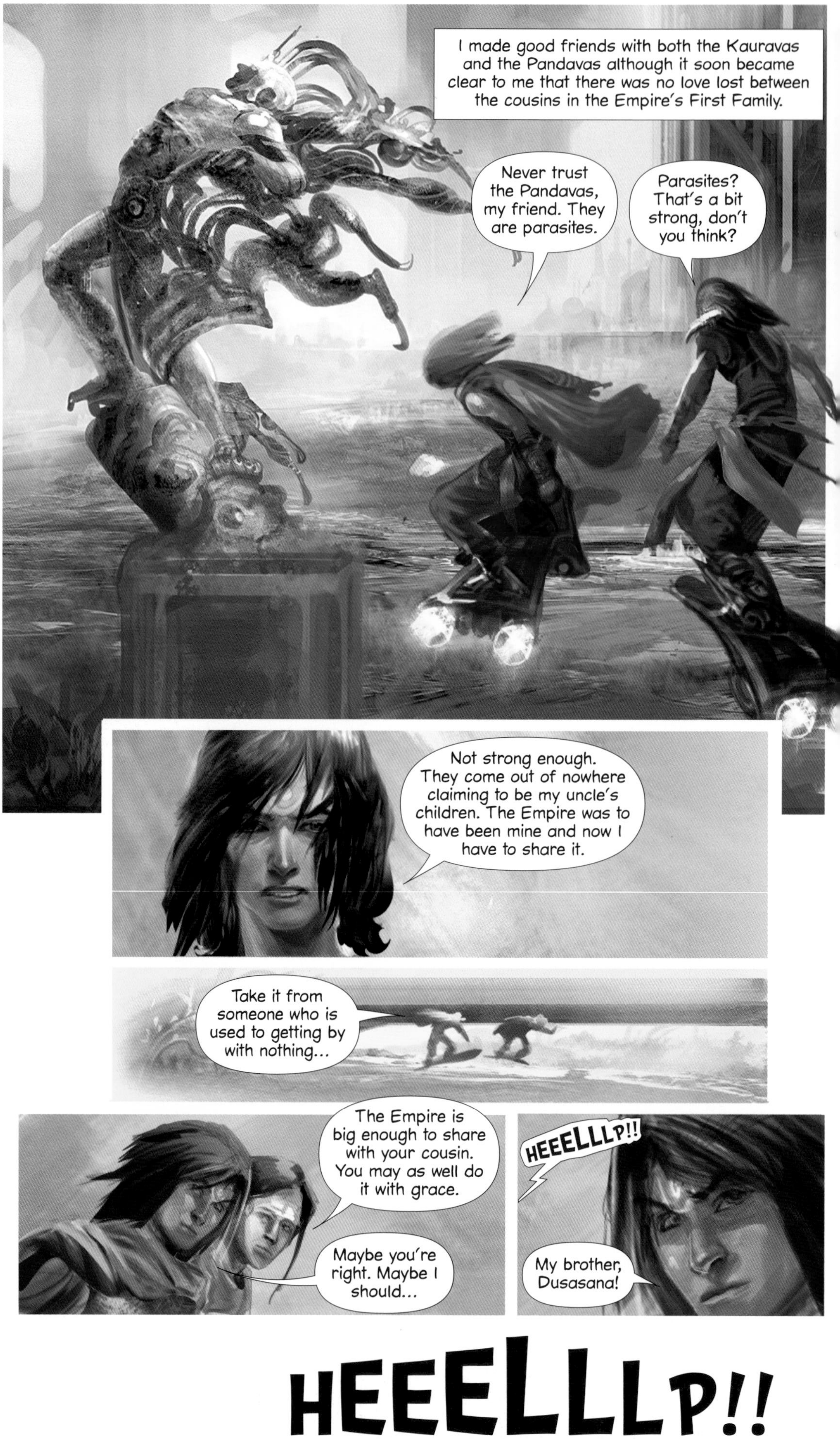
I made good friends with both the Kauravas and the Pandavas although it soon became clear to me that there was no love lost between the cousins in the Empire's First Family.
Never trust the Pandavas, my friend. They are parasites.
Parasites? That's a bit strong, don't you think?
Not strong enough. They come out of nowhere claiming to be my uncle's children. The Empire was to have been mine and now I have to share it.
Take it from someone who is used to getting by with nothing...
The Empire is big enough to share with your cousin. You may as well do it with grace.
Maybe you're right. Maybe I should...
HEEELLLP!!
My brother, Dusasana!
HEEELLLP!!

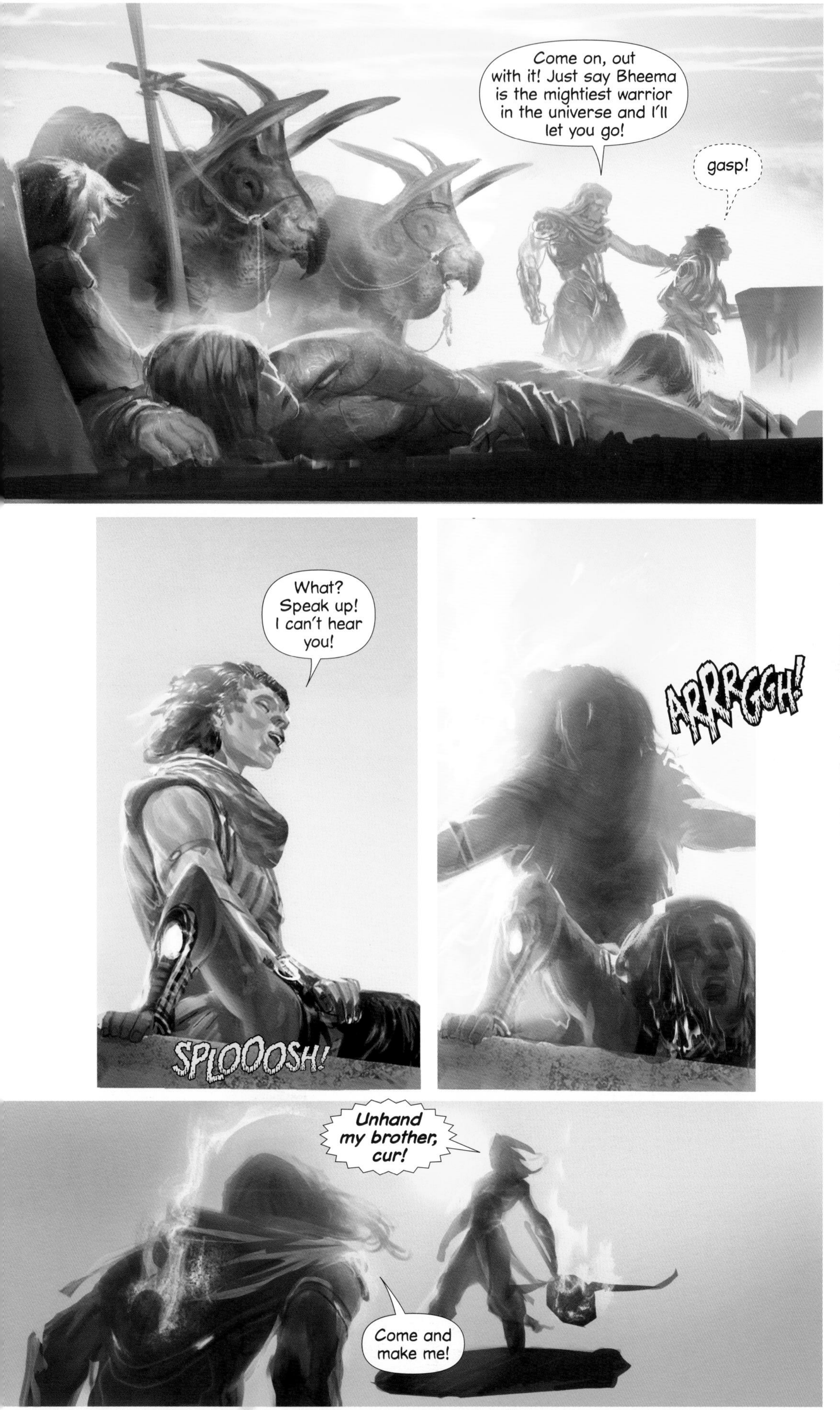
Come on, out with it! Just say Bheema is the mightiest warrior in the universe and I'll let you go!
gasp!
What? Speak up! I can't hear you!
SPLOOOSH!
ARRRGGH!
Unhand my brother, cur!
Come and make me!

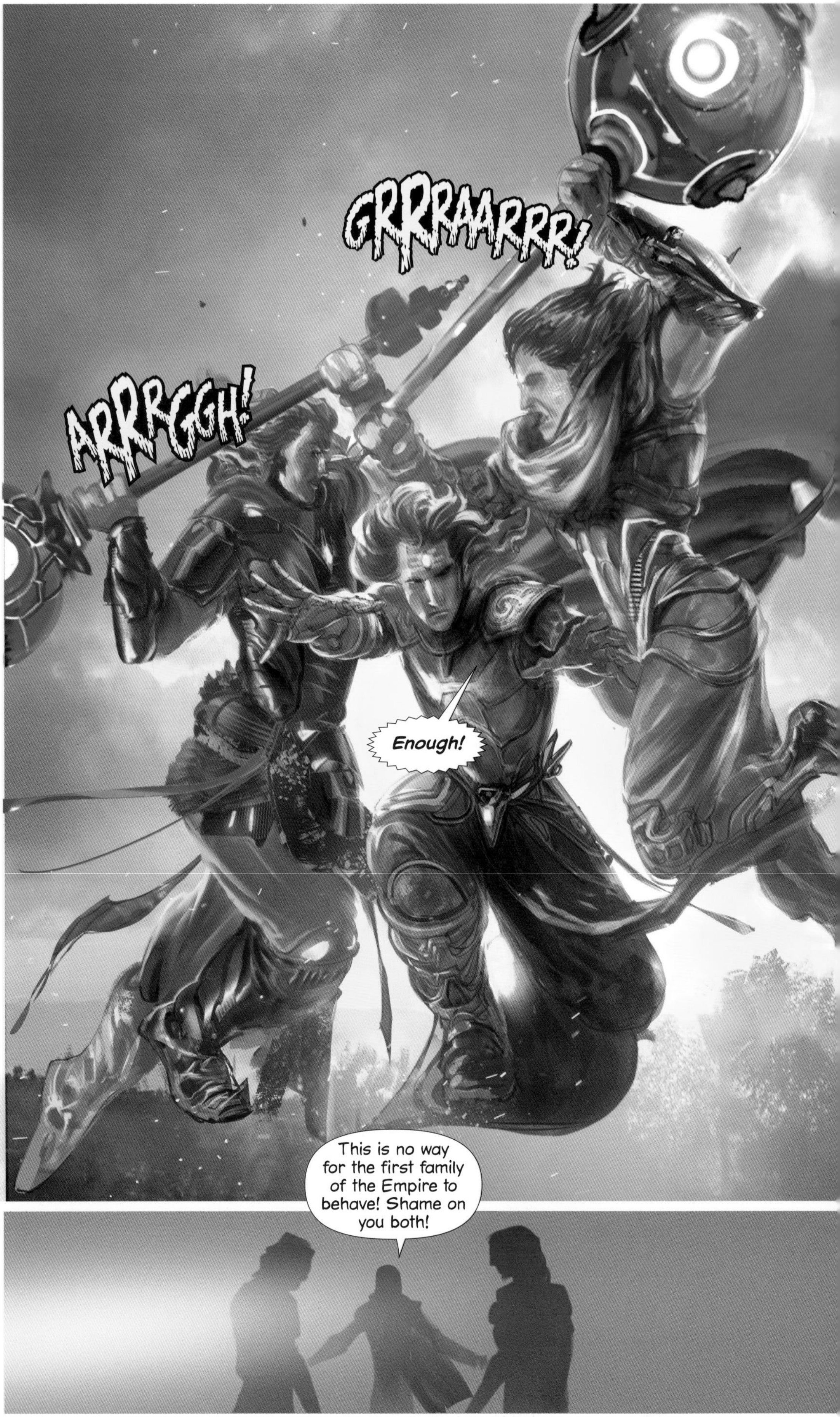
GRRRAARRR!
ARRRGGH!
Enough!
This is no way for the first family of the Empire to behave! Shame on you both!

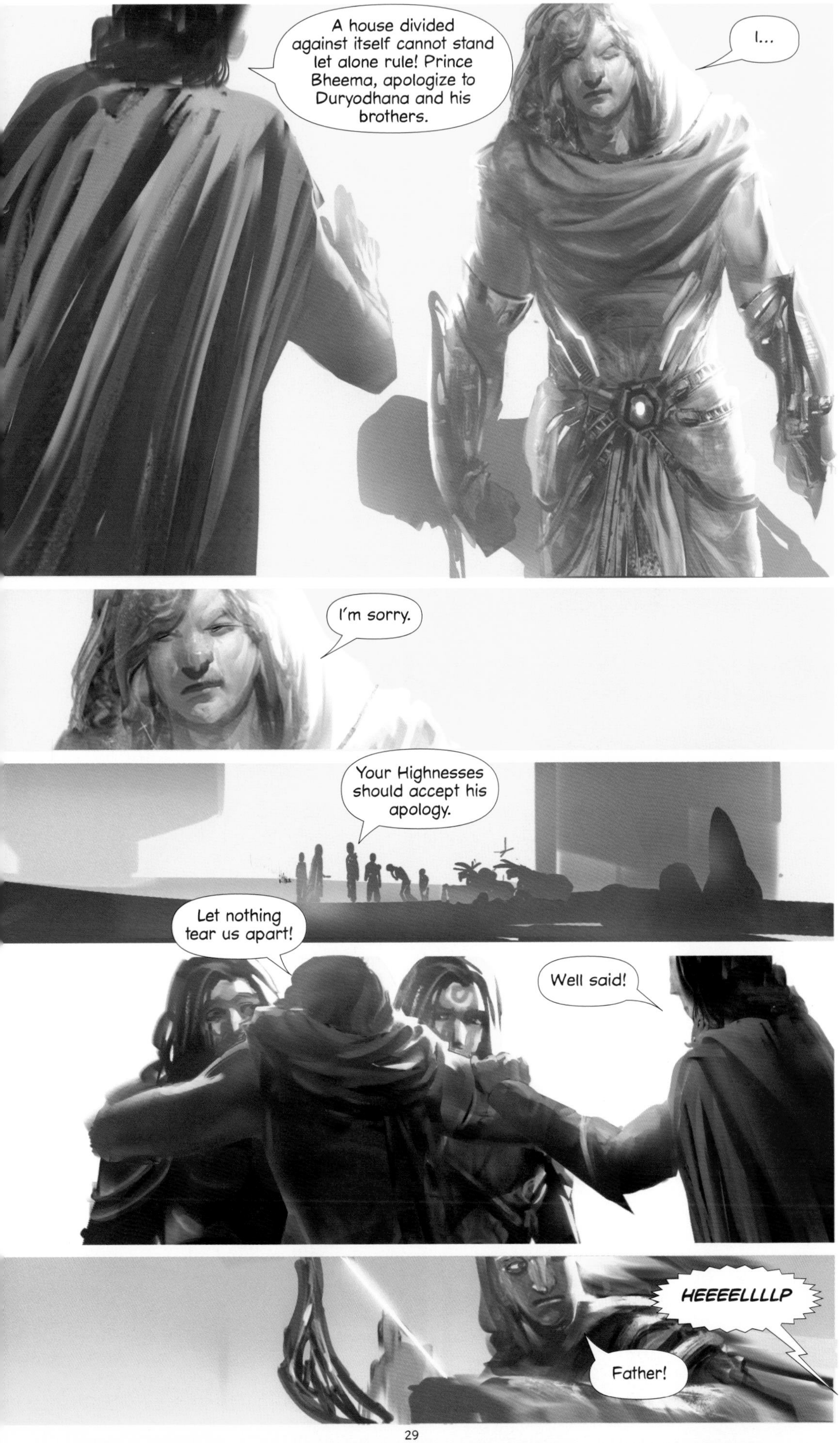
A house divided against itself cannot stand let alone rule! Prince Bheema, apologize to Duryodhana and his brothers.
I...
I'm sorry.
Your Highnesses should accept his apology.
Let nothing tear us apart!
Well said!
HEEEELLLLP
Father!

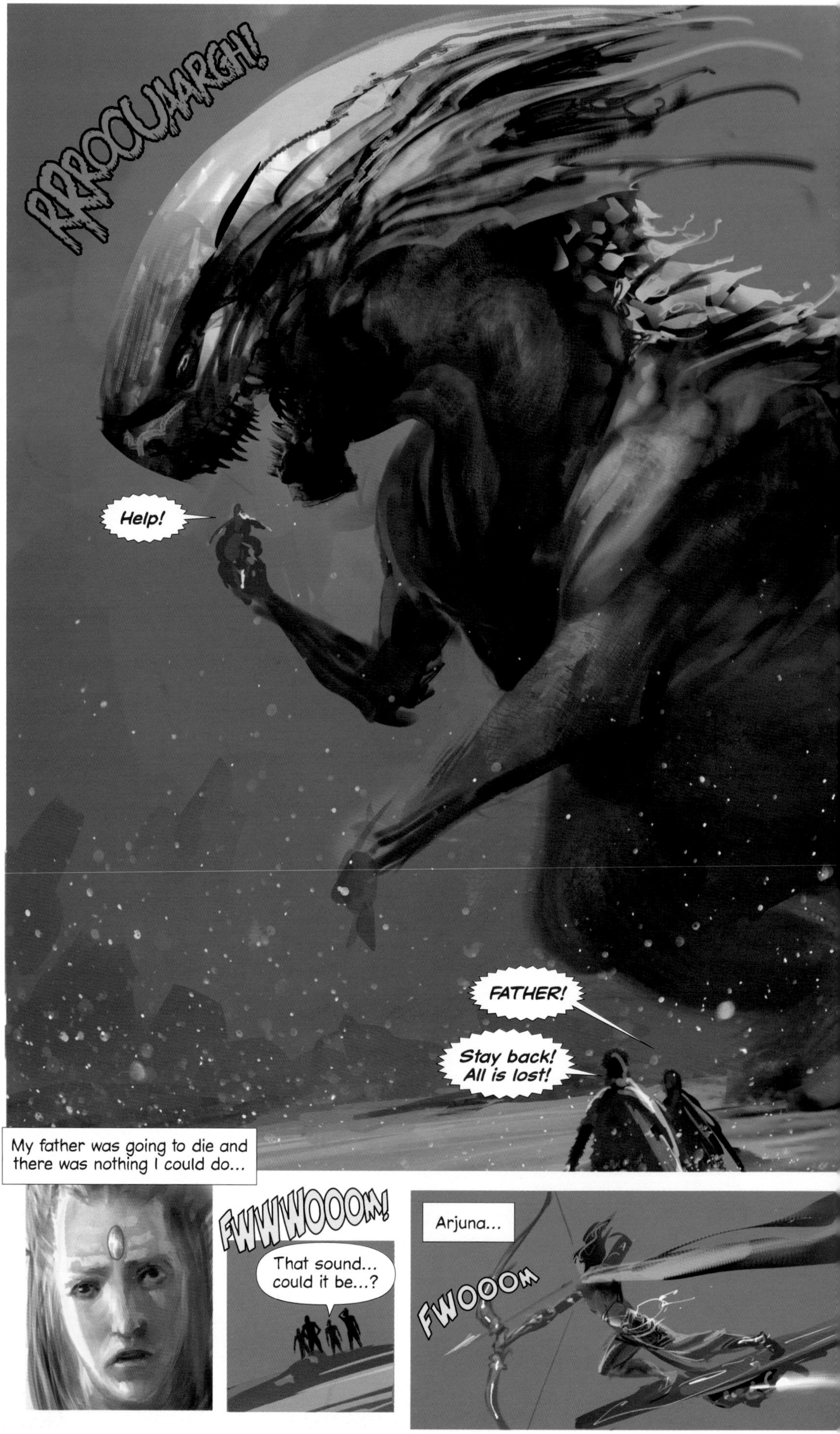
RRROOUARGH!
Help!
FATHER!
Stay back! All is lost!
My father was going to die and there was nothing I could do...
FWWWOOOM!
That sound... could it be...?
Arjuna...
FWOOOM

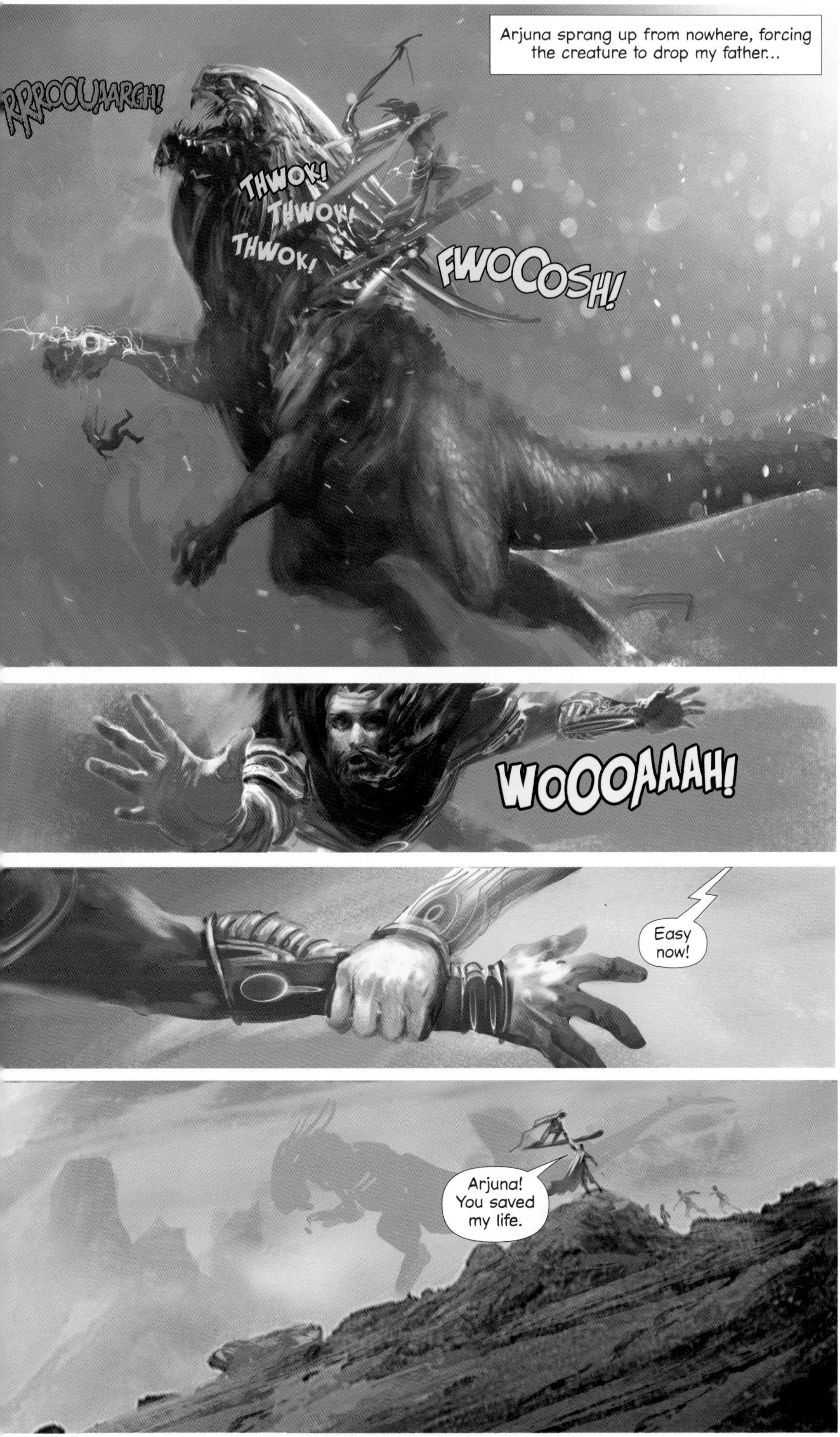
Arjuna sprang up from nowhere, forcing the creature to drop my father...
RRROOUAARGH!
THWOK!
THWOK!
THWOK!
FWOOOSH!
WOOOAAAH!
Easy now!
Arjuna! You saved my life.

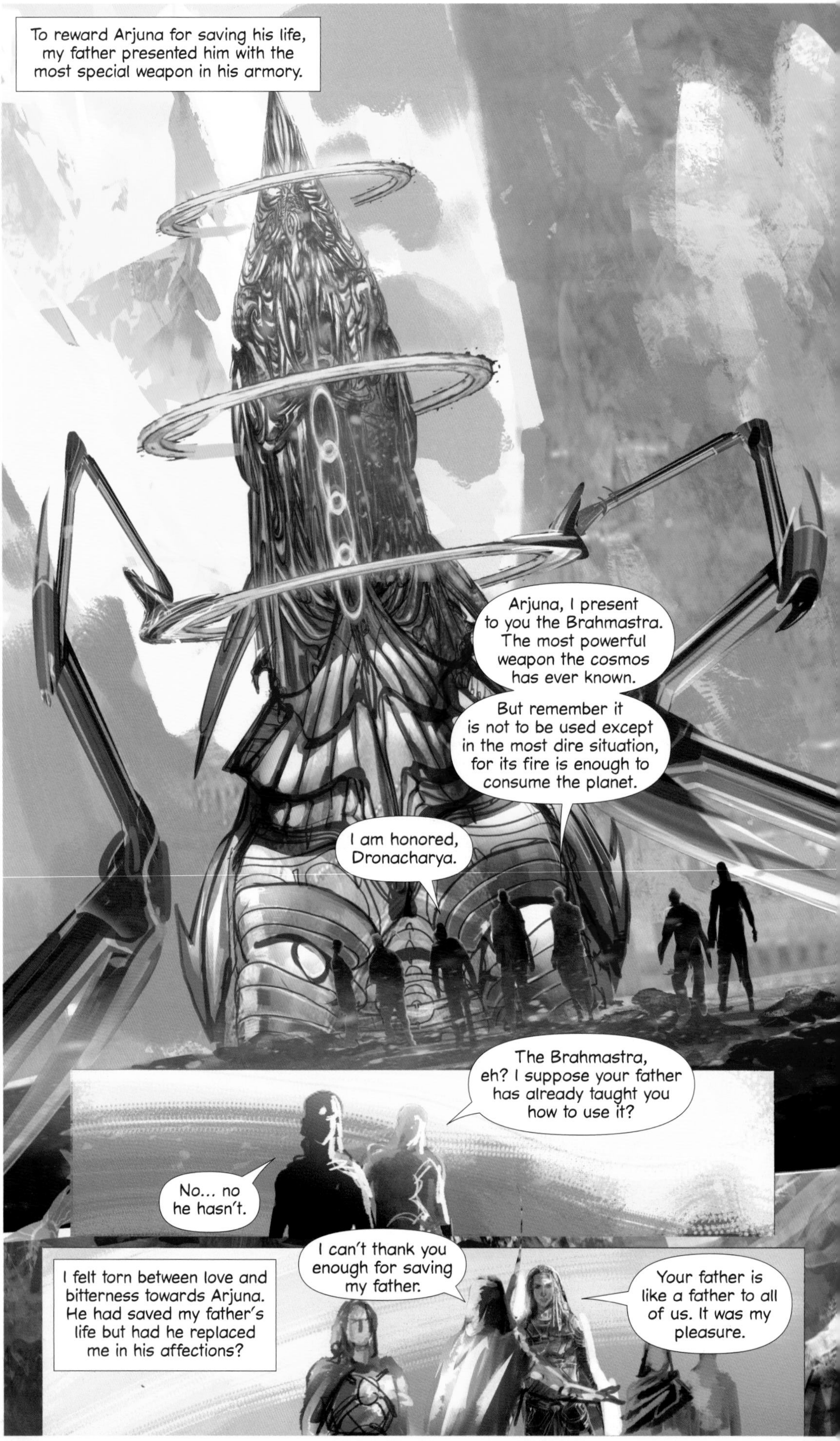
To reward Arjuna for saving his life, my father presented him with the most special weapon in his armory.
Arjuna, I present to you the Brahmastra. The most powerful weapon the cosmos has ever known.
But remember it is not to be used except in the most dire situation, for its fire is enough to consume the planet.
I am honored, Dronacharya.
The Brahmastra, eh? I suppose your father has already taught you how to use it?
No... no he hasn't.
I felt torn between love and bitterness towards Arjuna. He had saved my father's life but had he replaced me in his affections?
I can't thank you enough for saving my father.
Your father is like a father to all of us. It was my pleasure.

Arjuna and my father became inseparable. After classes, they would spend time examining and modifying the latest technology the Kaurava Empire had to offer.

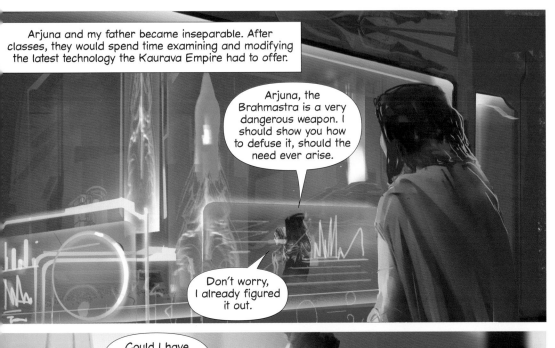

Arjuna, the Brahmastra is a very dangerous weapon. I should show you how to defuse it, should the need ever arise.

Don't worry, I already figured it out.

Could I have a word, please... alone. Without your shadow.

I take it I'm the shadow? As you wish. I'll see you all tomorrow.

What has got into you, boy? That's no way to speak to...

Please, Father! You show Arjuna more love than you ever showed me. It is too hard to take. I...

But I love you as a son. I love Arjuna as a genius on the battlefield. The two are completely different.

Arjuna is my greatest achievement as a teacher. But you are my greatest achievement as a man. You are my son and I love nothing better.

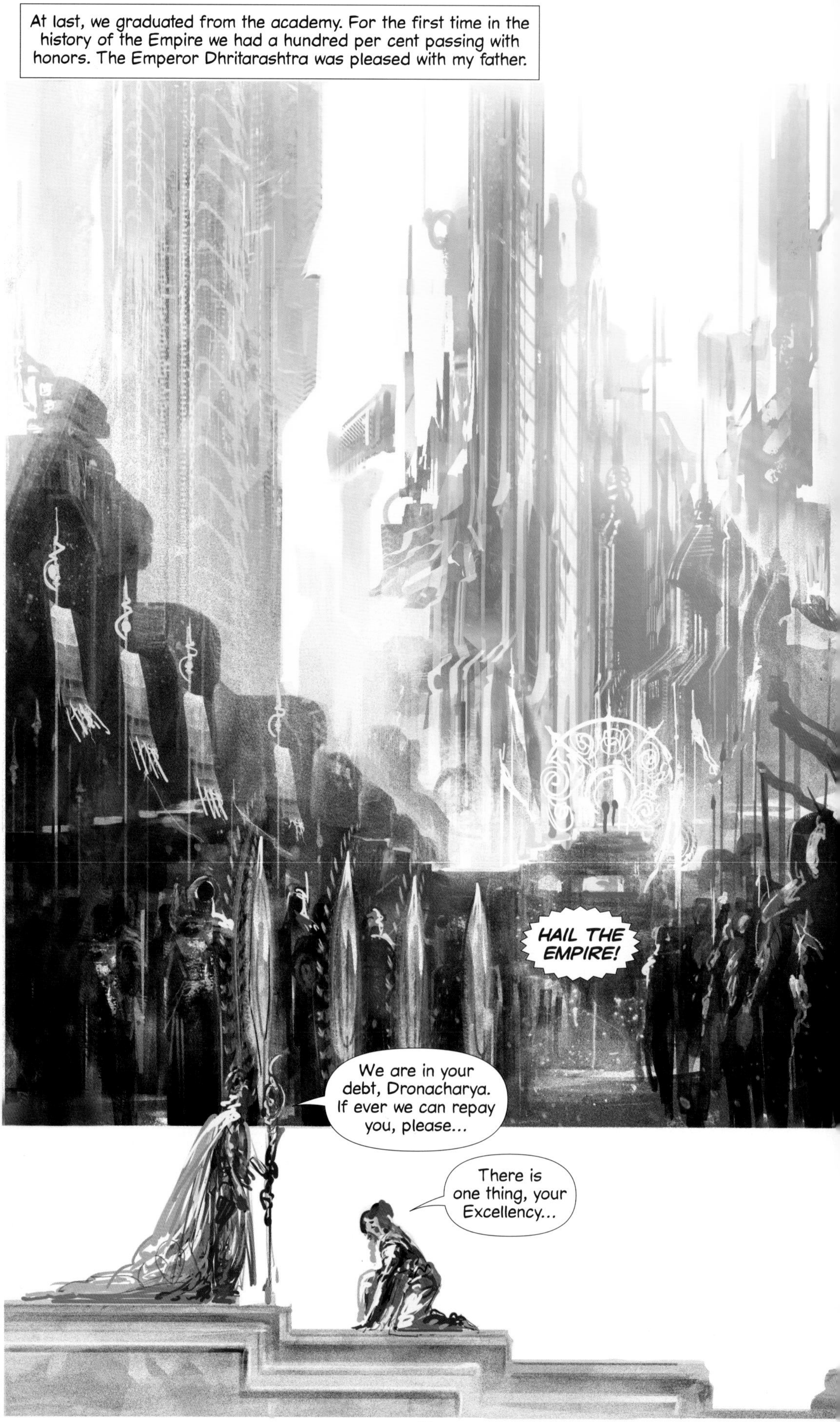
At last, we graduated from the academy. For the first time in the history of the Empire we had a hundred per cent passing with honors. The Emperor Dhritarashtra was pleased with my father.
HAIL THE EMPIRE!
We are in your debt, Dronacharya. If ever we can repay you, please...
There is one thing, your Excellency...

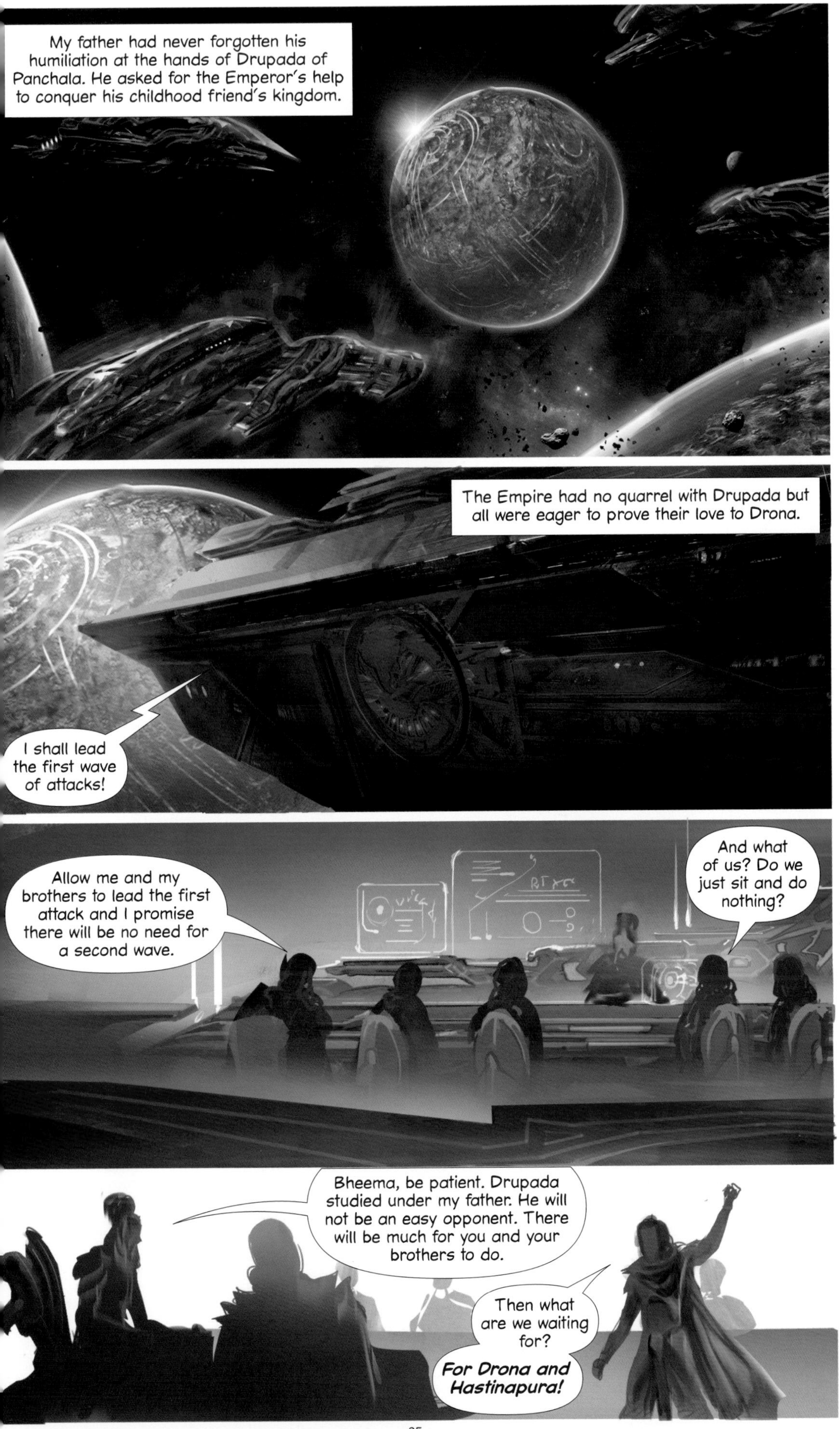

My father had never forgotten his humiliation at the hands of Drupada of Panchala. He asked for the Emperor's help to conquer his childhood friend's kingdom.
The Empire had no quarrel with Drupada but all were eager to prove their love to Drona.
I shall lead the first wave of attacks!
Allow me and my brothers to lead the first attack and I promise there will be no need for a second wave.
And what of us? Do we just sit and do nothing?
Bheema, be patient. Drupada studied under my father. He will not be an easy opponent. There will be much for you and your brothers to do.
Then what are we waiting for?
For Drona and Hastinapura!

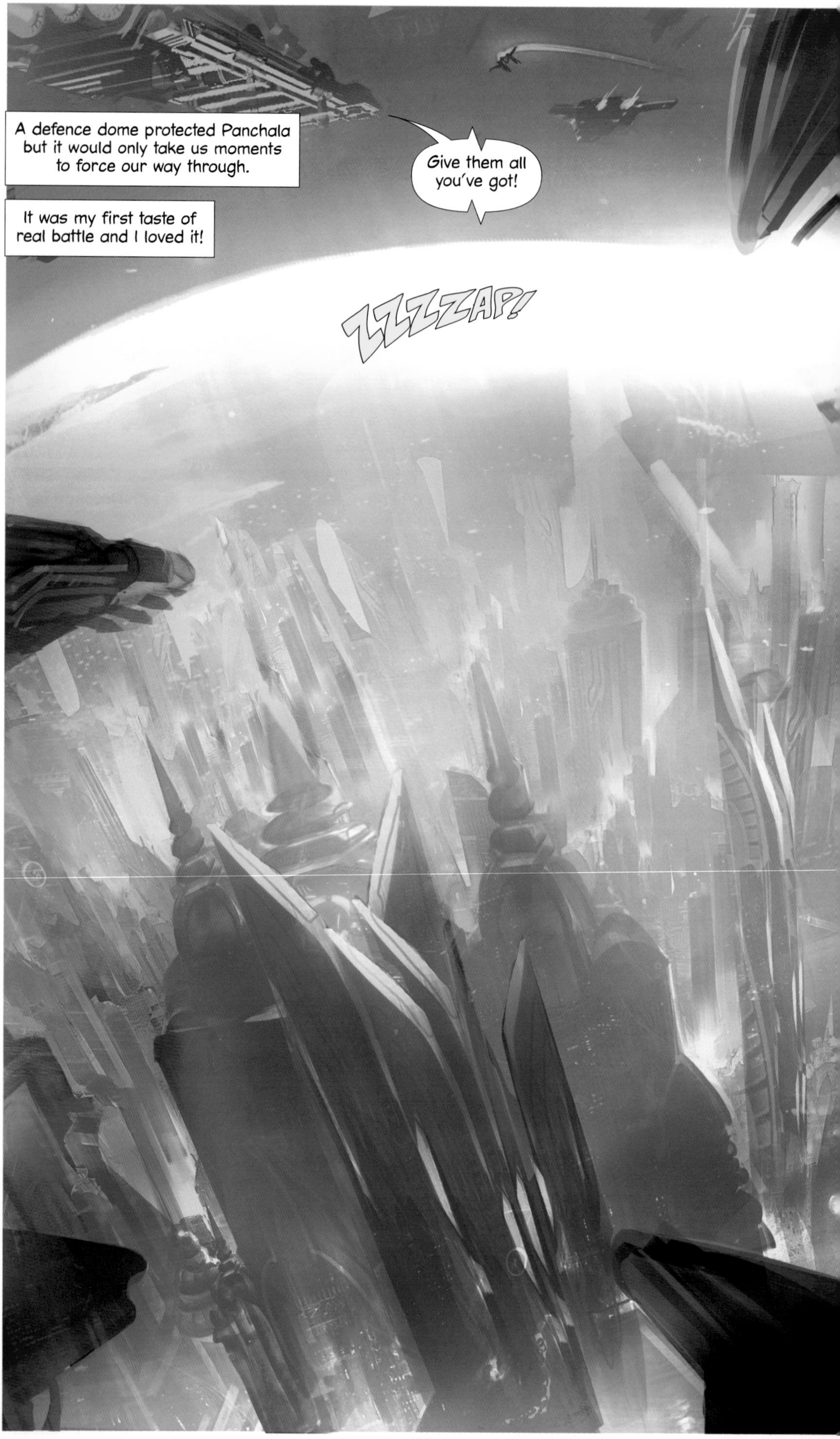
A defence dome protected Panchala but it would only take us moments to force our way through.
It was my first taste of real battle and I loved it!
Give them all you've got!
ZZZZAP!

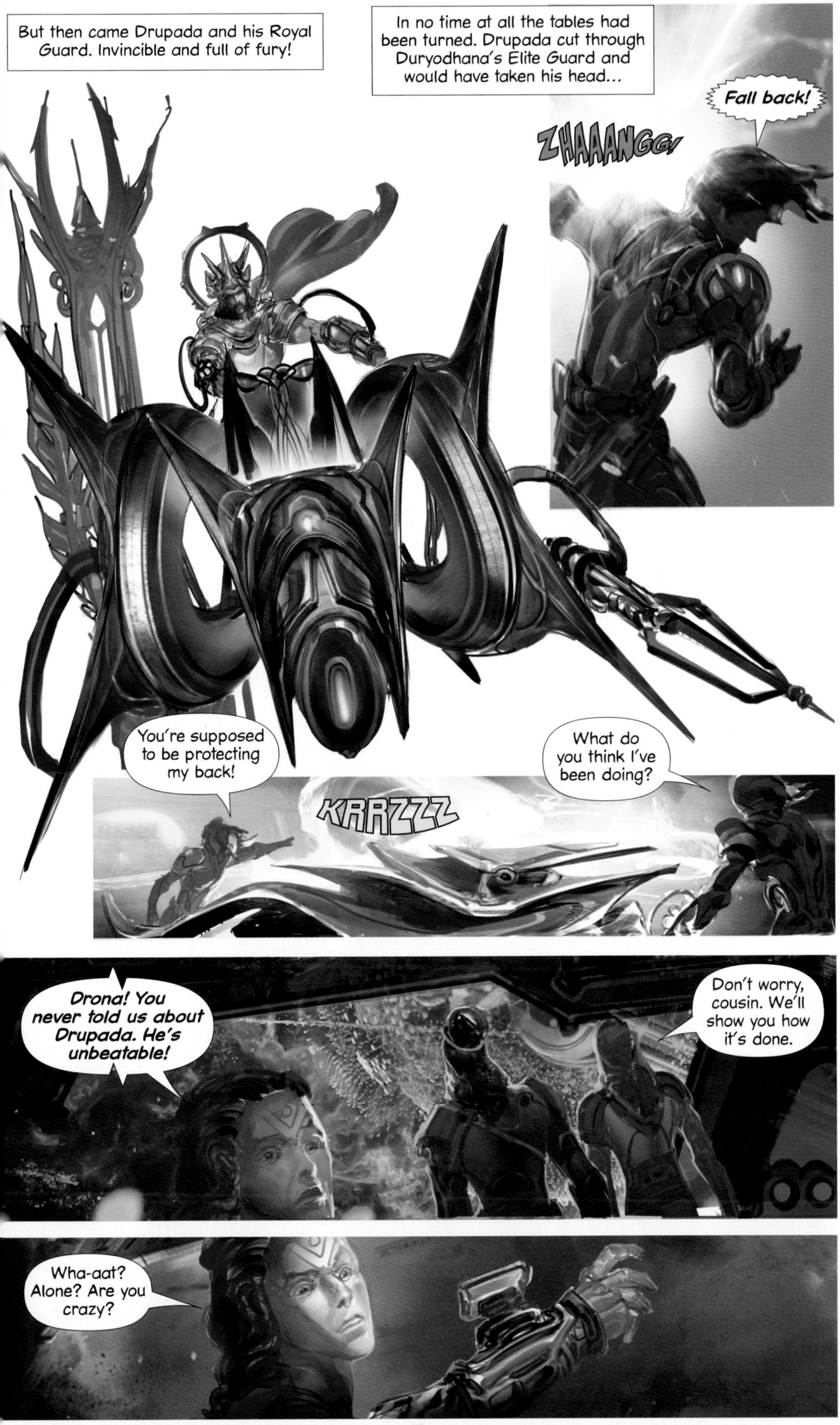

But then came Drupada and his Royal Guard. Invincible and full of fury!
In no time at all the tables had been turned. Drupada cut through Duryodhana's Elite Guard and would have taken his head...
Fall back!
ZHAAANGG!
You're supposed to be protecting my back!
What do you think I've been doing?
KRRZZZ
Drona! You never told us about Drupada. He's unbeatable!
Don't worry, cousin. We'll show you how it's done.
Wha-aat? Alone? Are you crazy?

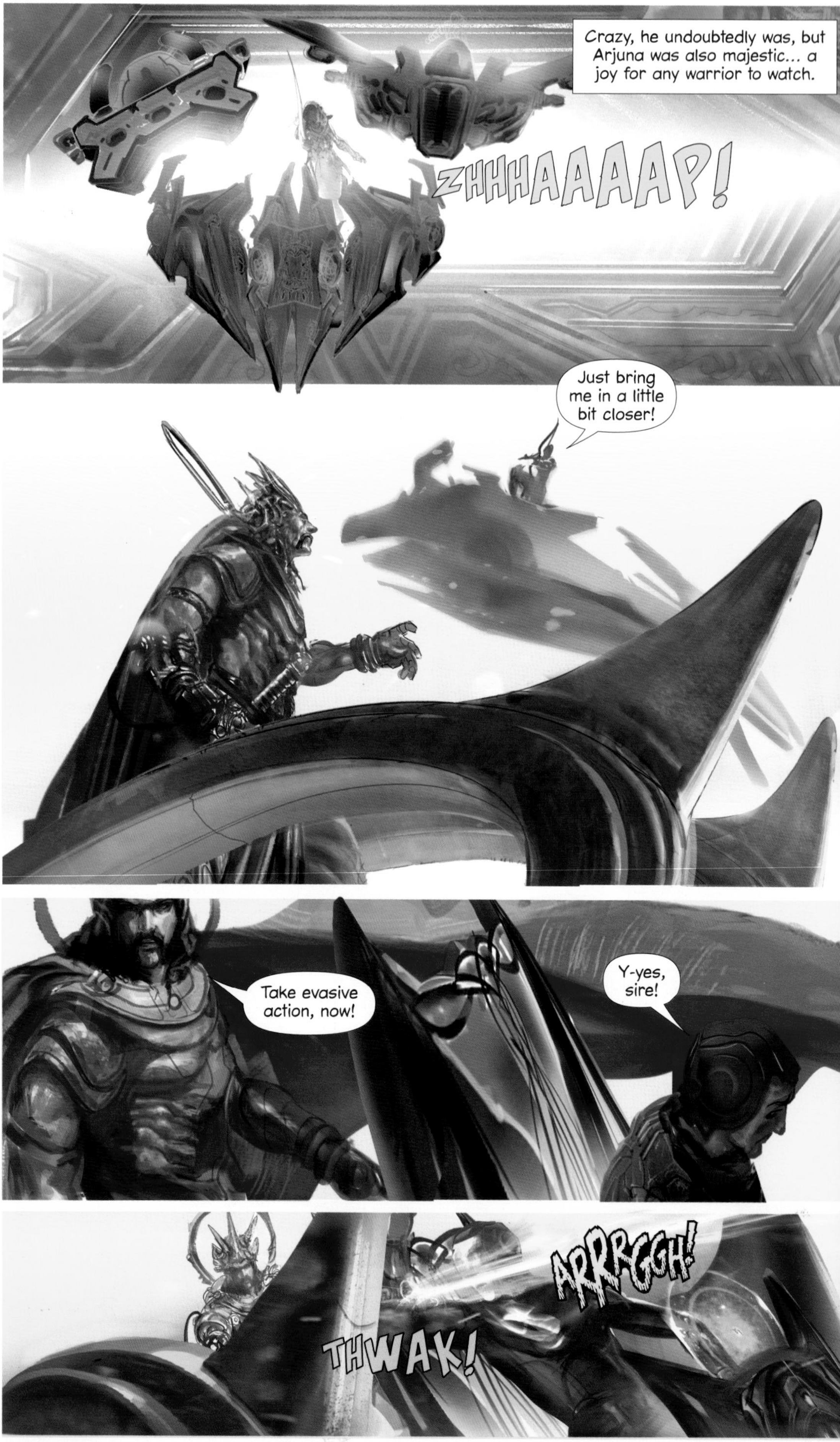
Crazy, he undoubtedly was, but Arjuna was also majestic... a joy for any warrior to watch.
ZHHHAAAAAP!
Just bring me in a little bit closer!
Take evasive action, now!
Y-yes, sire!
ARRRGGH!
THWAK!

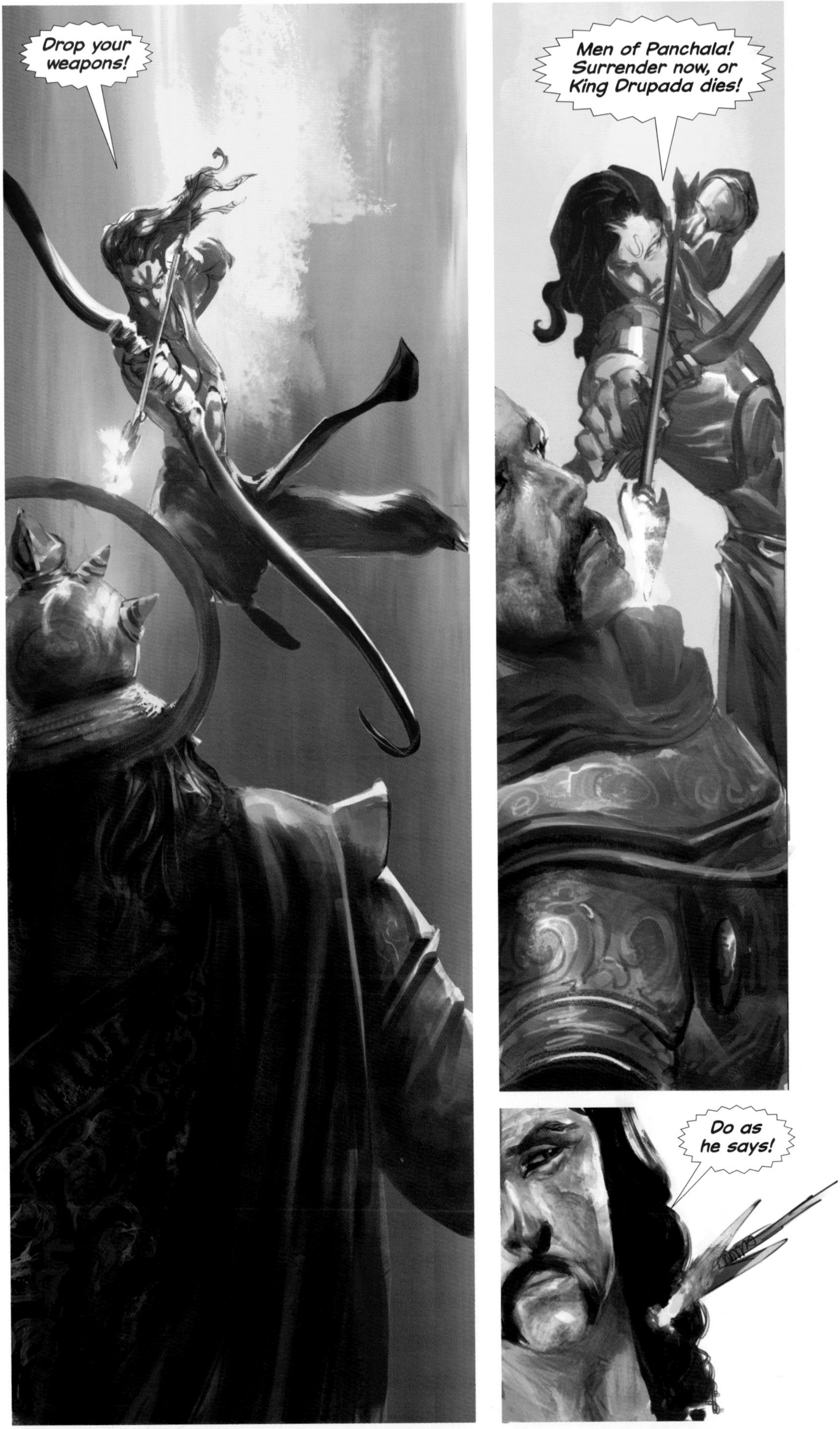
Drop your weapons!
Men of Panchala! Surrender now, or King Drupada dies!
Do as he says!

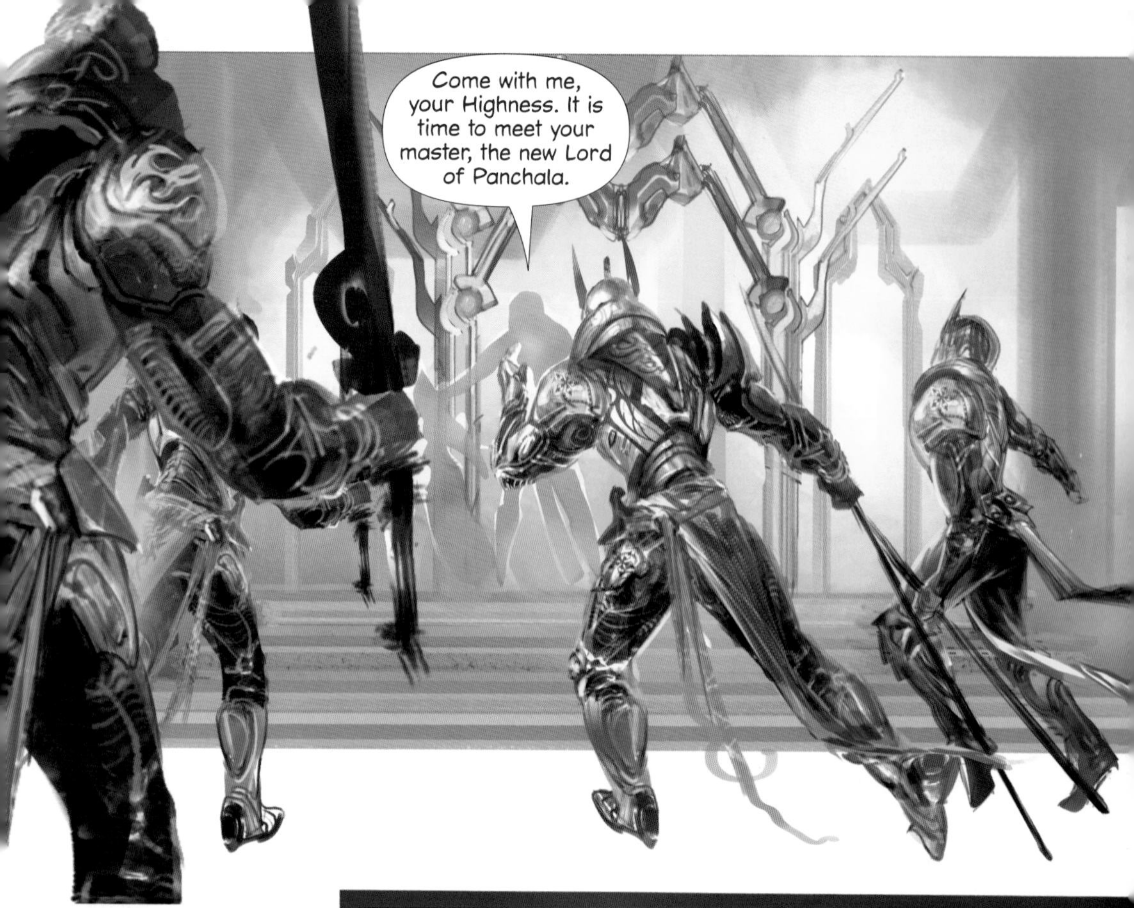
Come with me, your Highness. It is time to meet your master, the new Lord of Panchala.

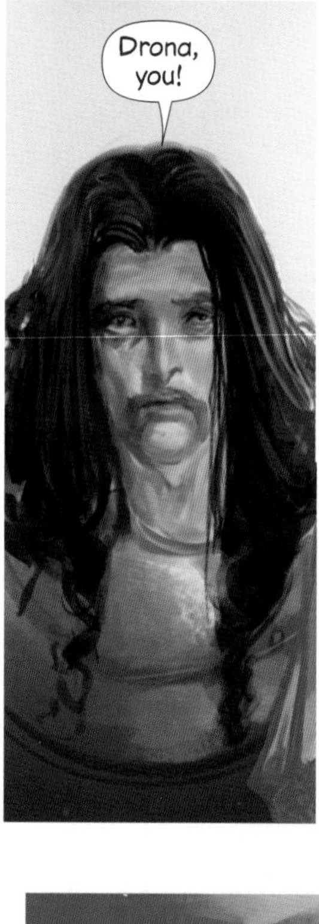
Drona, you!

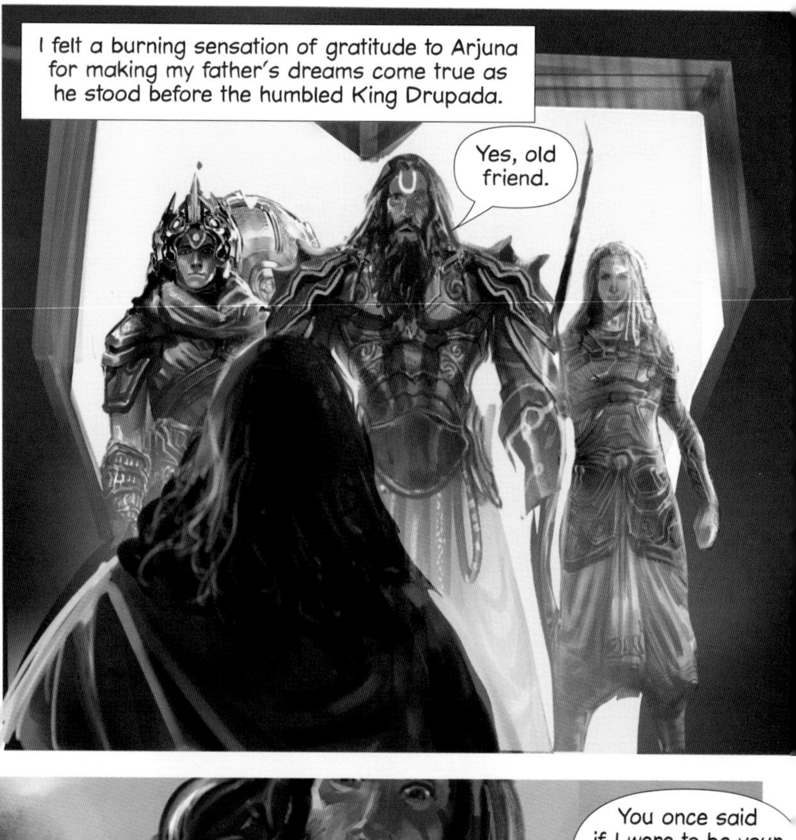
I felt a burning sensation of gratitude to Arjuna for making my father's dreams come true as he stood before the humbled King Drupada.
Yes, old friend.

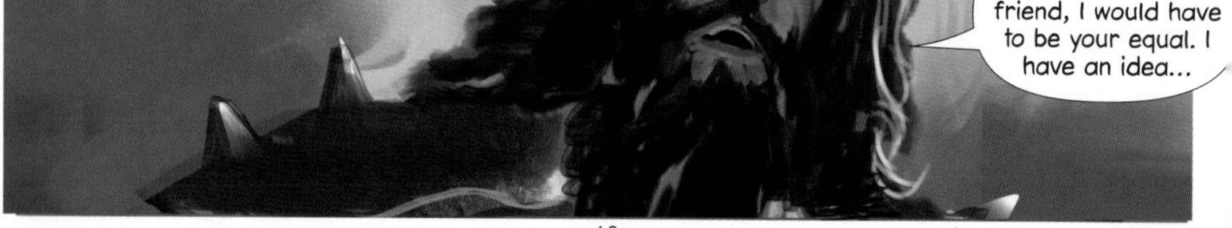
You once said if I were to be your friend, I would have to be your equal. I have an idea...

I will return half your lands and wealth. We shall rule as equals... on one condition.

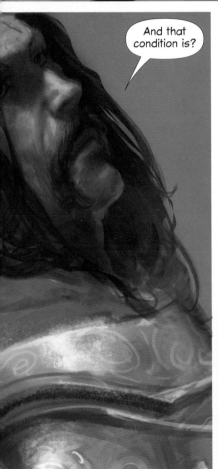

And that condition is?

That we swear undying friendship and loyalty to each other from this day on.

Of course Drupada agreed, but it was the one foolish act my father ever committed.

Old friend... forgive my foolish arrogance.

I don't trust Drupada. I would watch him closely if I were you.

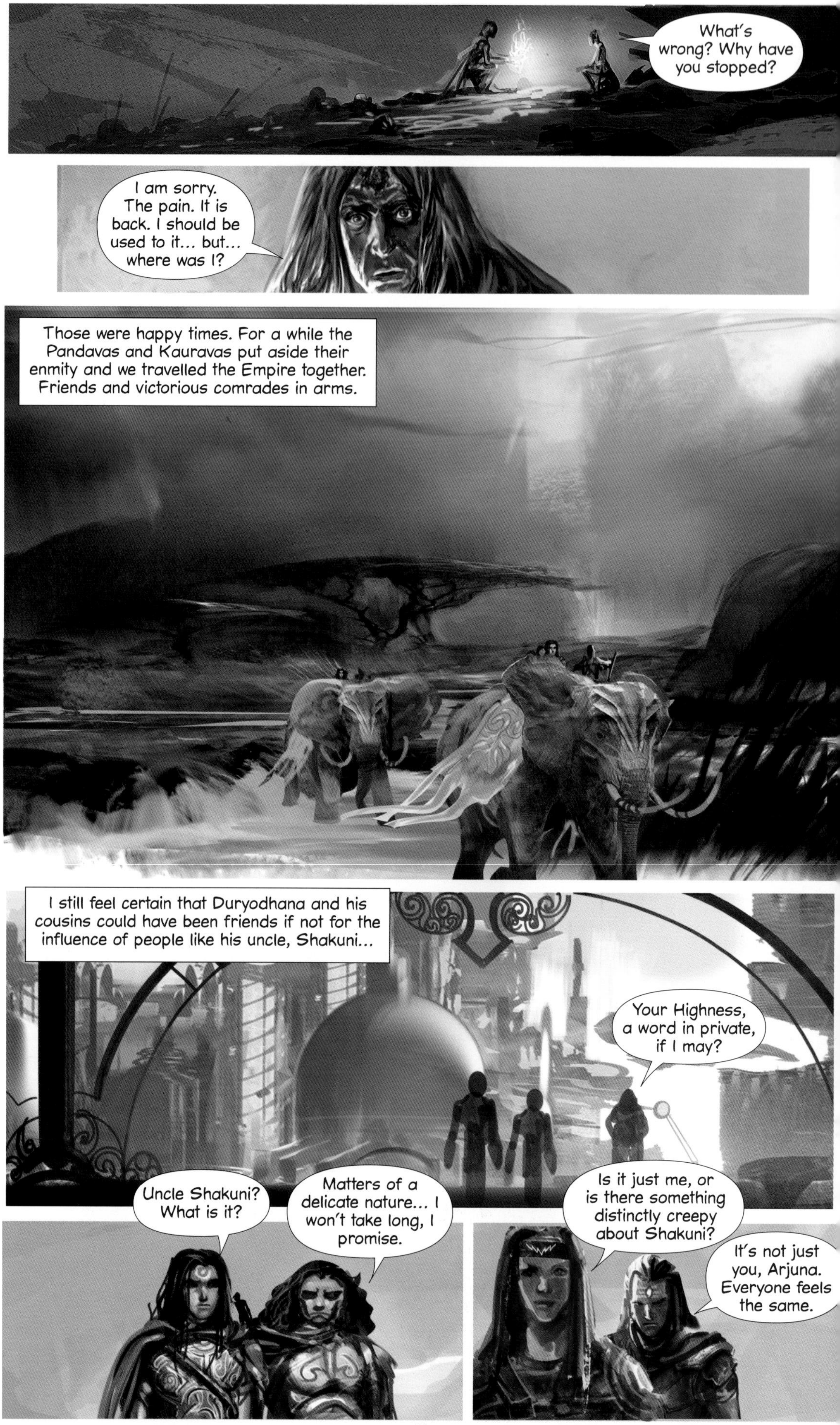
What's wrong? Why have you stopped?
I am sorry. The pain. It is back. I should be used to it... but... where was I?
Those were happy times. For a while the Pandavas and Kauravas put aside their enmity and we travelled the Empire together. Friends and victorious comrades in arms.
I still feel certain that Duryodhana and his cousins could have been friends if not for the influence of people like his uncle, Shakuni...
Your Highness, a word in private, if I may?
Uncle Shakuni? What is it?
Matters of a delicate nature... I won't take long, I promise.
Is it just me, or is there something distinctly creepy about Shakuni?
It's not just you, Arjuna. Everyone feels the same.

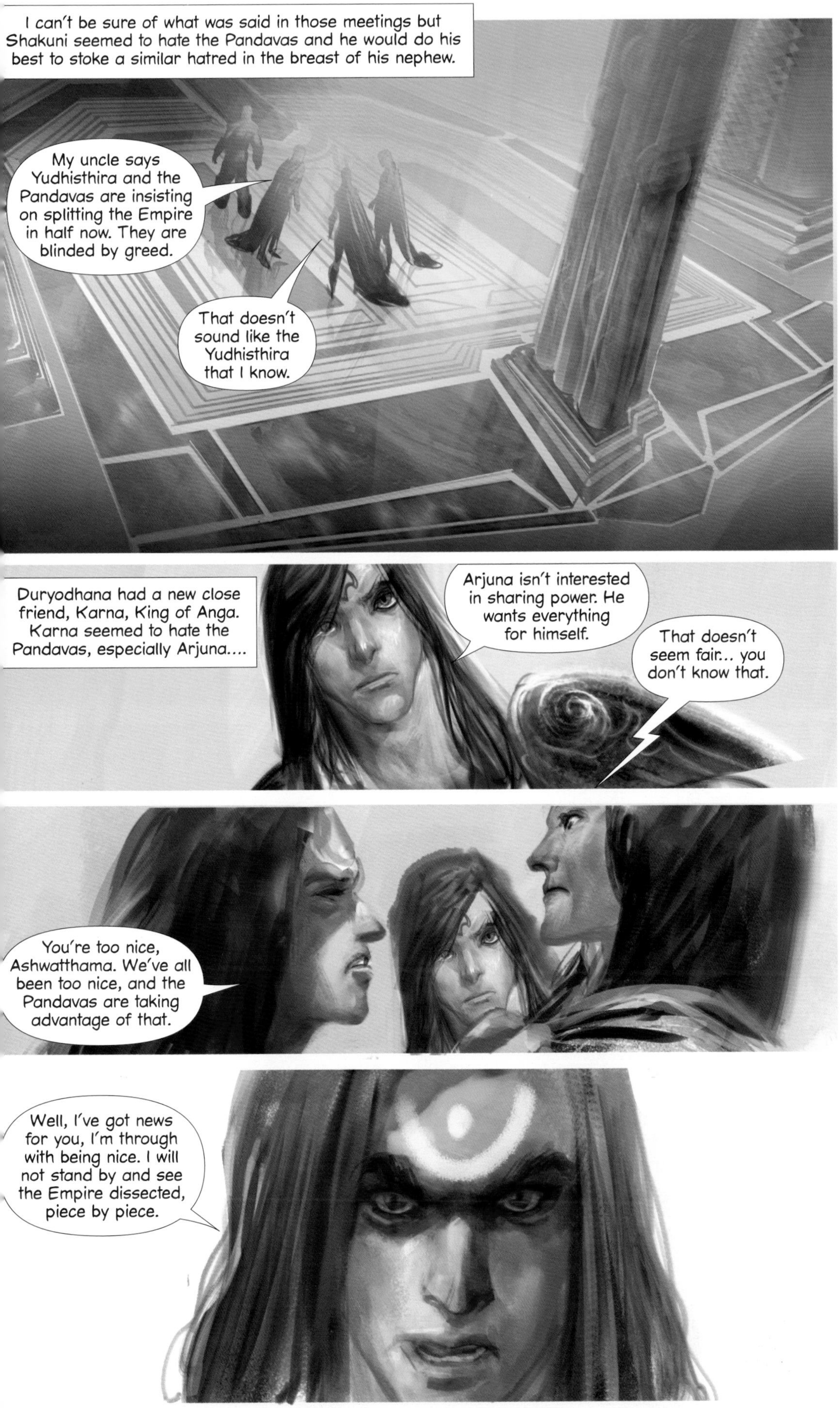
I can't be sure of what was said in those meetings but Shakuni seemed to hate the Pandavas and he would do his best to stoke a similar hatred in the breast of his nephew.
My uncle says Yudhisthira and the Pandavas are insisting on splitting the Empire in half now. They are blinded by greed.
That doesn't sound like the Yudhisthira that I know.
Duryodhana had a new close friend, Karna, King of Anga. Karna seemed to hate the Pandavas, especially Arjuna....
Arjuna isn't interested in sharing power. He wants everything for himself.
That doesn't seem fair... you don't know that.
You're too nice, Ashwatthama. We've all been too nice, and the Pandavas are taking advantage of that.
Well, I've got news for you, I'm through with being nice. I will not stand by and see the Empire dissected, piece by piece.

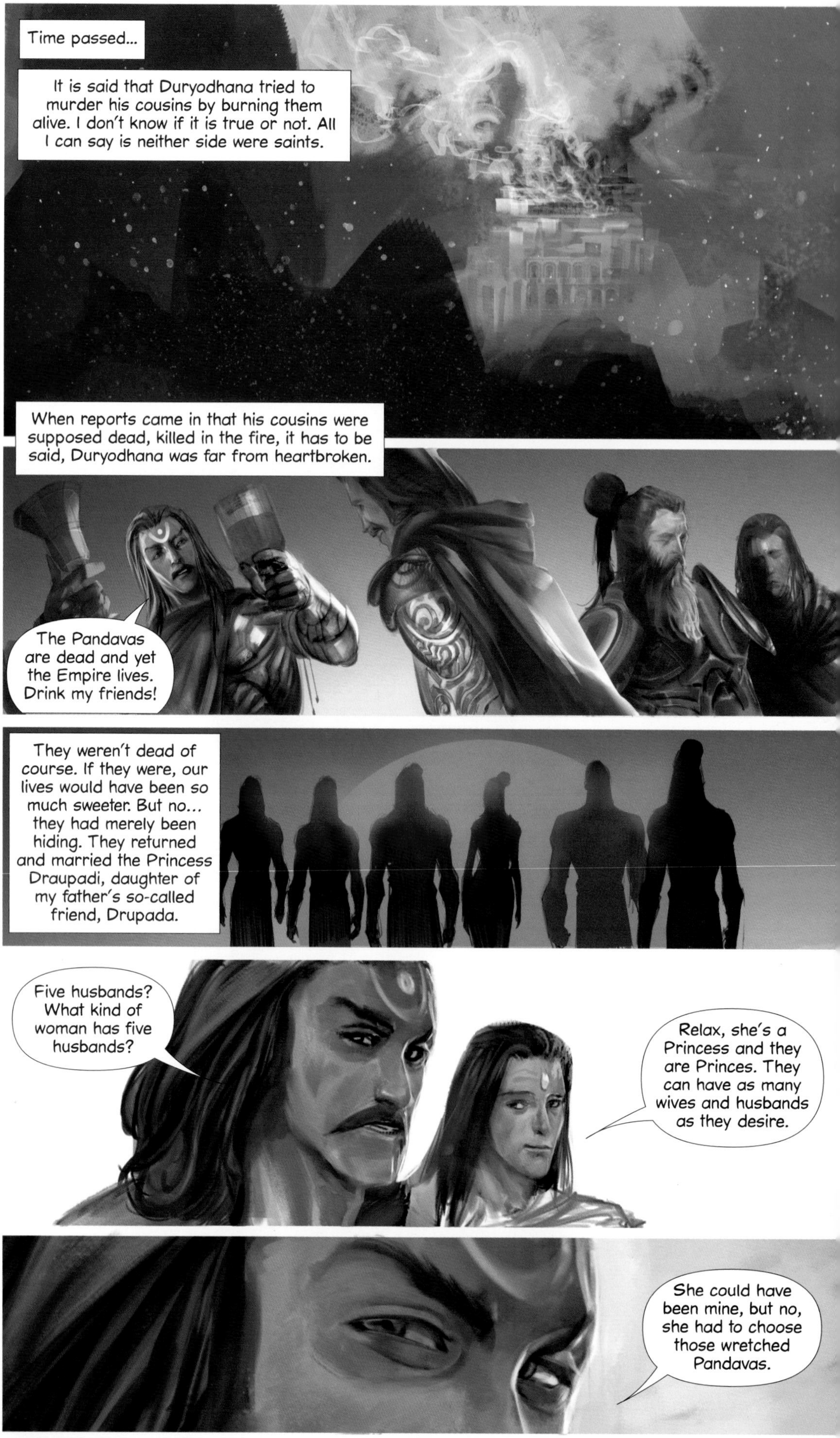
Time passed...
It is said that Duryodhana tried to murder his cousins by burning them alive. I don't know if it is true or not. All I can say is neither side were saints.
When reports came in that his cousins were supposed dead, killed in the fire, it has to be said, Duryodhana was far from heartbroken.
The Pandavas are dead and yet the Empire lives. Drink my friends!
They weren't dead of course. If they were, our lives would have been so much sweeter. But no... they had merely been hiding. They returned and married the Princess Draupadi, daughter of my father's so-called friend, Drupada.
Five husbands? What kind of woman has five husbands?
Relax, she's a Princess and they are Princes. They can have as many wives and husbands as they desire.
She could have been mine, but no, she had to choose those wretched Pandavas.

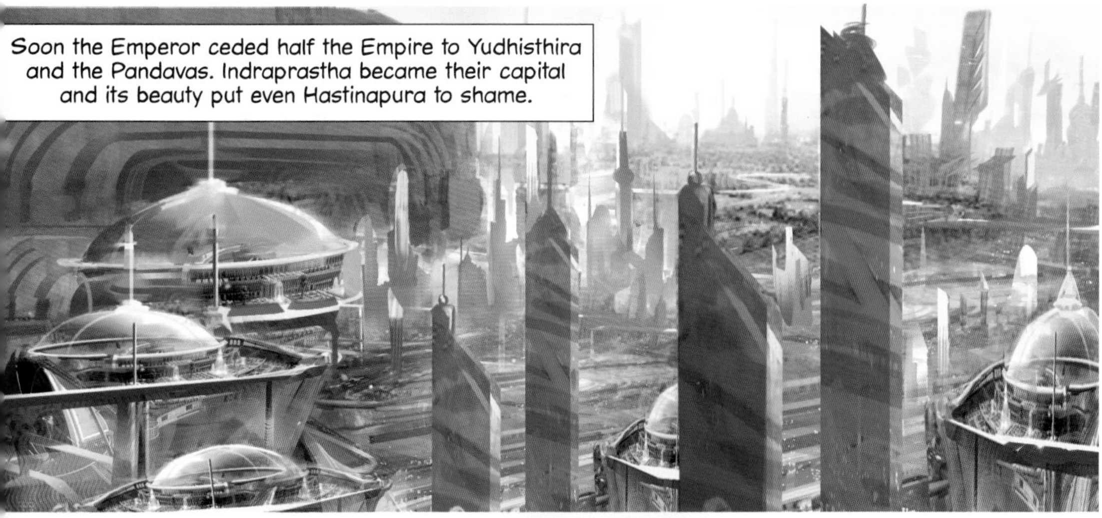
Soon the Emperor ceded half the Empire to Yudhisthira and the Pandavas. Indraprastha became their capital and its beauty put even Hastinapura to shame.

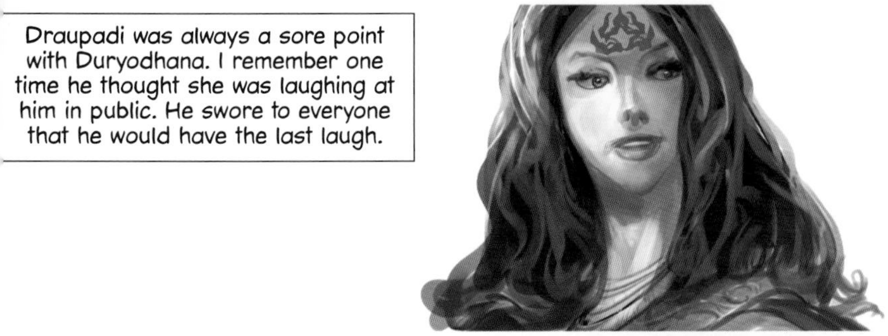
Draupadi was always a sore point with Duryodhana. I remember one time he thought she was laughing at him in public. He swore to everyone that he would have the last laugh.

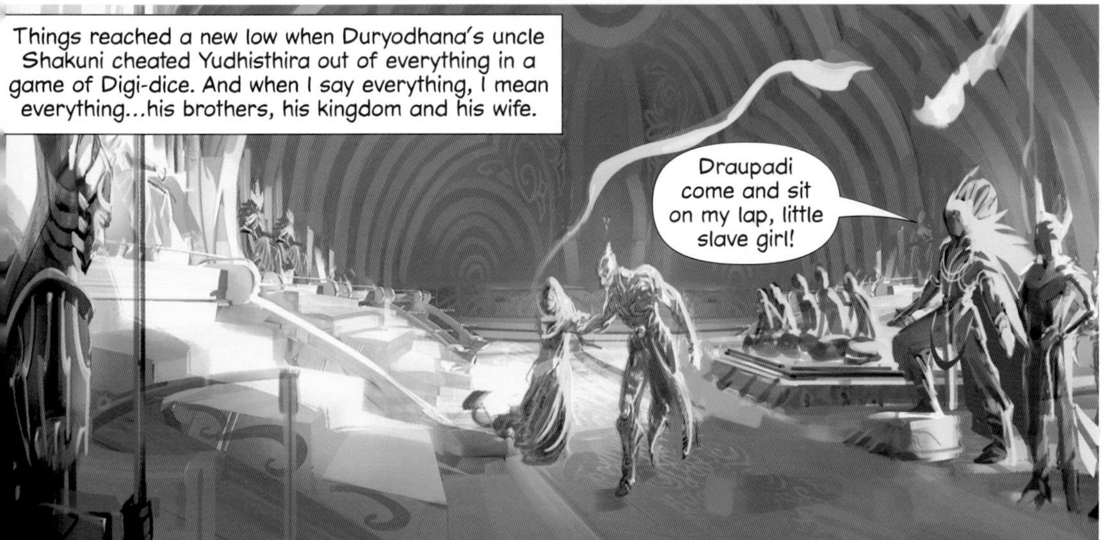
Things reached a new low when Duryodhana's uncle Shakuni cheated Yudhisthira out of everything in a game of Digi-dice. And when I say everything, I mean everything...his brothers, his kingdom and his wife.
Draupadi come and sit on my lap, little slave girl!

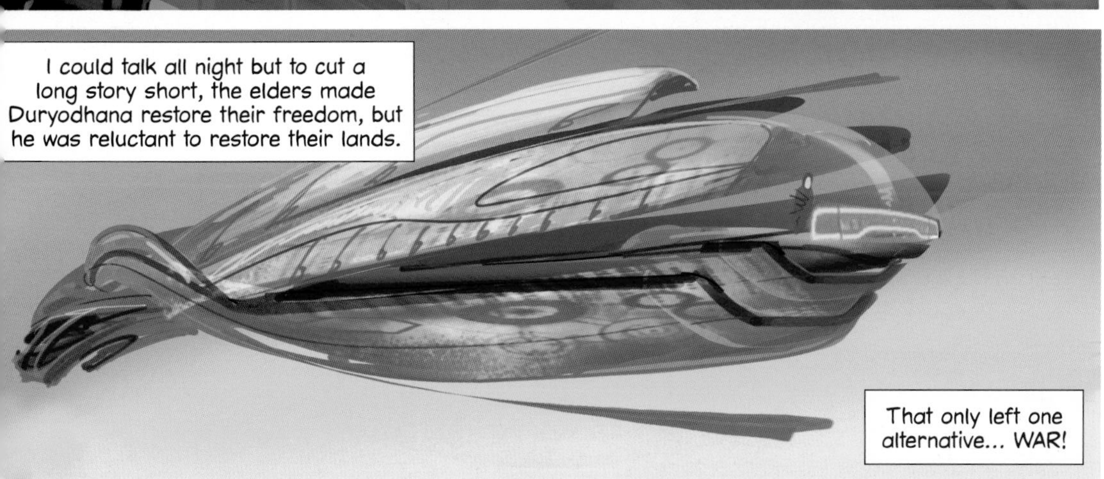
I could talk all night but to cut a long story short, the elders made Duryodhana restore their freedom, but he was reluctant to restore their lands.
That only left one alternative... WAR!

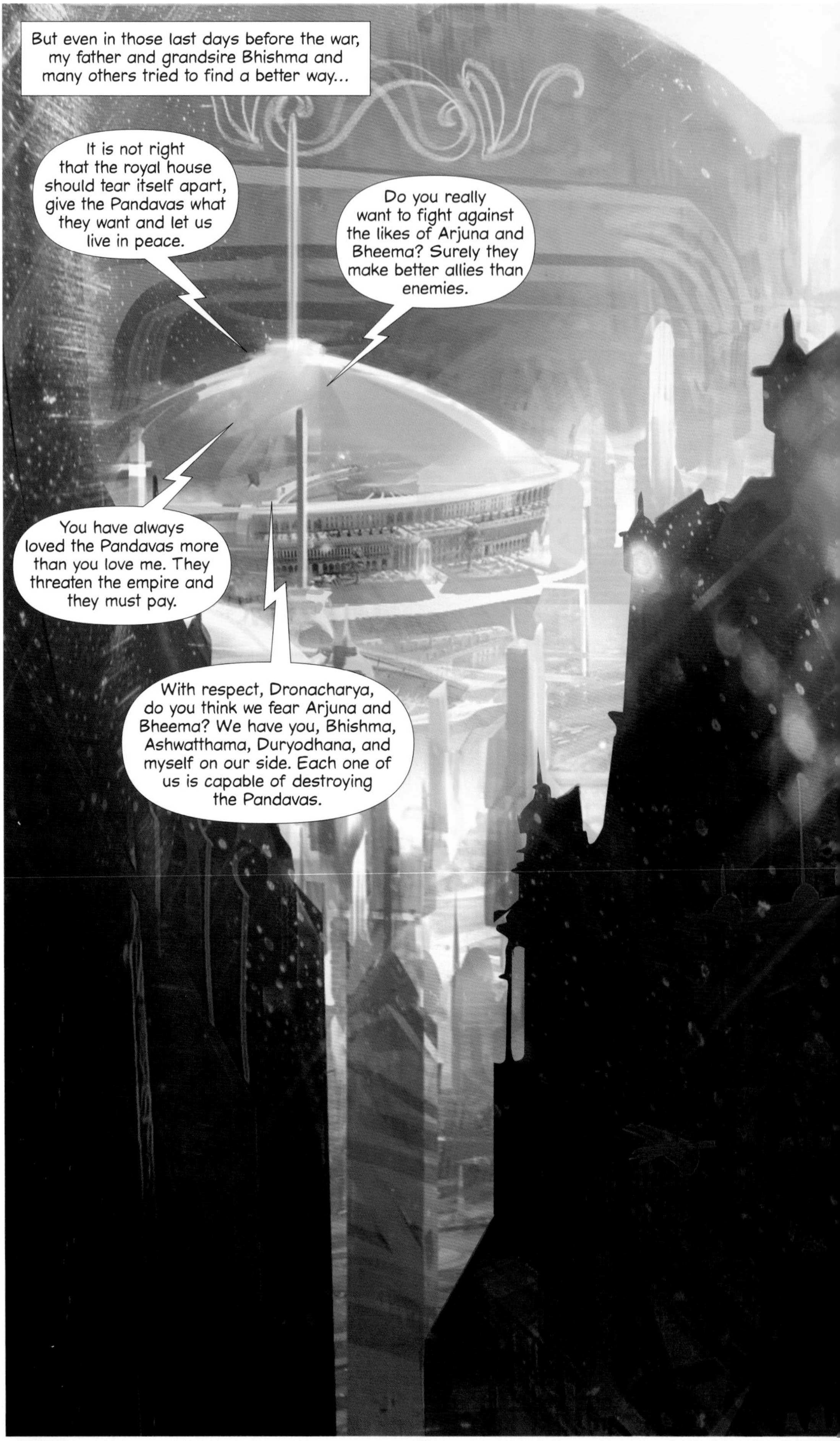

But even in those last days before the war, my father and grandsire Bhishma and many others tried to find a better way...
It is not right that the royal house should tear itself apart, give the Pandavas what they want and let us live in peace.
Do you really want to fight against the likes of Arjuna and Bheema? Surely they make better allies than enemies.
You have always loved the Pandavas more than you love me. They threaten the empire and they must pay.
With respect, Dronacharya, do you think we fear Arjuna and Bheema? We have you, Bhishma, Ashwatthama, Duryodhana, and myself on our side. Each one of us is capable of destroying the Pandavas.

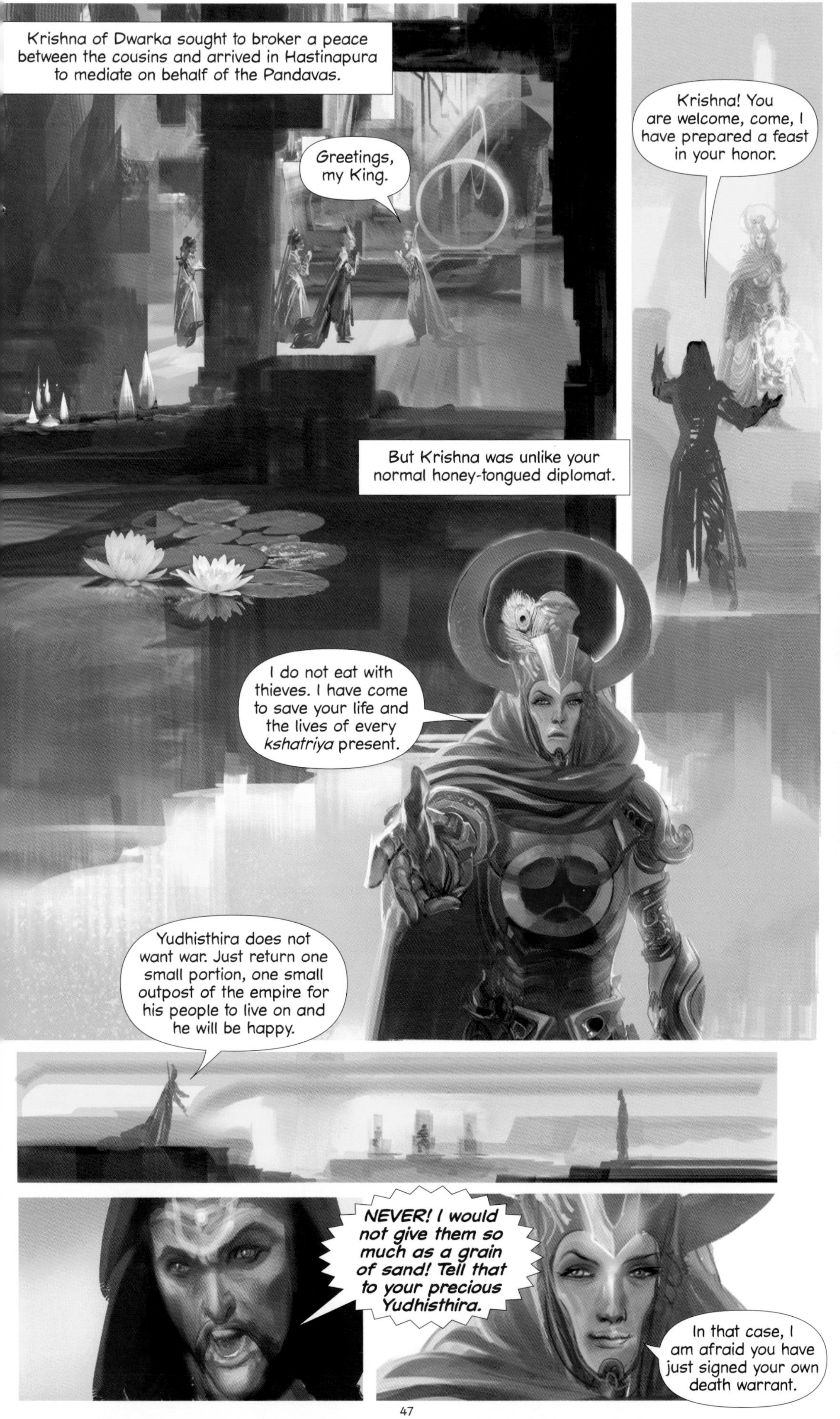

Krishna of Dwarka sought to broker a peace between the cousins and arrived in Hastinapura to mediate on behalf of the Pandavas.
Greetings, my King.
Krishna! You are welcome, come, I have prepared a feast in your honor.
But Krishna was unlike your normal honey-tongued diplomat.
I do not eat with thieves. I have come to save your life and the lives of every *kshatriya* present.
Yudhisthira does not want war. Just return one small portion, one small outpost of the empire for his people to live on and he will be happy.
NEVER! I would not give them so much as a grain of sand! Tell that to your precious Yudhisthira.
In that case, I am afraid you have just signed your own death warrant.

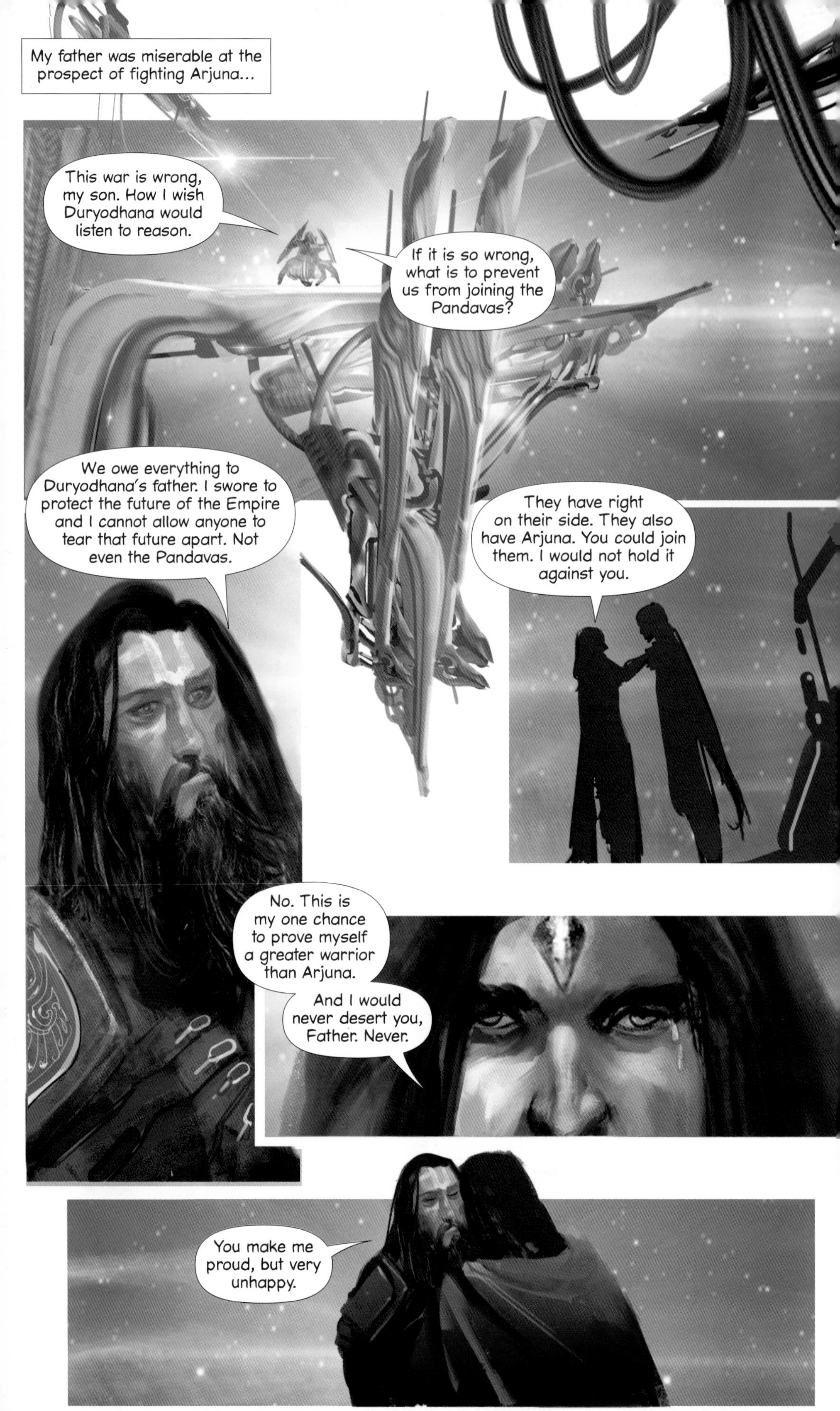
My father was miserable at the prospect of fighting Arjuna...
This war is wrong, my son. How I wish Duryodhana would listen to reason.
If it is so wrong, what is to prevent us from joining the Pandavas?
We owe everything to Duryodhana's father. I swore to protect the future of the Empire and I cannot allow anyone to tear that future apart. Not even the Pandavas.
They have right on their side. They also have Arjuna. You could join them. I would not hold it against you.
No. This is my one chance to prove myself a greater warrior than Arjuna.
And I would never desert you, Father. Never.
You make me proud, but very unhappy.

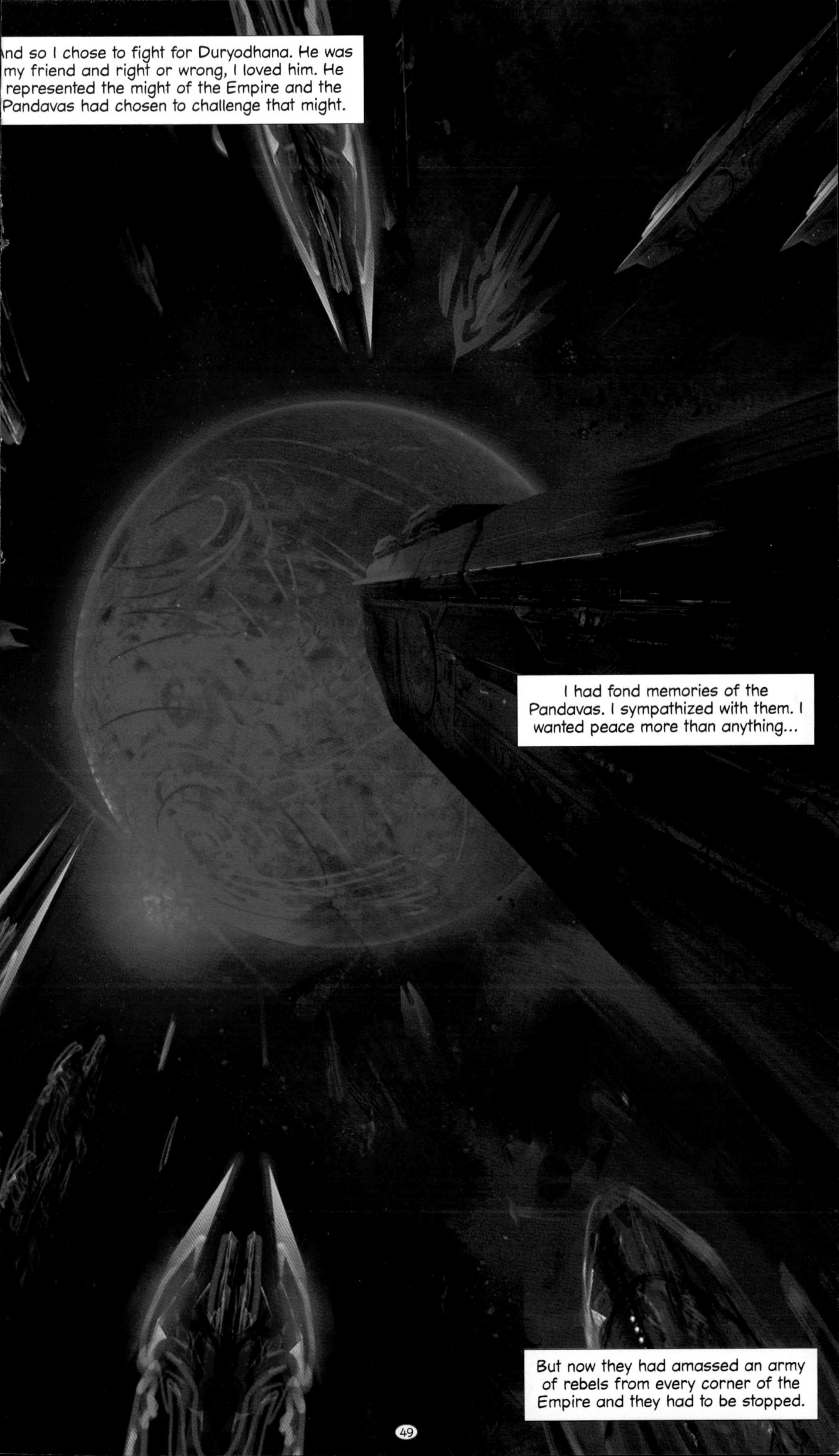

And so I chose to fight for Duryodhana. He was my friend and right or wrong, I loved him. He represented the might of the Empire and the Pandavas had chosen to challenge that might.
I had fond memories of the Pandavas. I sympathized with them. I wanted peace more than anything...
But now they had amassed an army of rebels from every corner of the Empire and they had to be stopped.

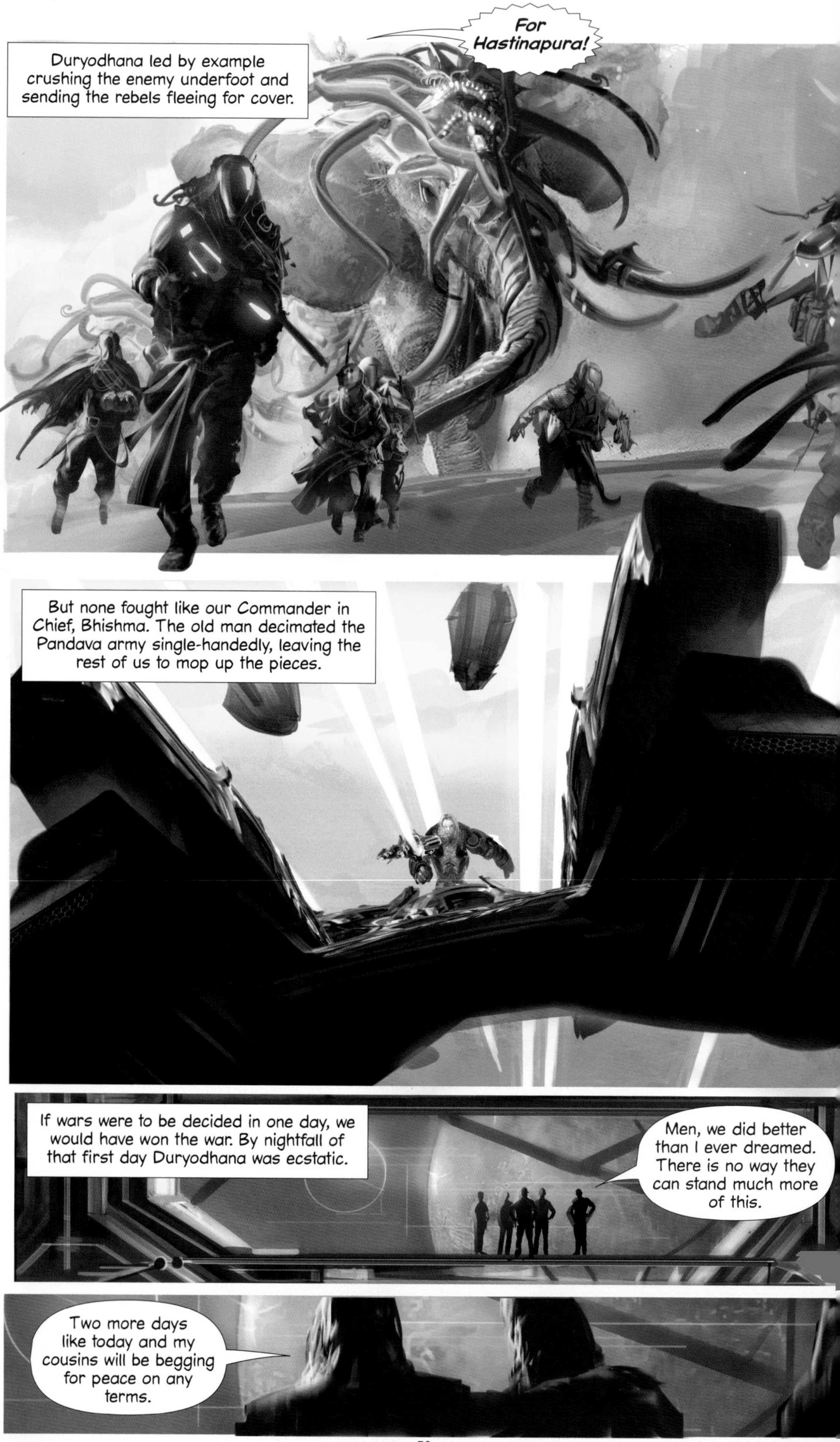
Duryodhana led by example crushing the enemy underfoot and sending the rebels fleeing for cover.
For Hastinapura!
But none fought like our Commander in Chief, Bhishma. The old man decimated the Pandava army single-handedly, leaving the rest of us to mop up the pieces.
If wars were to be decided in one day, we would have won the war. By nightfall of that first day Duryodhana was ecstatic.
Men, we did better than I ever dreamed. There is no way they can stand much more of this.
Two more days like today and my cousins will be begging for peace on any terms.

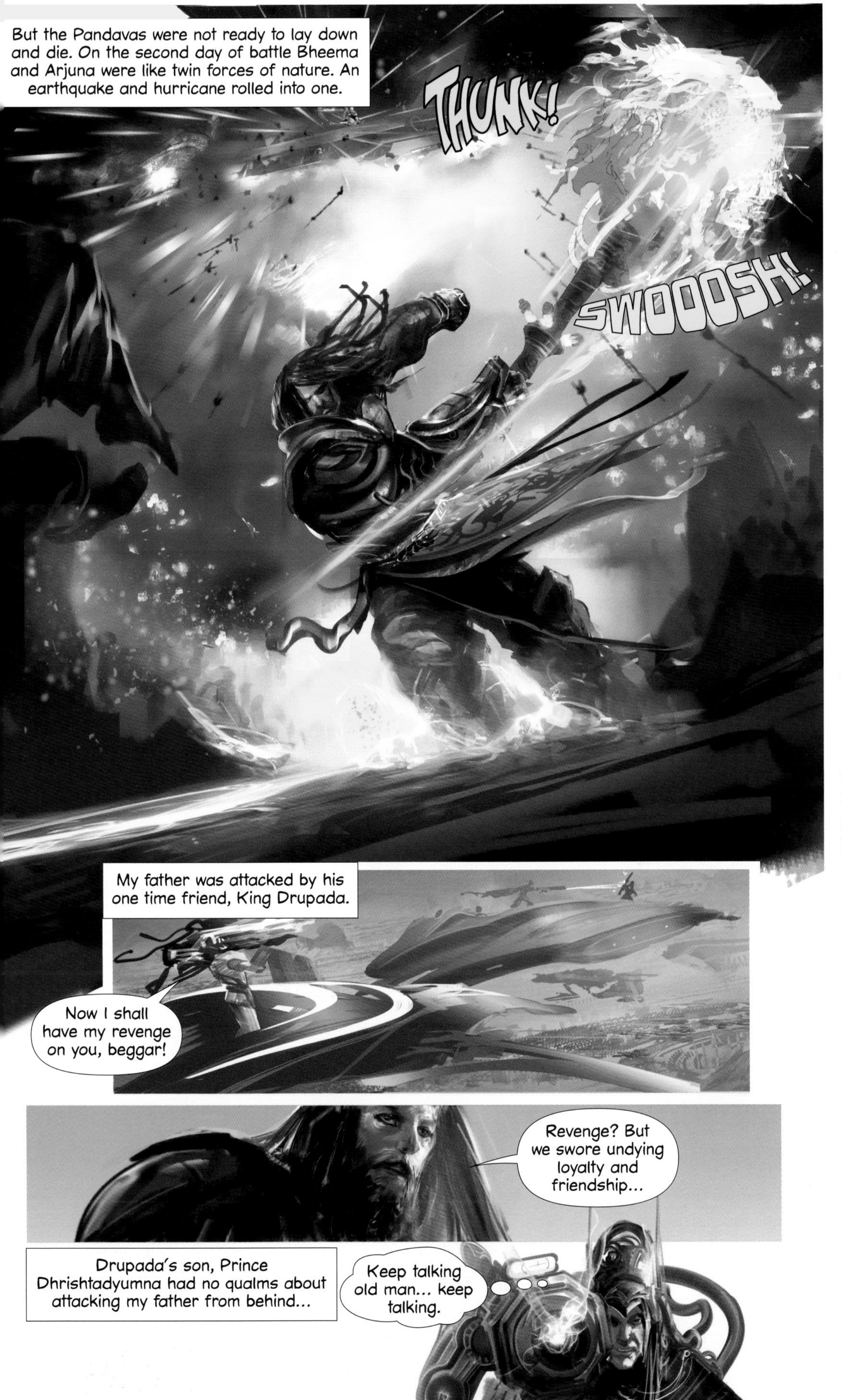
But the Pandavas were not ready to lay down and die. On the second day of battle Bheema and Arjuna were like twin forces of nature. An earthquake and hurricane rolled into one.
THUNK!
SWOOOSH!
My father was attacked by his one time friend, King Drupada.
Now I shall have my revenge on you, beggar!
Revenge? But we swore undying loyalty and friendship...
Drupada's son, Prince Dhrishtadyumna had no qualms about attacking my father from behind...
Keep talking old man... keep talking.

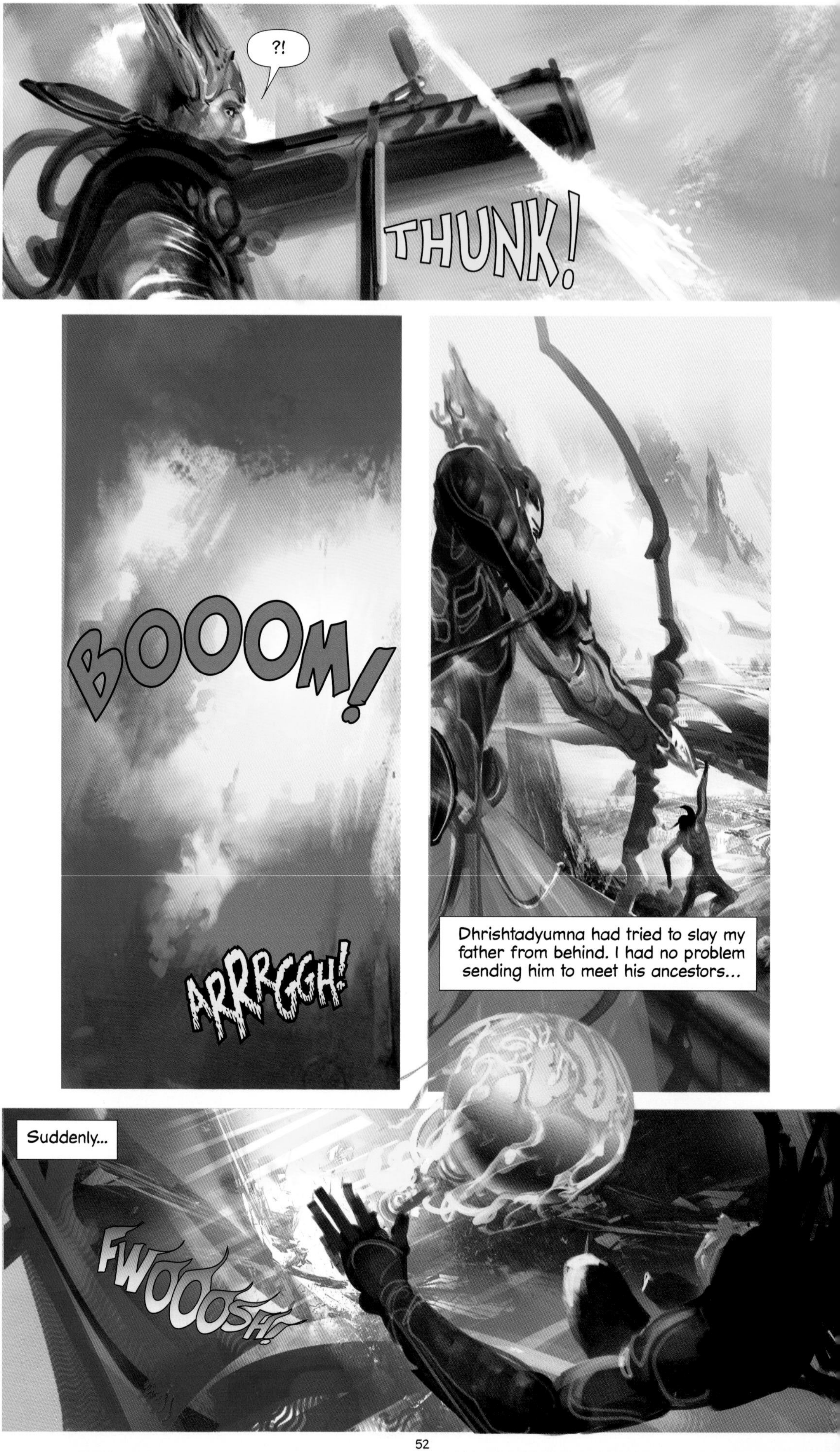
?!
THUNK!
BOOOM!
ARRRGGH!
Dhrishtadyumna had tried to slay my father from behind. I had no problem sending him to meet his ancestors...
Suddenly...
FWOOOOSH!

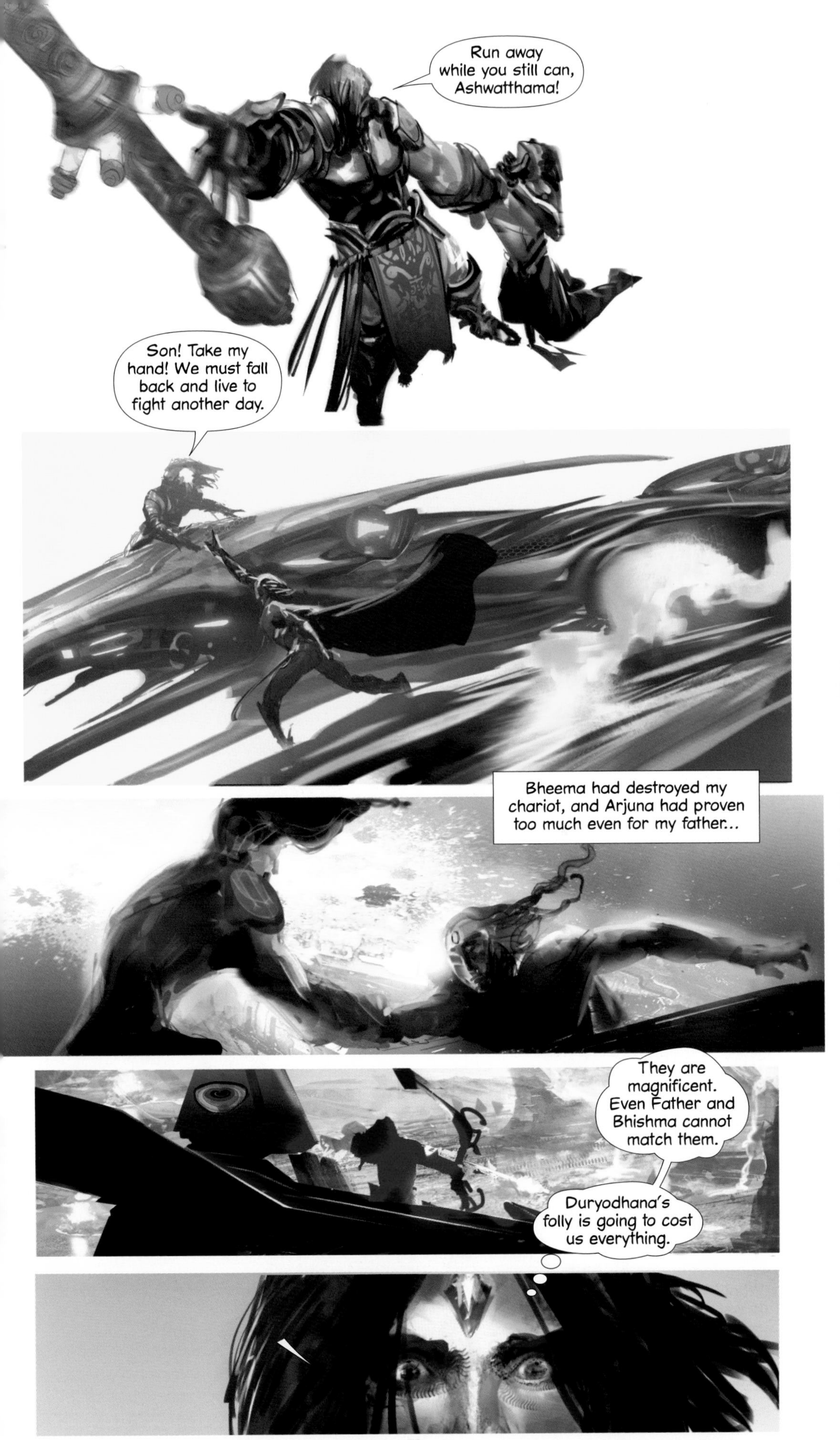
Run away while you still can, Ashwatthama!
Son! Take my hand! We must fall back and live to fight another day.
Bheema had destroyed my chariot, and Arjuna had proven too much even for my father...
They are magnificent. Even Father and Bhishma cannot match them.
Duryodhana's folly is going to cost us everything.

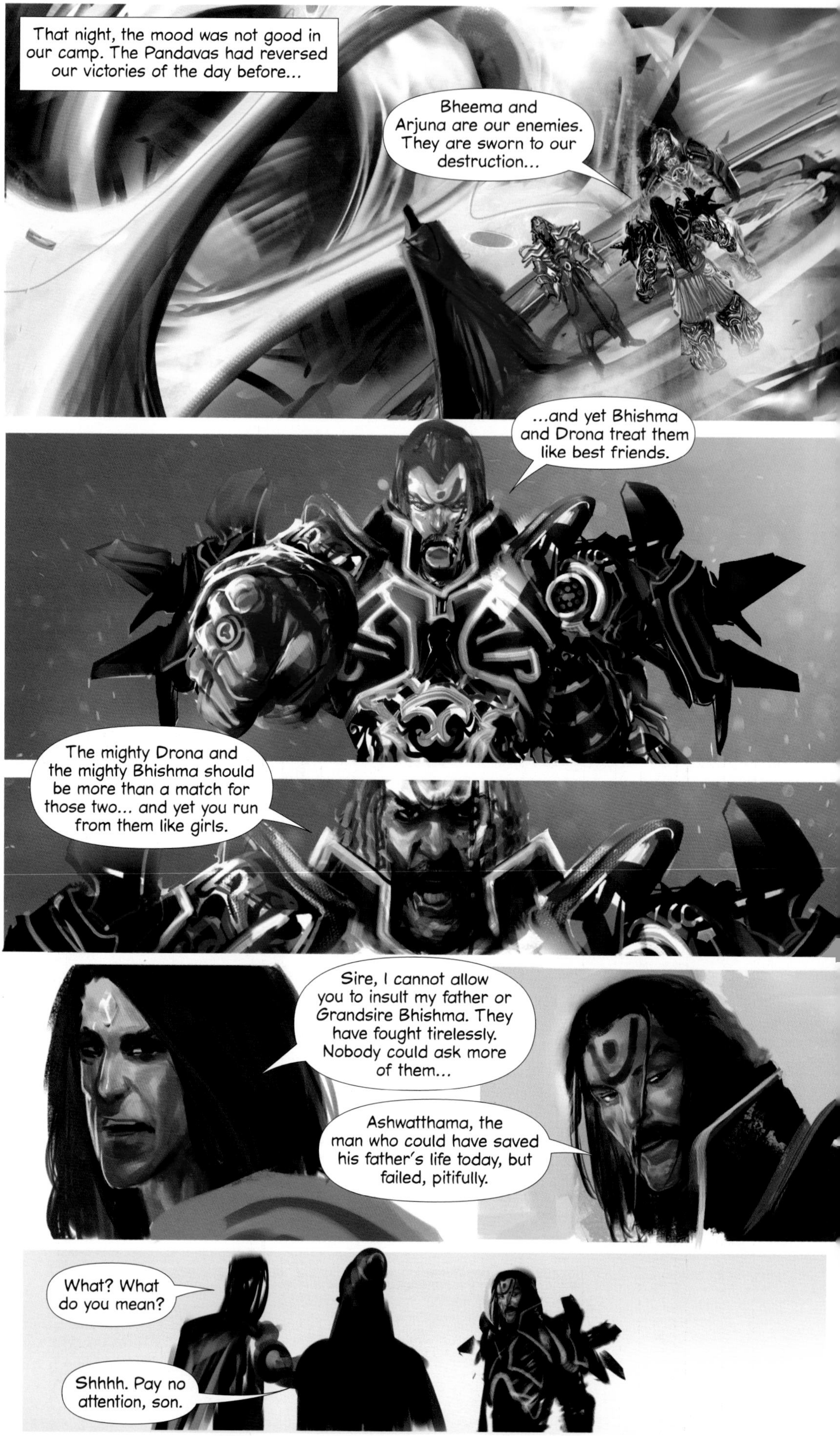
That night, the mood was not good in our camp. The Pandavas had reversed our victories of the day before...
Bheema and Arjuna are our enemies. They are sworn to our destruction...
...and yet Bhishma and Drona treat them like best friends.
The mighty Drona and the mighty Bhishma should be more than a match for those two... and yet you run from them like girls.
Sire, I cannot allow you to insult my father or Grandsire Bhishma. They have fought tirelessly. Nobody could ask more of them...
Ashwatthama, the man who could have saved his father's life today, but failed, pitifully.
What? What do you mean?
Shhhh. Pay no attention, son.

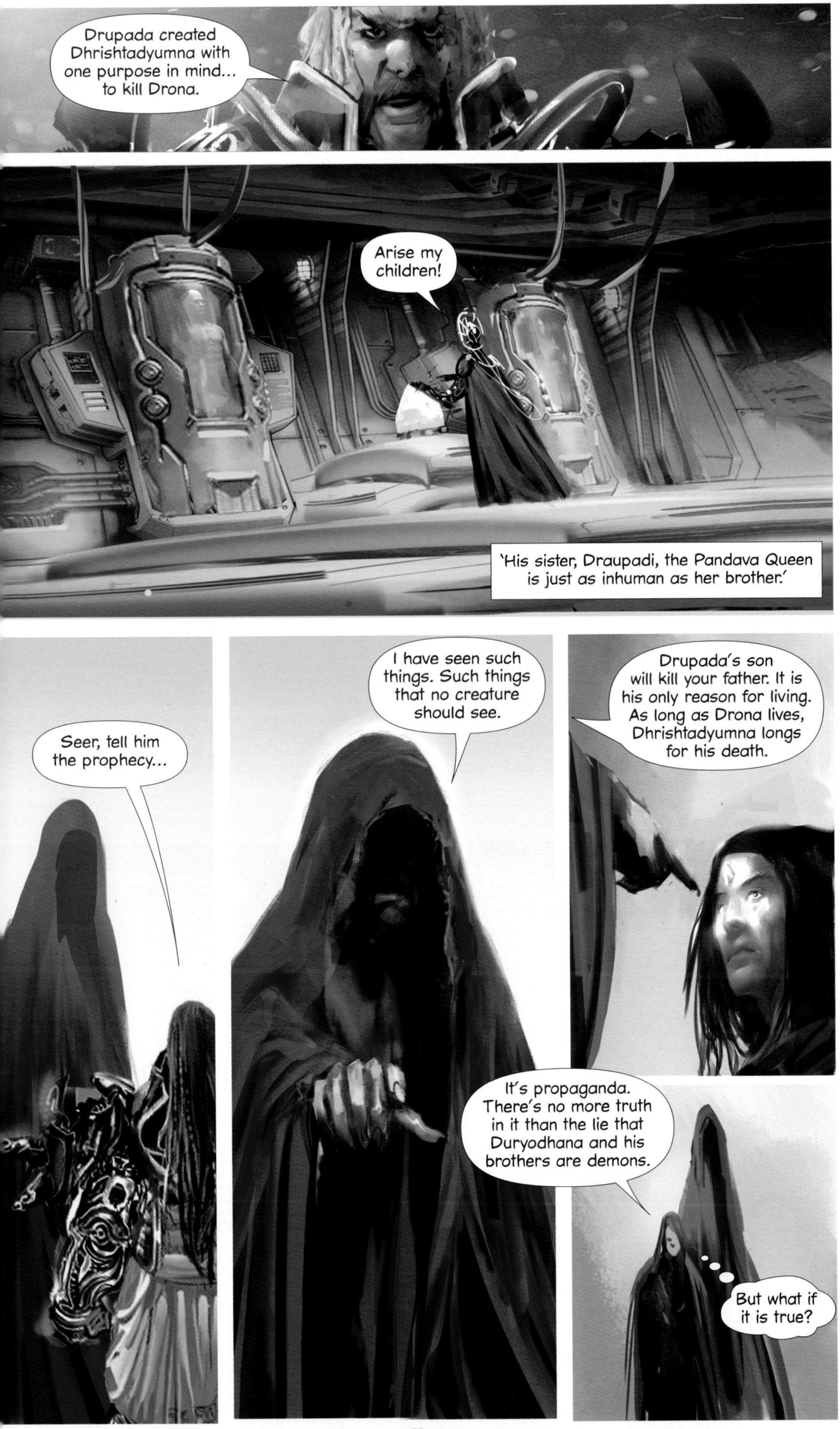
Drupada created Dhrishtadyumna with one purpose in mind... to kill Drona.
Arise my children!
'His sister, Draupadi, the Pandava Queen is just as inhuman as her brother.'
Seer, tell him the prophecy...
I have seen such things. Such things that no creature should see.
Drupada's son will kill your father. It is his only reason for living. As long as Drona lives, Dhrishtadyumna longs for his death.
It's propaganda. There's no more truth in it than the lie that Duryodhana and his brothers are demons.
But what if it is true?

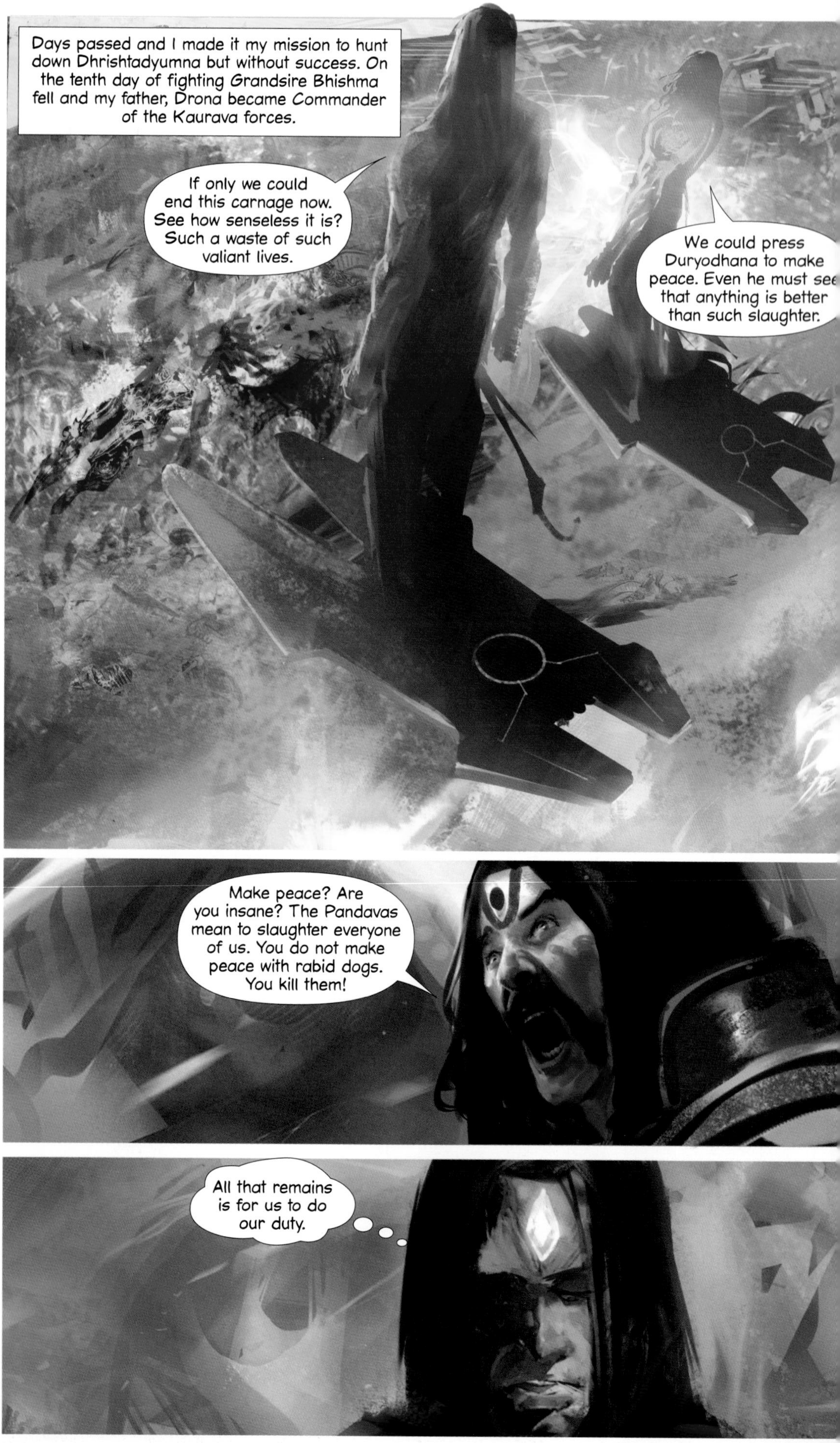
Days passed and I made it my mission to hunt down Dhrishtadyumna but without success. On the tenth day of fighting Grandsire Bhishma fell and my father, Drona became Commander of the Kaurava forces.
If only we could end this carnage now. See how senseless it is? Such a waste of such valiant lives.
We could press Duryodhana to make peace. Even he must see that anything is better than such slaughter.
Make peace? Are you insane? The Pandavas mean to slaughter everyone of us. You do not make peace with rabid dogs. You kill them!
All that remains is for us to do our duty.

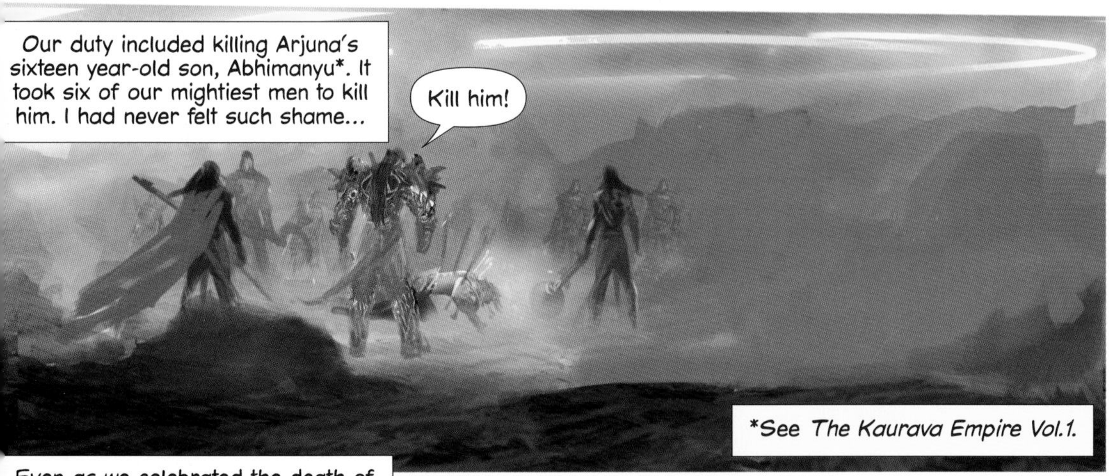
Our duty included killing Arjuna's sixteen year-old son, Abhimanyu*. It took six of our mightiest men to kill him. I had never felt such shame...
Kill him!
*See The Kaurava Empire Vol.1.

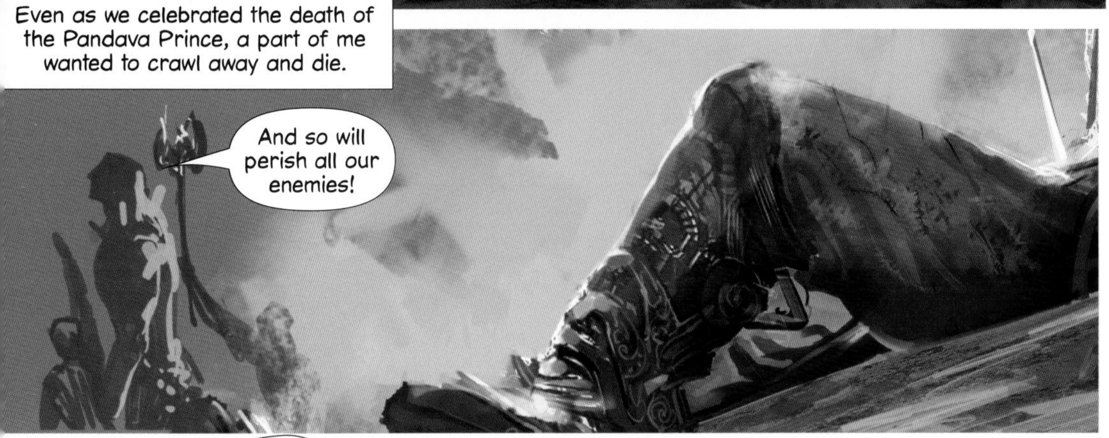
Even as we celebrated the death of the Pandava Prince, a part of me wanted to crawl away and die.
And so will perish all our enemies!

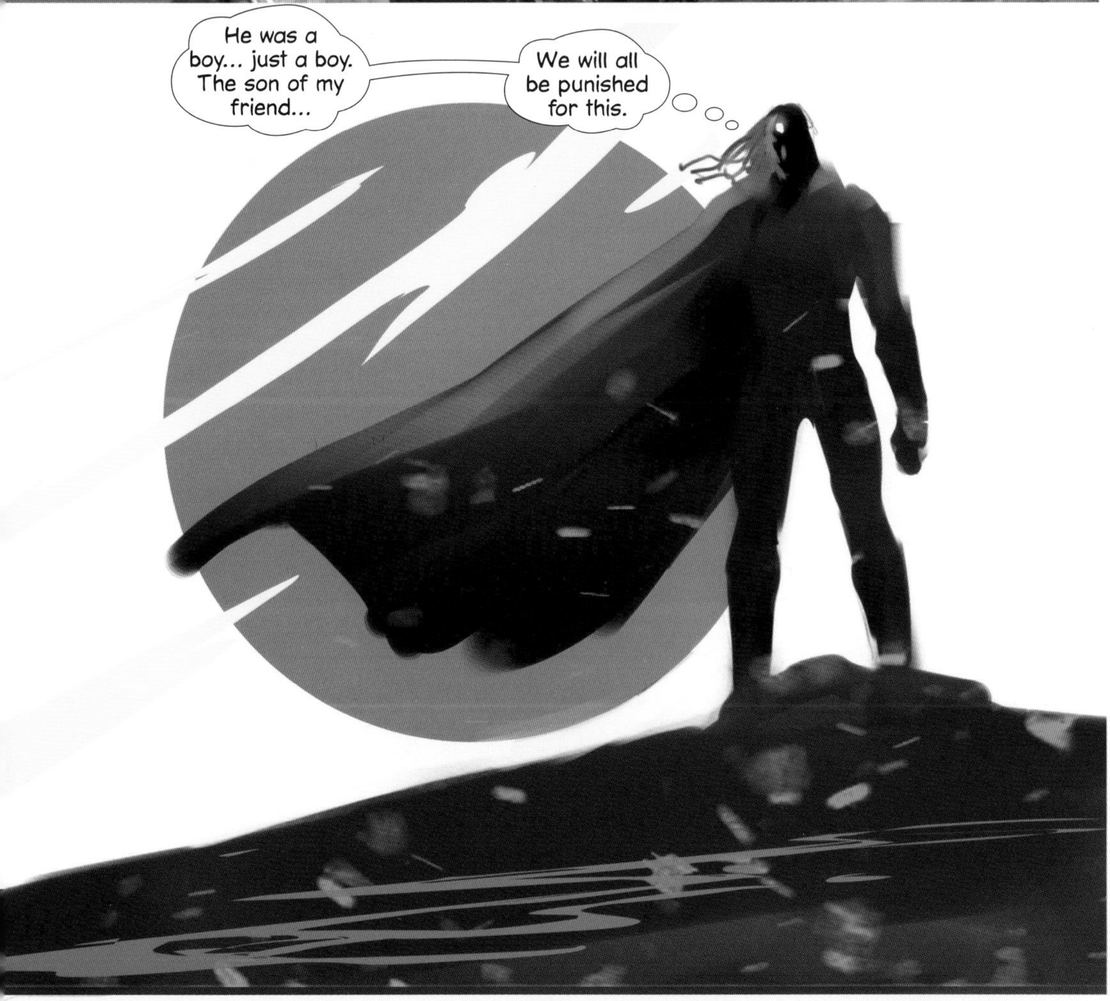
He was a boy... just a boy. The son of my friend...
We will all be punished for this.

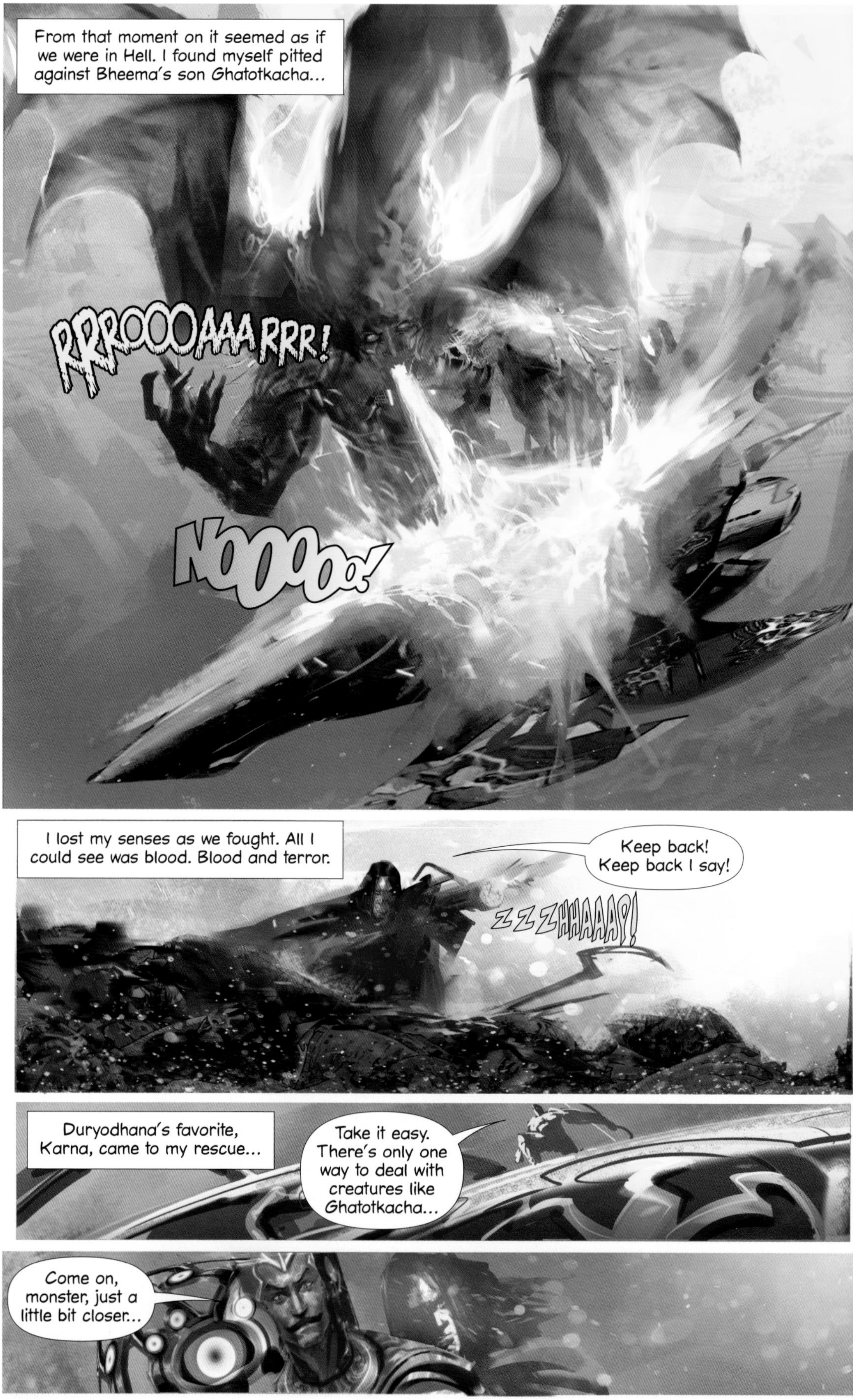
From that moment on it seemed as if we were in Hell. I found myself pitted against Bheema's son Ghatotkacha...
RRROOOAAARRR!
NOOOOO!
I lost my senses as we fought. All I could see was blood. Blood and terror.
Keep back! Keep back I say!
ZZZHHAAAP!
Duryodhana's favorite, Karna, came to my rescue...
Take it easy. There's only one way to deal with creatures like Ghatotkacha...
Come on, monster, just a little bit closer...

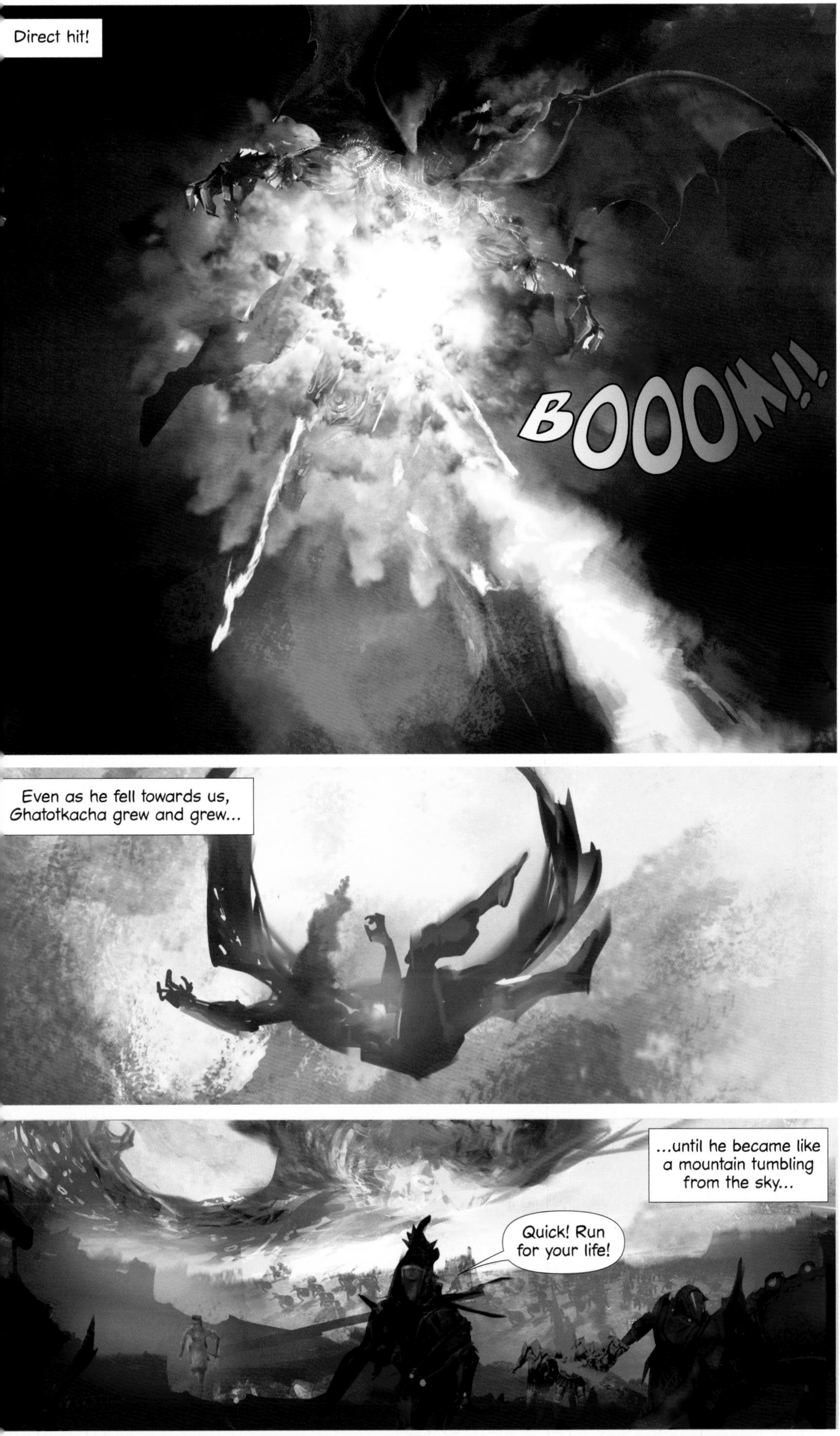
Direct hit!
BOOOM!!
Even as he fell towards us, Ghatotkacha grew and grew...
...until he became like a mountain tumbling from the sky...
Quick! Run for your life!

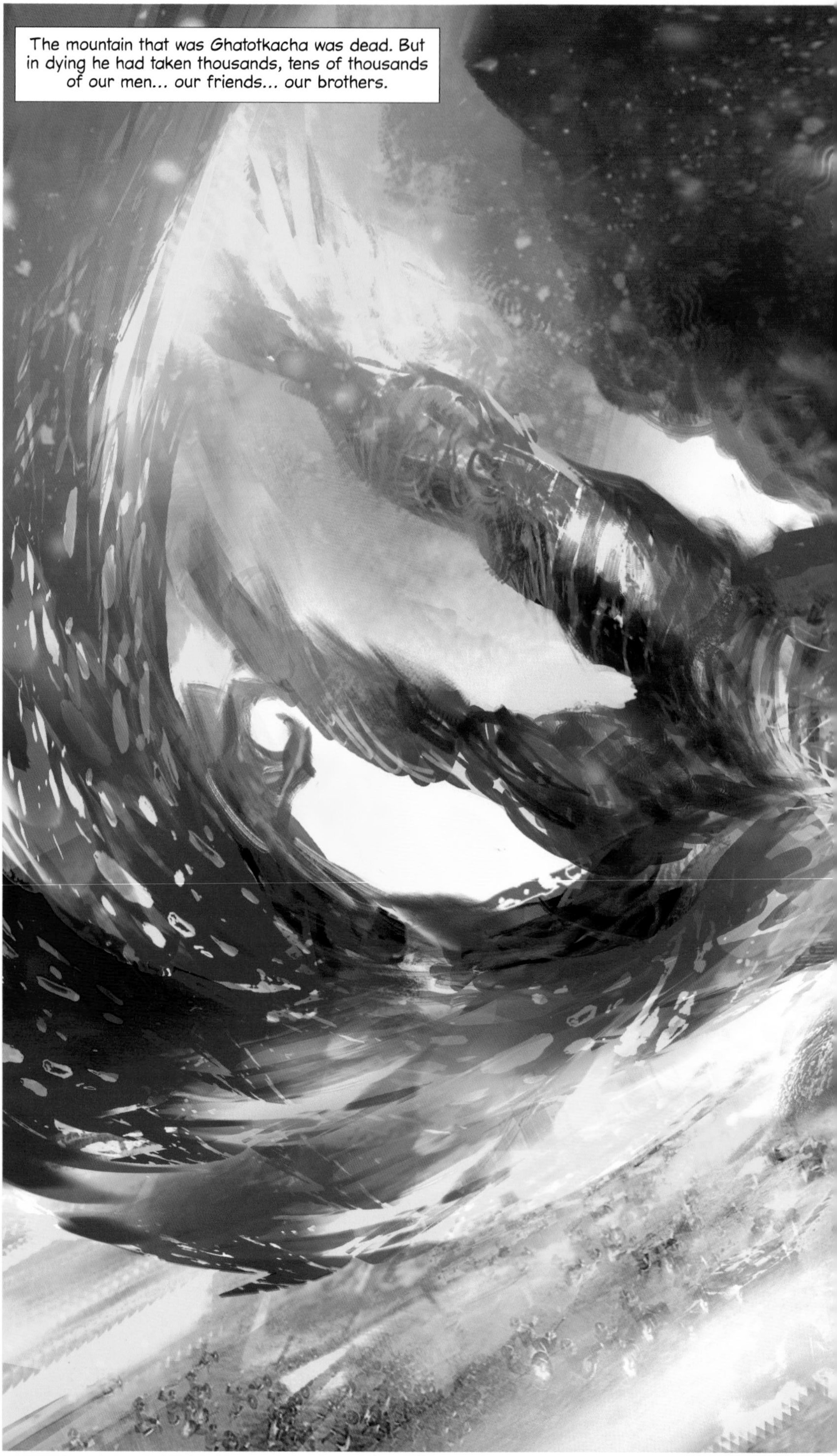
The mountain that was Ghatotkacha was dead. But in dying he had taken thousands, tens of thousands of our men... our friends... our brothers.

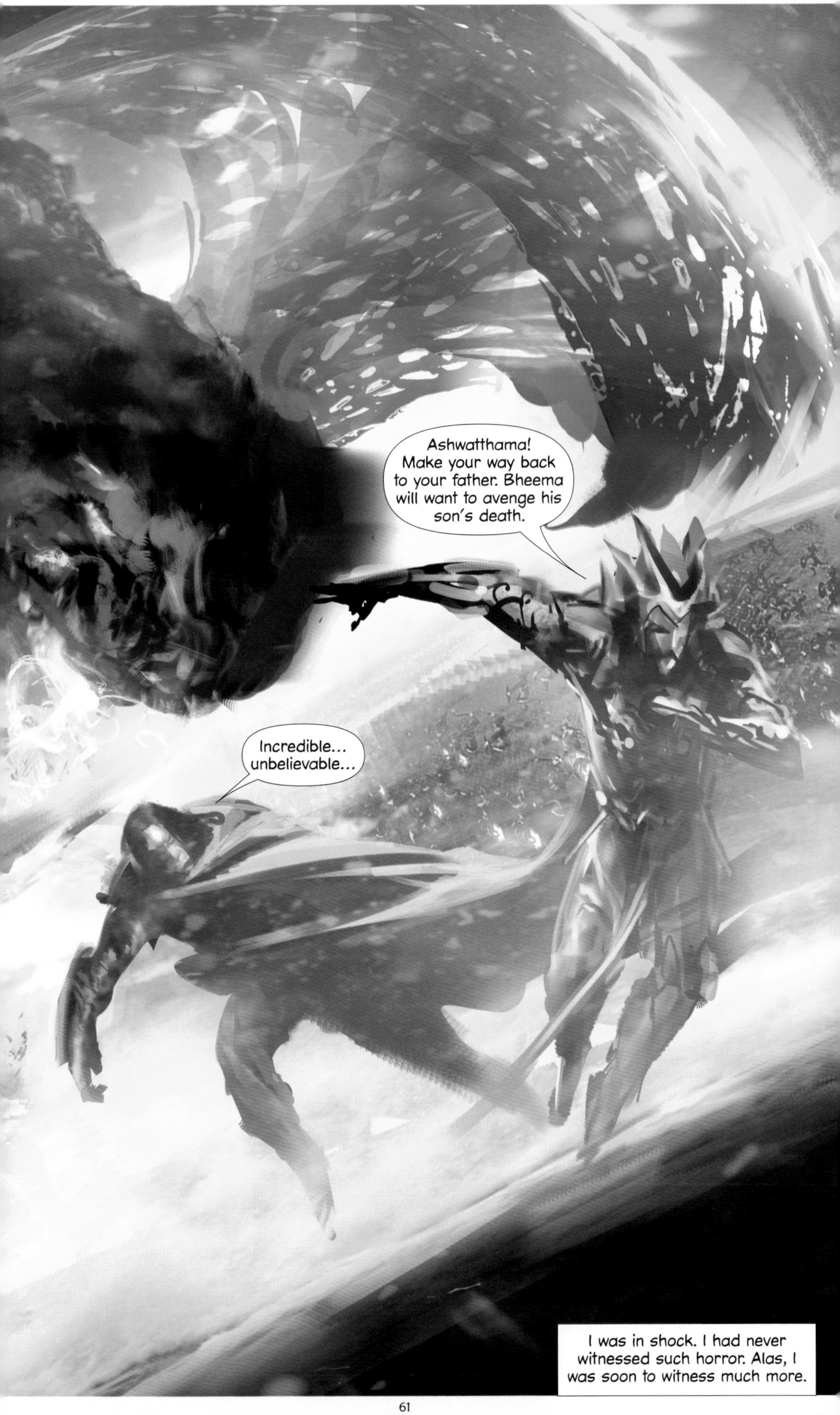
Ashwatthama! Make your way back to your father. Bheema will want to avenge his son's death.
Incredible... unbelievable...
I was in shock. I had never witnessed such horror. Alas, I was soon to witness much more.

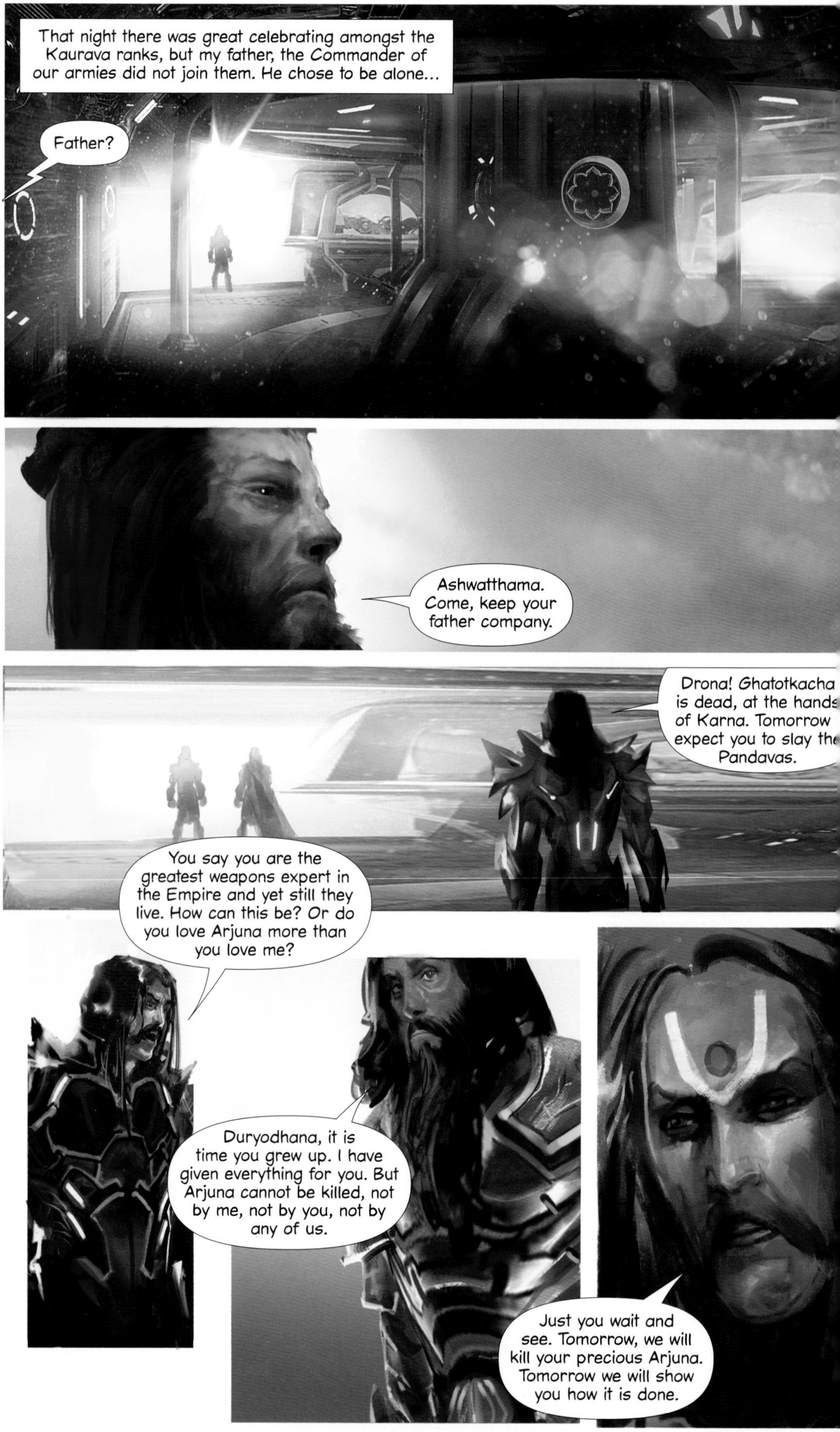
That night there was great celebrating amongst the Kaurava ranks, but my father, the Commander of our armies did not join them. He chose to be alone...
Father?
Ashwatthama. Come, keep your father company.
Drona! Ghatotkacha is dead, at the hands of Karna. Tomorrow I expect you to slay the Pandavas.
You say you are the greatest weapons expert in the Empire and yet still they live. How can this be? Or do you love Arjuna more than you love me?
Duryodhana, it is time you grew up. I have given everything for you. But Arjuna cannot be killed, not by me, not by you, not by any of us.
Just you wait and see. Tomorrow, we will kill your precious Arjuna. Tomorrow we will show you how it is done.

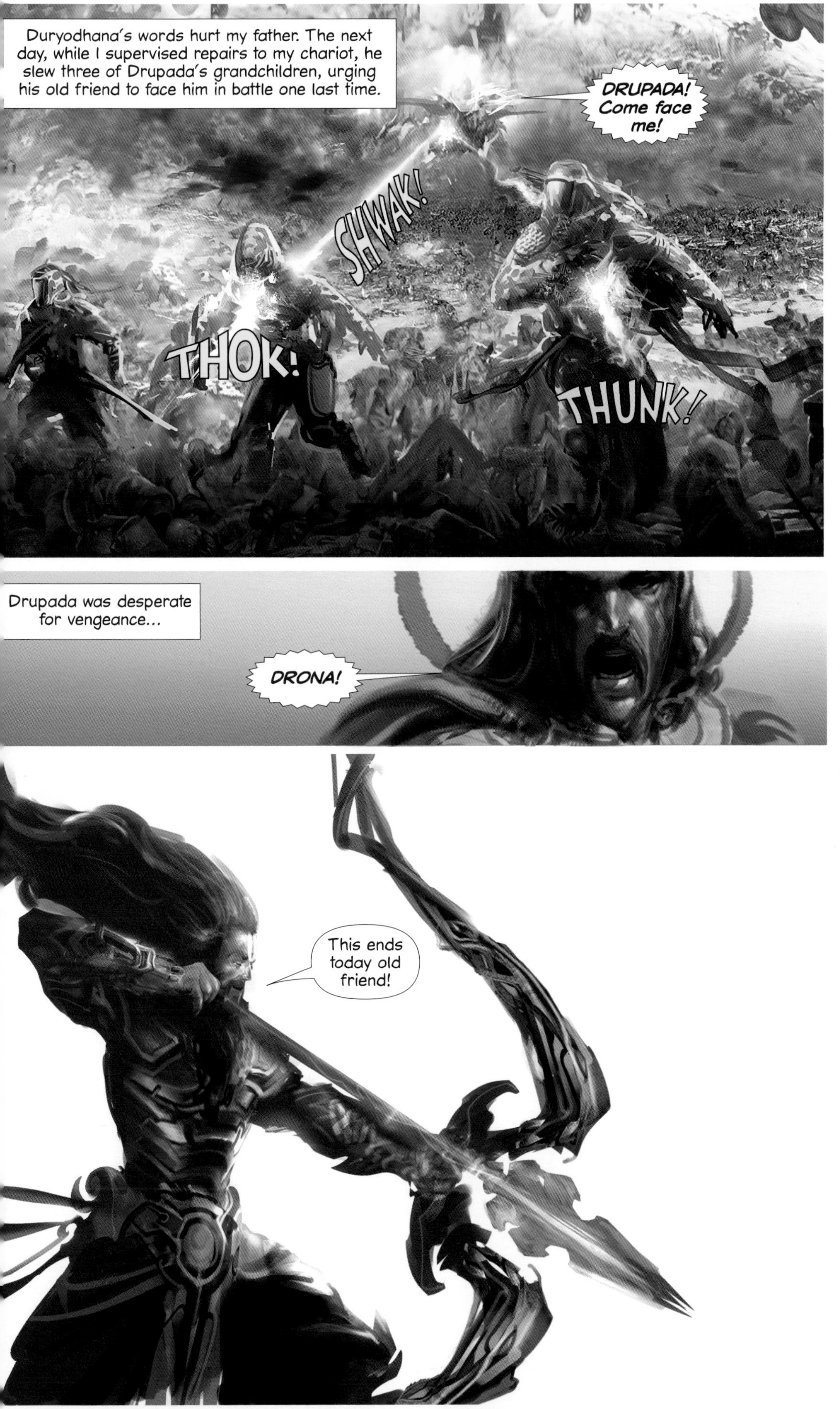

Duryodhana's words hurt my father. The next day, while I supervised repairs to my chariot, he slew three of Drupada's grandchildren, urging his old friend to face him in battle one last time.
DRUPADA! Come face me!
SHWAK!
THOK!
THUNK!
Drupada was desperate for vengeance...
DRONA!
This ends today old friend!

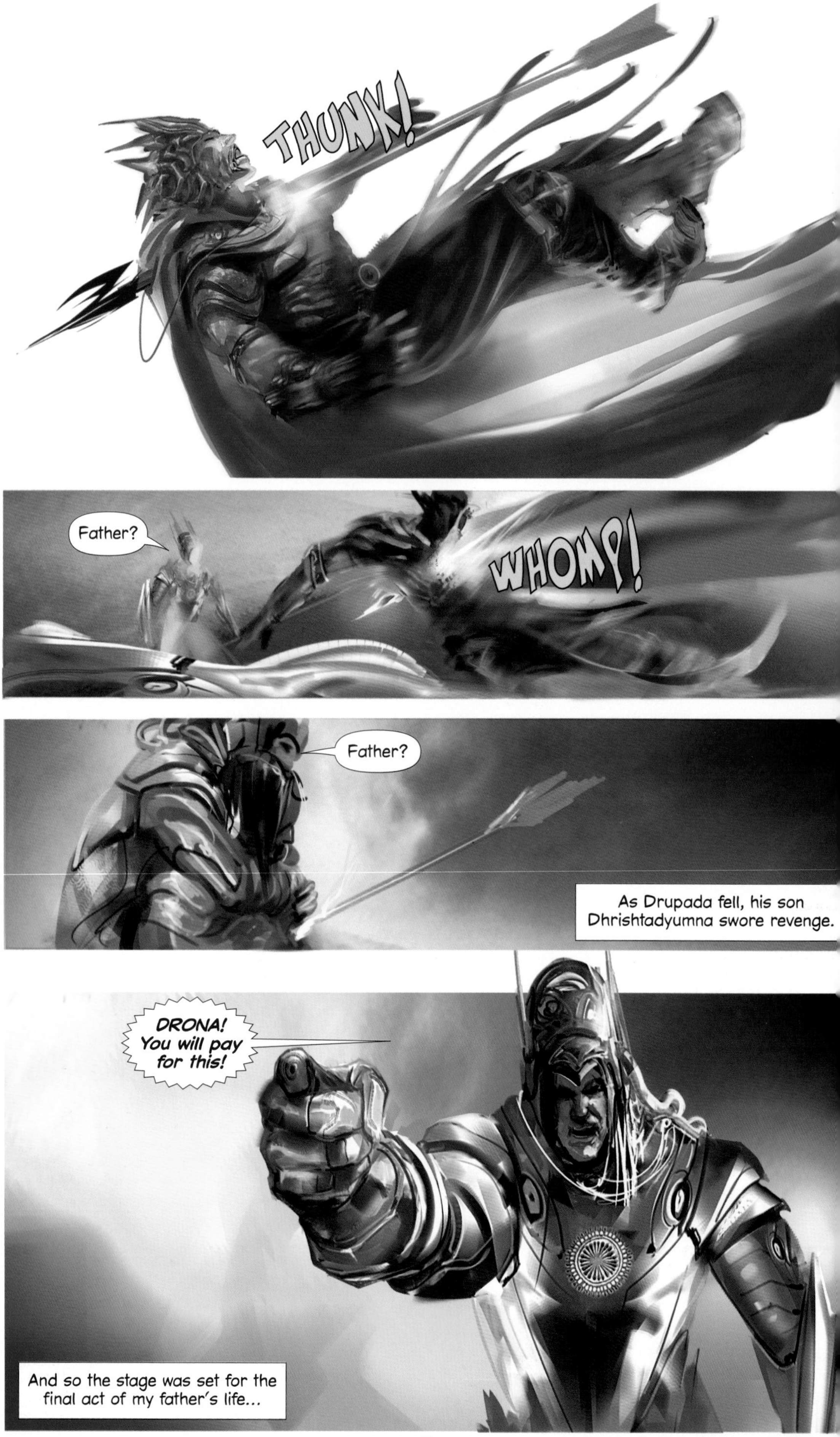
THUNK!
Father?
WHOMP!
Father?
As Drupada fell, his son Dhrishtadyumna swore revenge.
DRONA! You will pay for this!
And so the stage was set for the final act of my father's life...

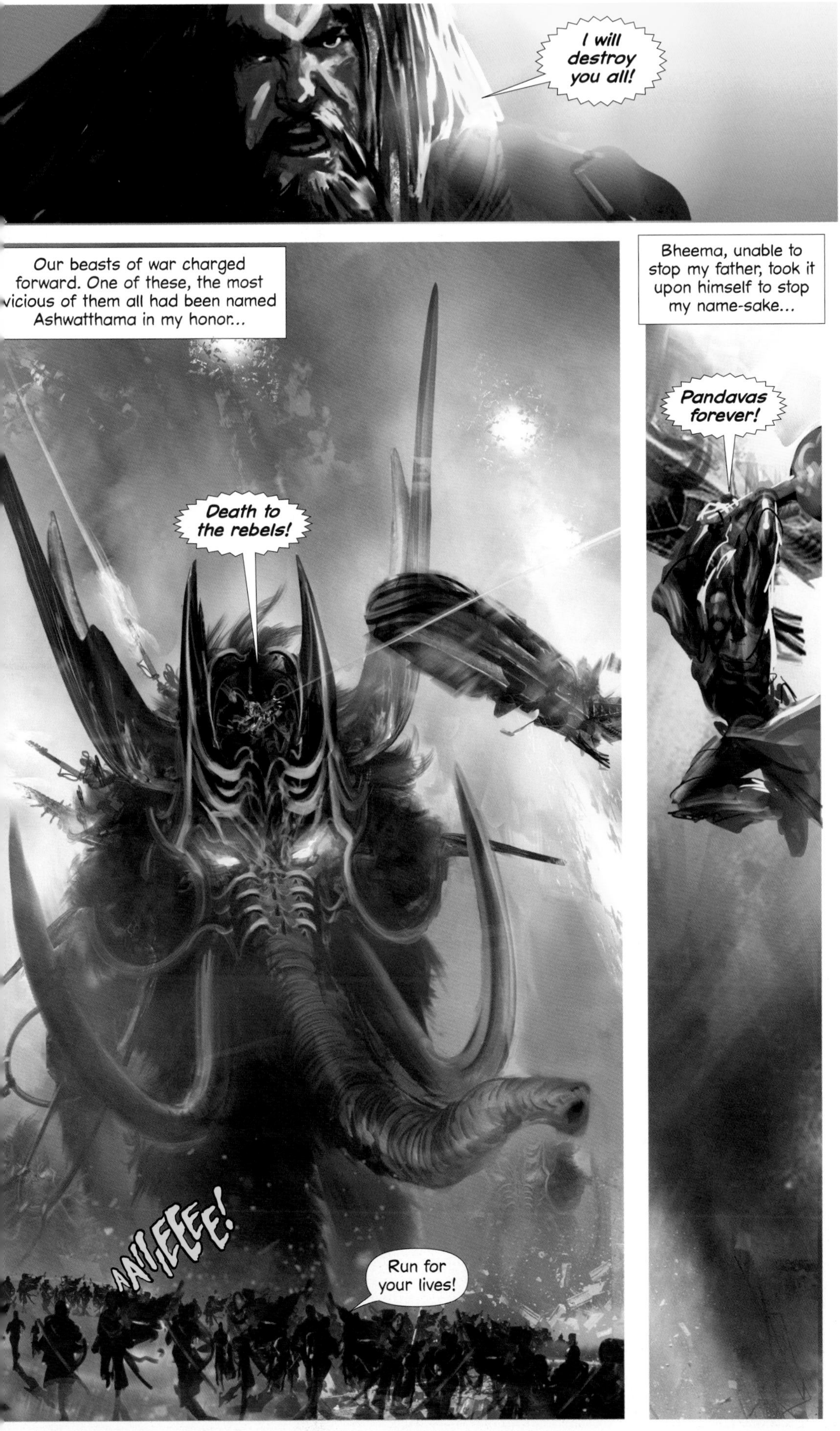
I will destroy you all!
Our beasts of war charged forward. One of these, the most vicious of them all had been named Ashwatthama in my honor...
Death to the rebels!
AAIIEEEE!
Run for your lives!
Bheema, unable to stop my father, took it upon himself to stop my name-sake...
Pandavas forever!

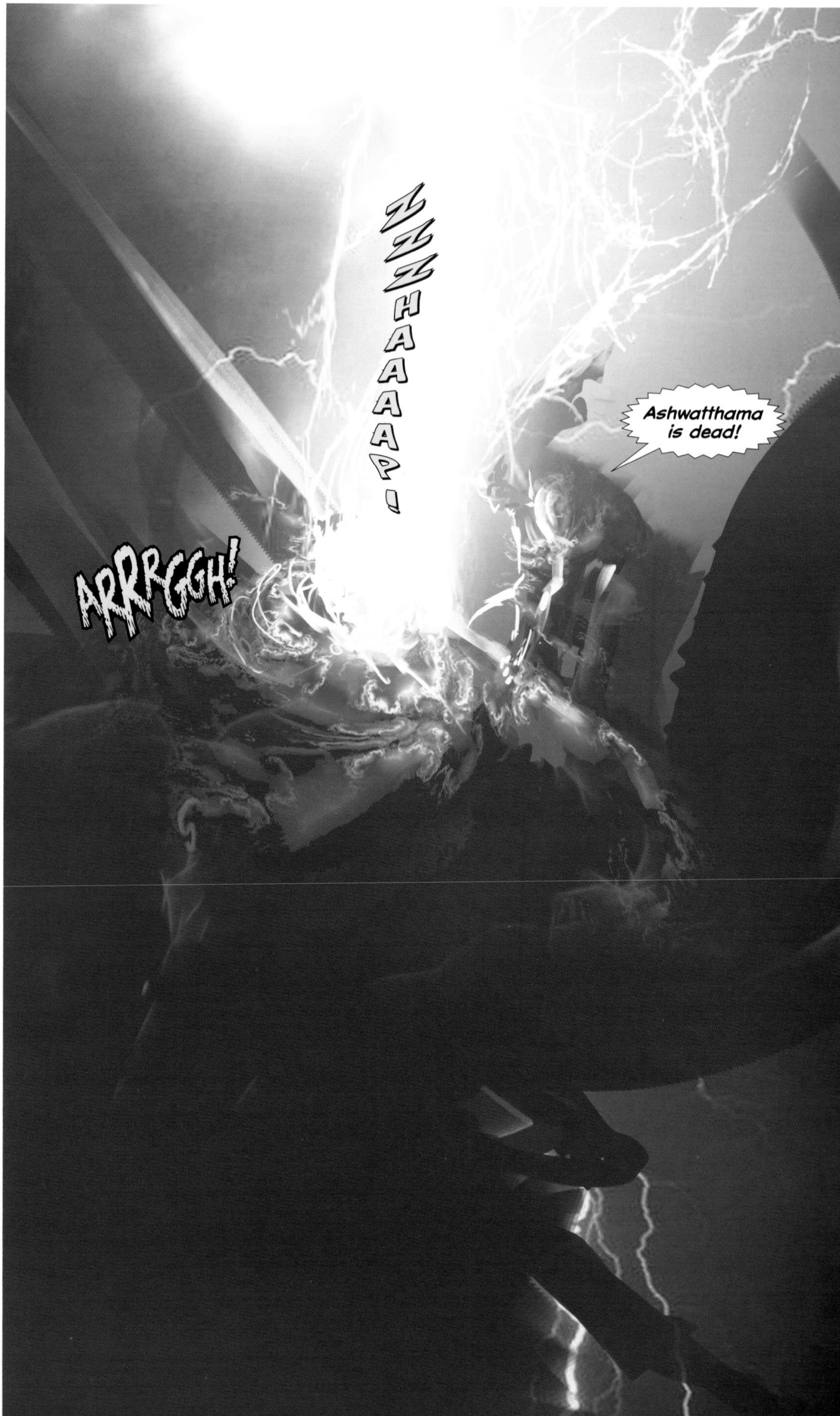
ZZZHAAAAAP!
Ashwatthama is dead!
ARRRGGH!

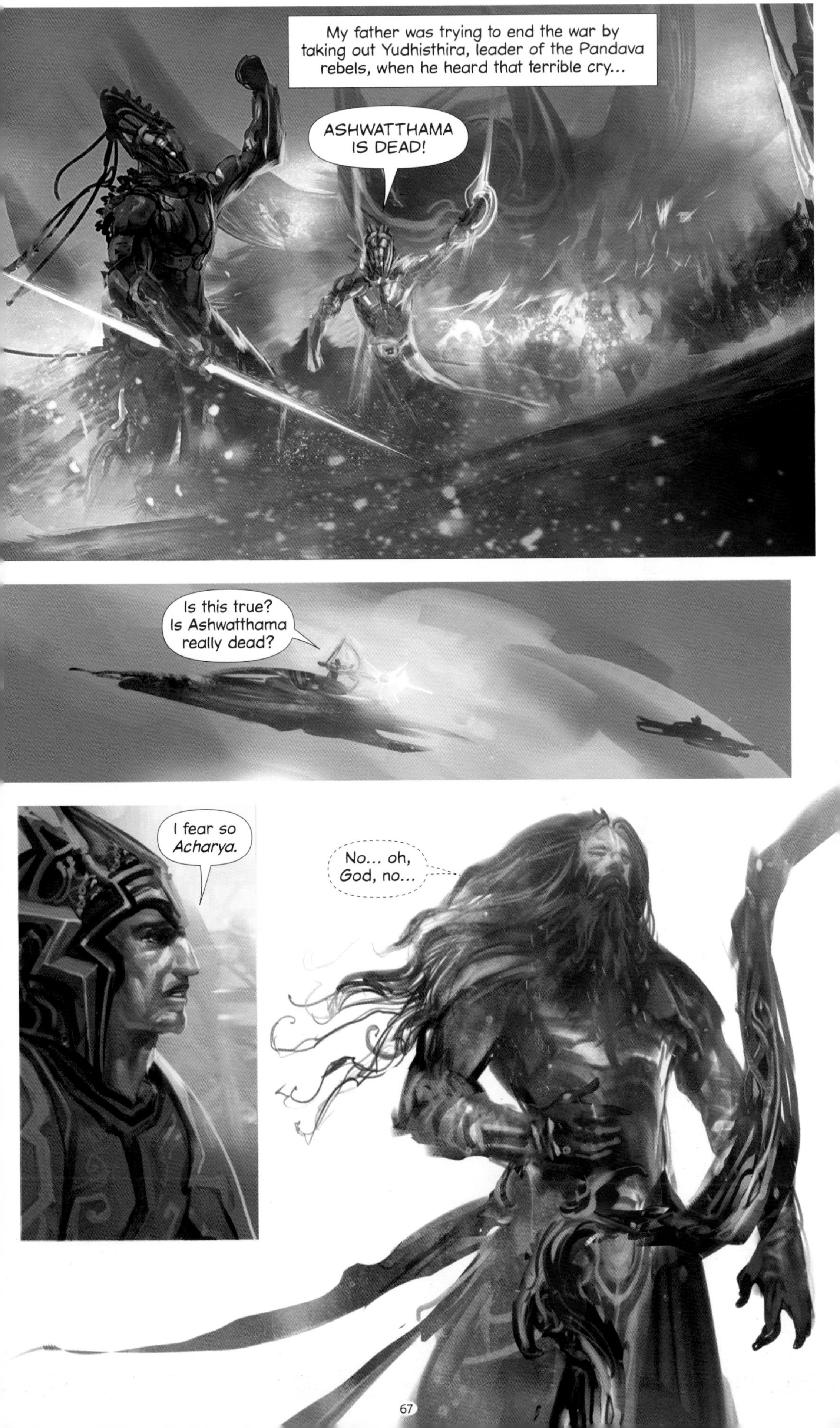

My father was trying to end the war by taking out Yudhisthira, leader of the Pandava rebels, when he heard that terrible cry...
ASHWATTHAMA IS DEAD!
Is this true? Is Ashwatthama really dead?
I fear so *Acharya.*
No... oh, God, no...

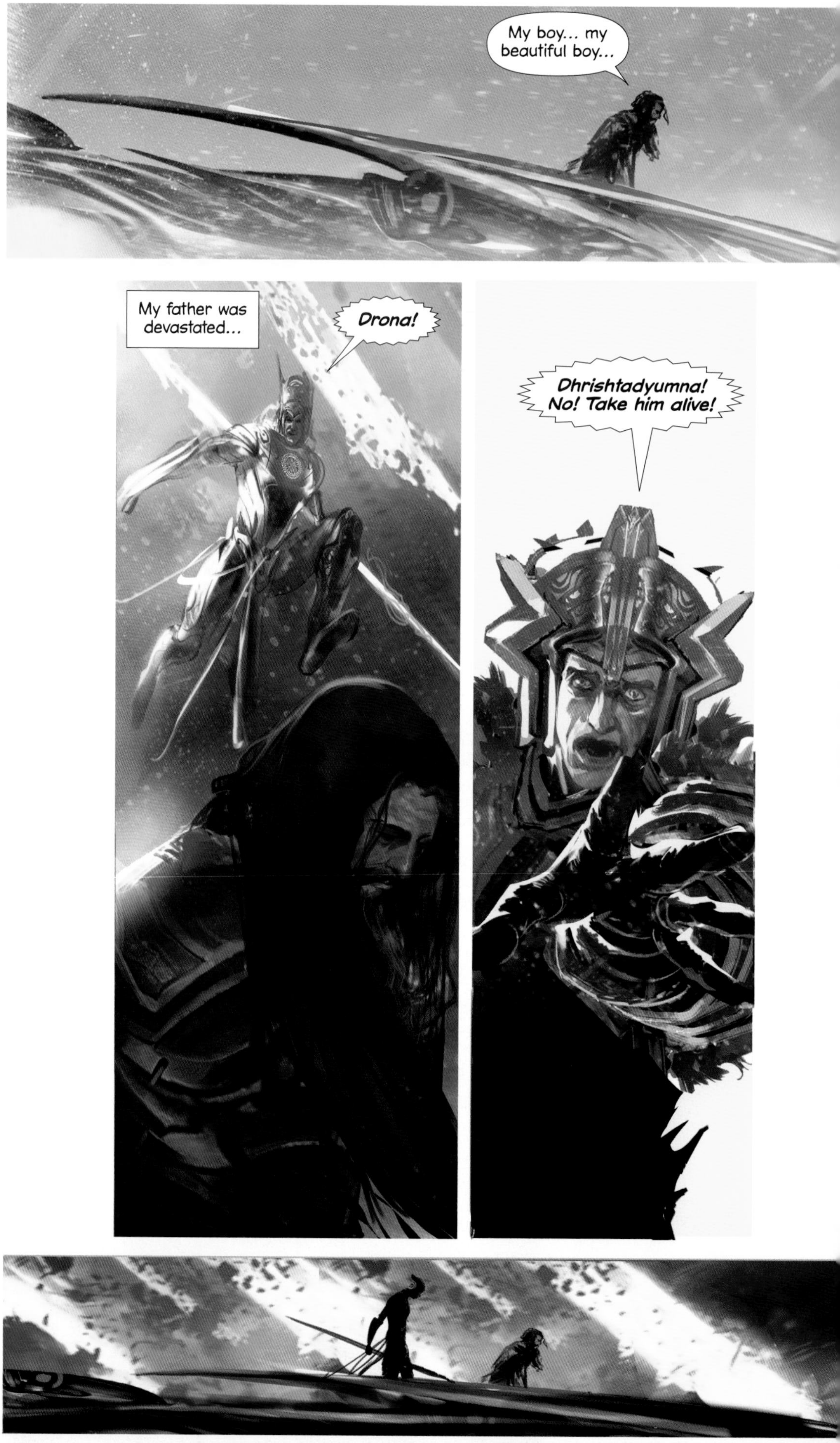
My boy... my beautiful boy...
My father was devastated...
Drona!
Dhrishtadyumna! No! Take him alive!

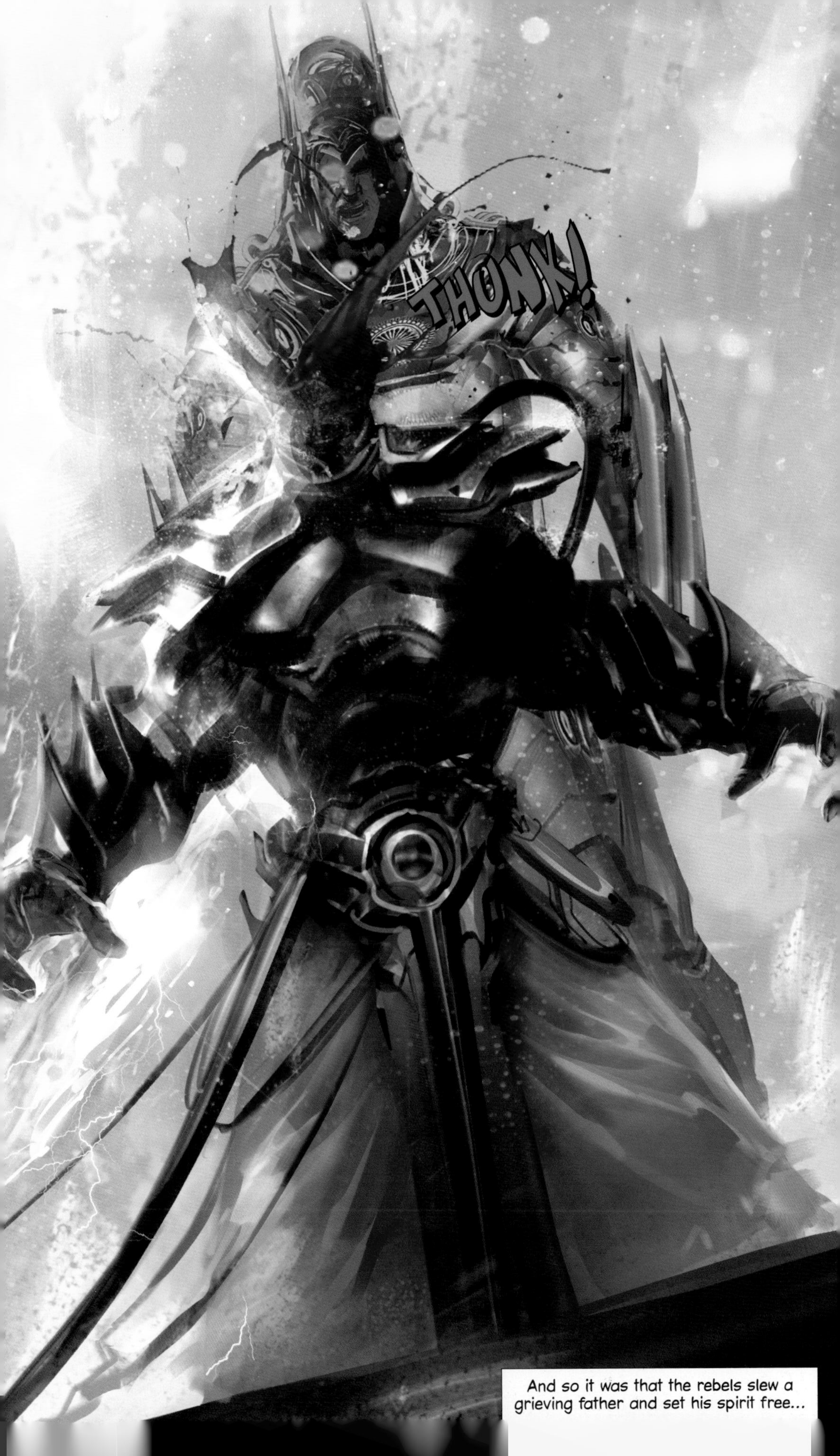
THONK!
And so it was that the rebels slew a grieving father and set his spirit free...

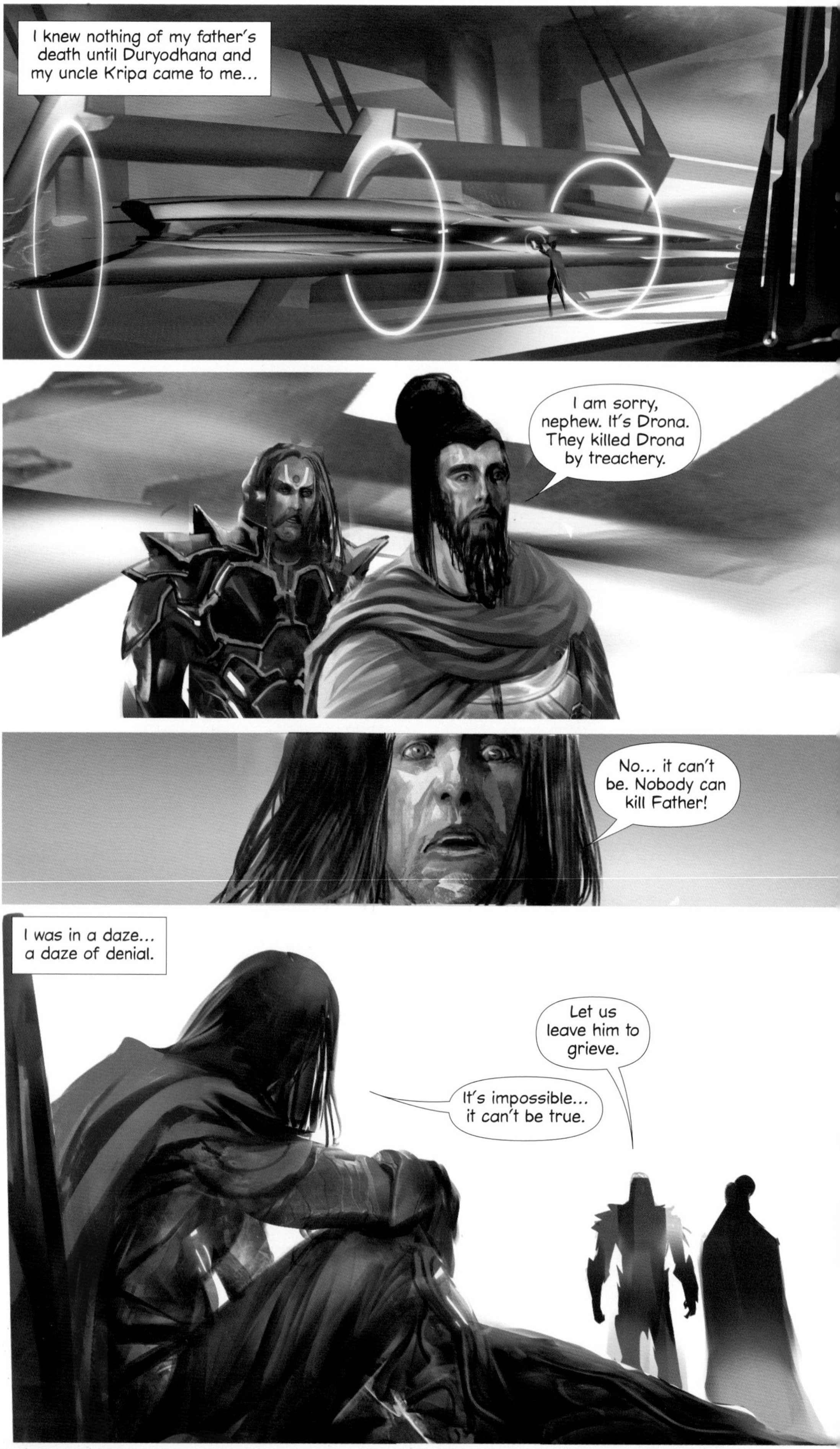
I knew nothing of my father's death until Duryodhana and my uncle Kripa came to me...
I am sorry, nephew. It's Drona. They killed Drona by treachery.
No... it can't be. Nobody can kill Father!
I was in a daze... a daze of denial.
Let us leave him to grieve.
It's impossible... it can't be true.

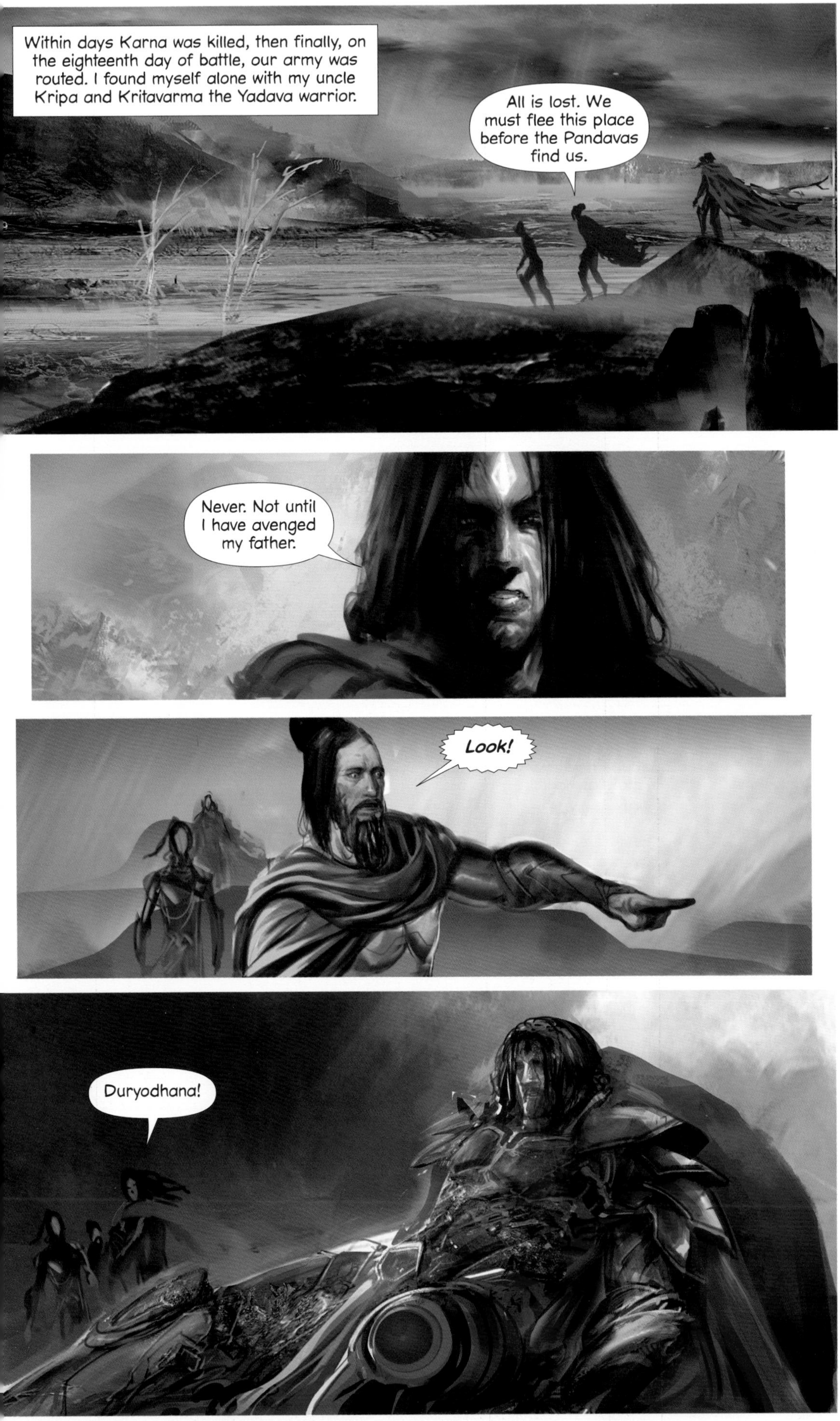
Within days Karna was killed, then finally, on the eighteenth day of battle, our army was routed. I found myself alone with my uncle Kripa and Kritavarma the Yadava warrior.
All is lost. We must flee this place before the Pandavas find us.
Never. Not until I have avenged my father.
Look!
Duryodhana!

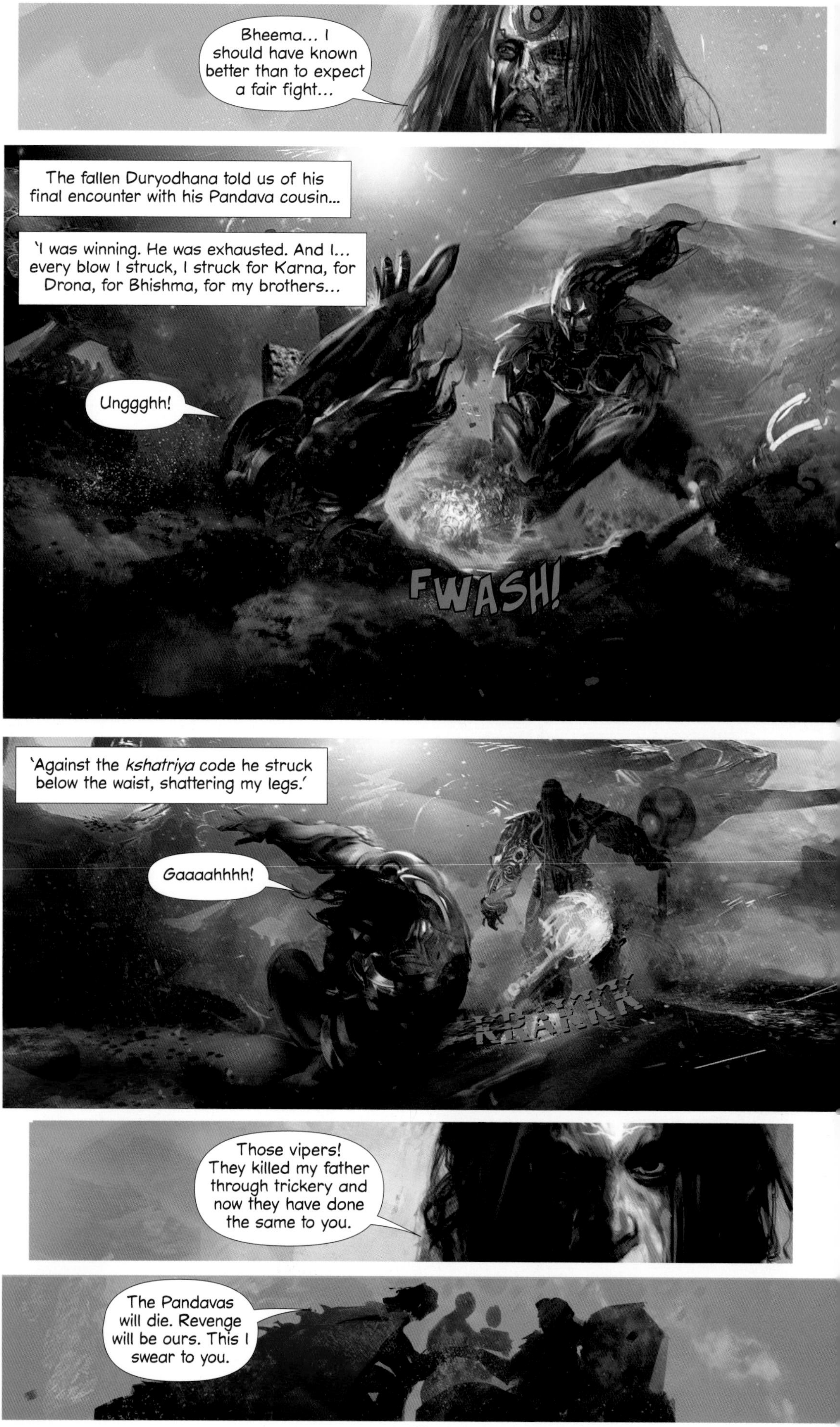
Bheema... I should have known better than to expect a fair fight...
The fallen Duryodhana told us of his final encounter with his Pandava cousin...
'I was winning. He was exhausted. And I... every blow I struck, I struck for Karna, for Drona, for Bhishma, for my brothers...
Ungggh!
FWASH!
'Against the *kshatriya* code he struck below the waist, shattering my legs.'
Gaaaahhhh!
Those vipers! They killed my father through trickery and now they have done the same to you.
The Pandavas will die. Revenge will be ours. This I swear to you.

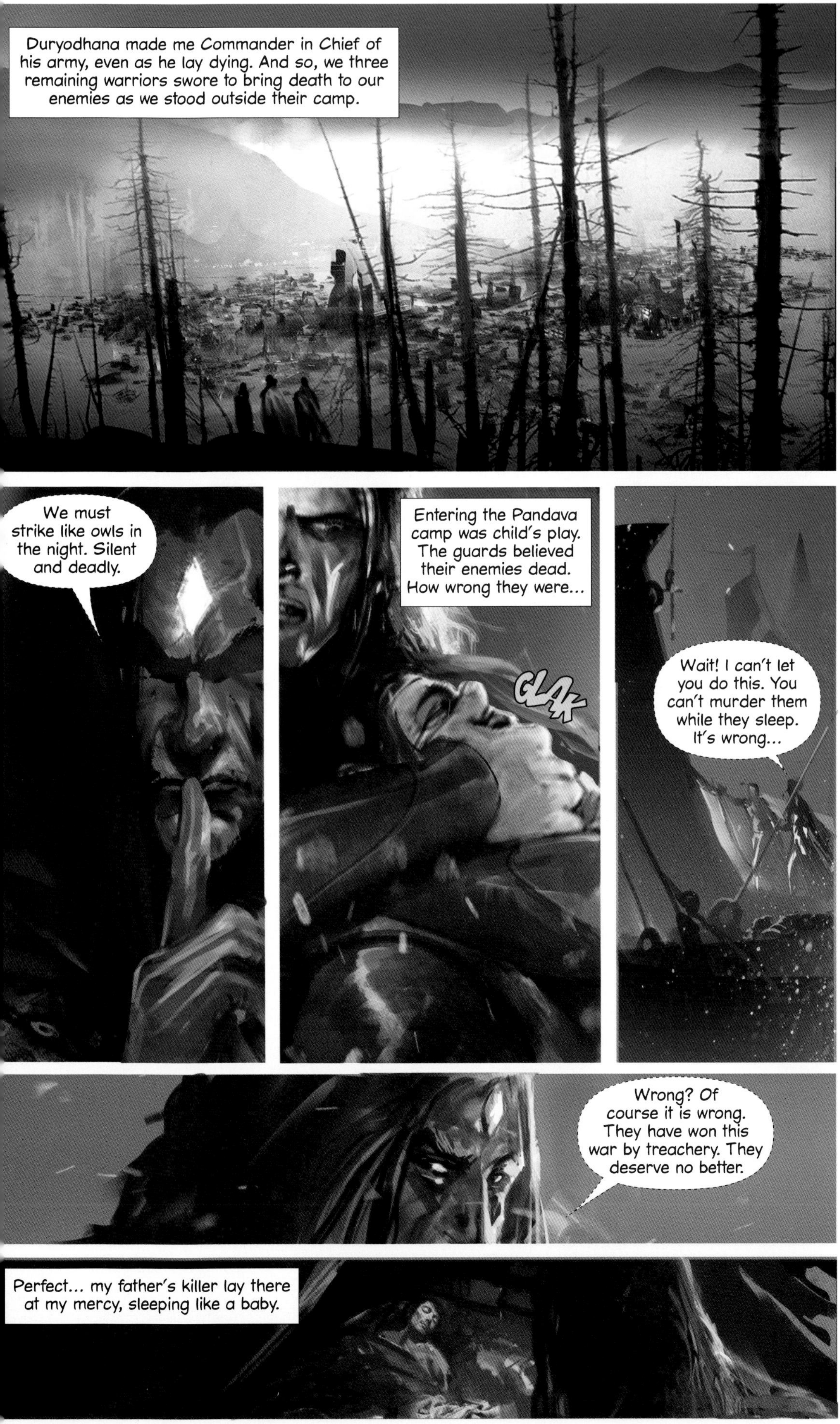
Duryodhana made me Commander in Chief of his army, even as he lay dying. And so, we three remaining warriors swore to bring death to our enemies as we stood outside their camp.
We must strike like owls in the night. Silent and deadly.
Entering the Pandava camp was child's play. The guards believed their enemies dead. How wrong they were...
GLAK
Wait! I can't let you do this. You can't murder them while they sleep. It's wrong...
Wrong? Of course it is wrong. They have won this war by treachery. They deserve no better.
Perfect... my father's killer lay there at my mercy, sleeping like a baby.

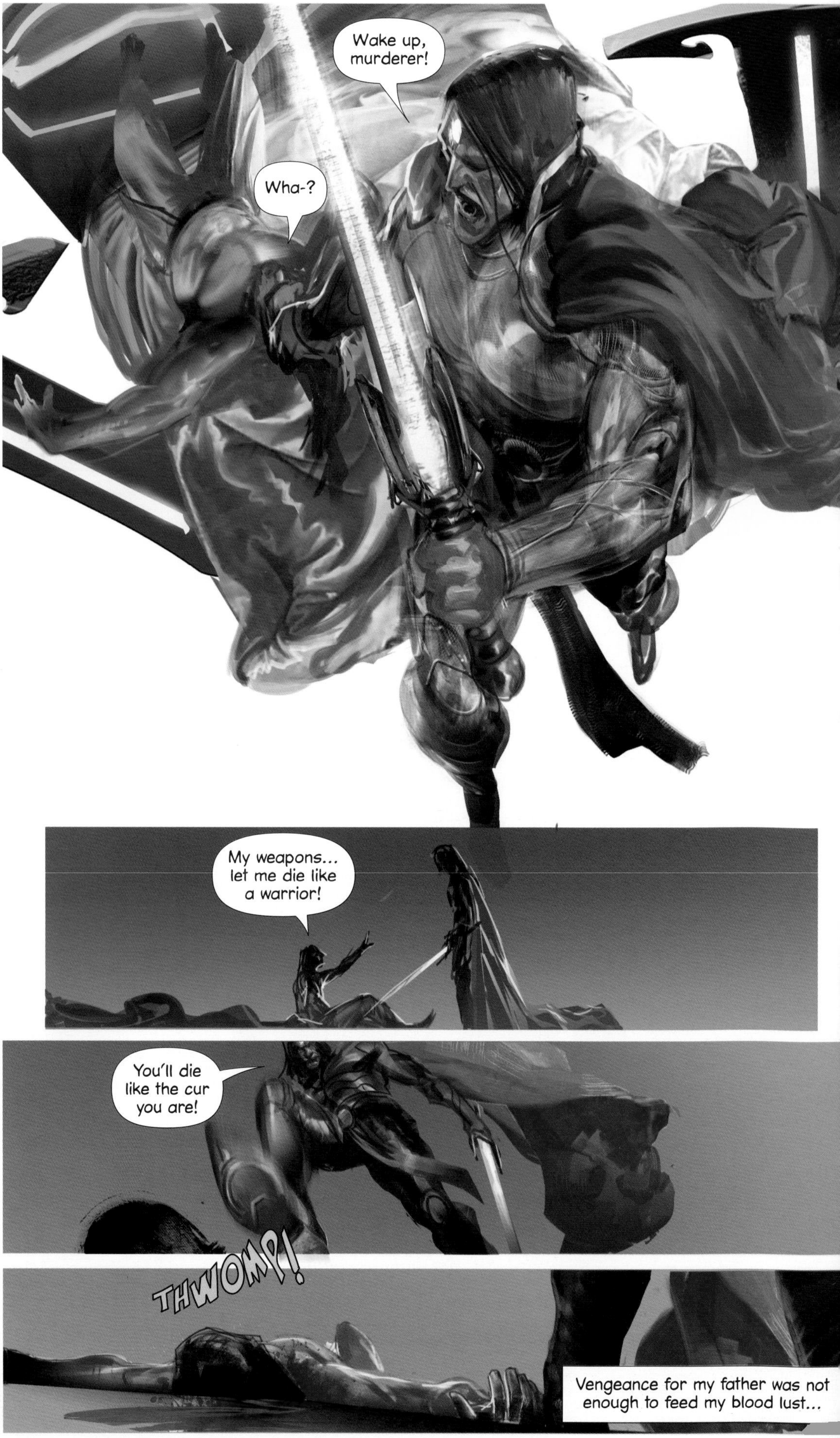
Wake up, murderer!
Wha-?
My weapons... let me die like a warrior!
You'll die like the cur you are!
THWOMP!
Vengeance for my father was not enough to feed my blood lust...

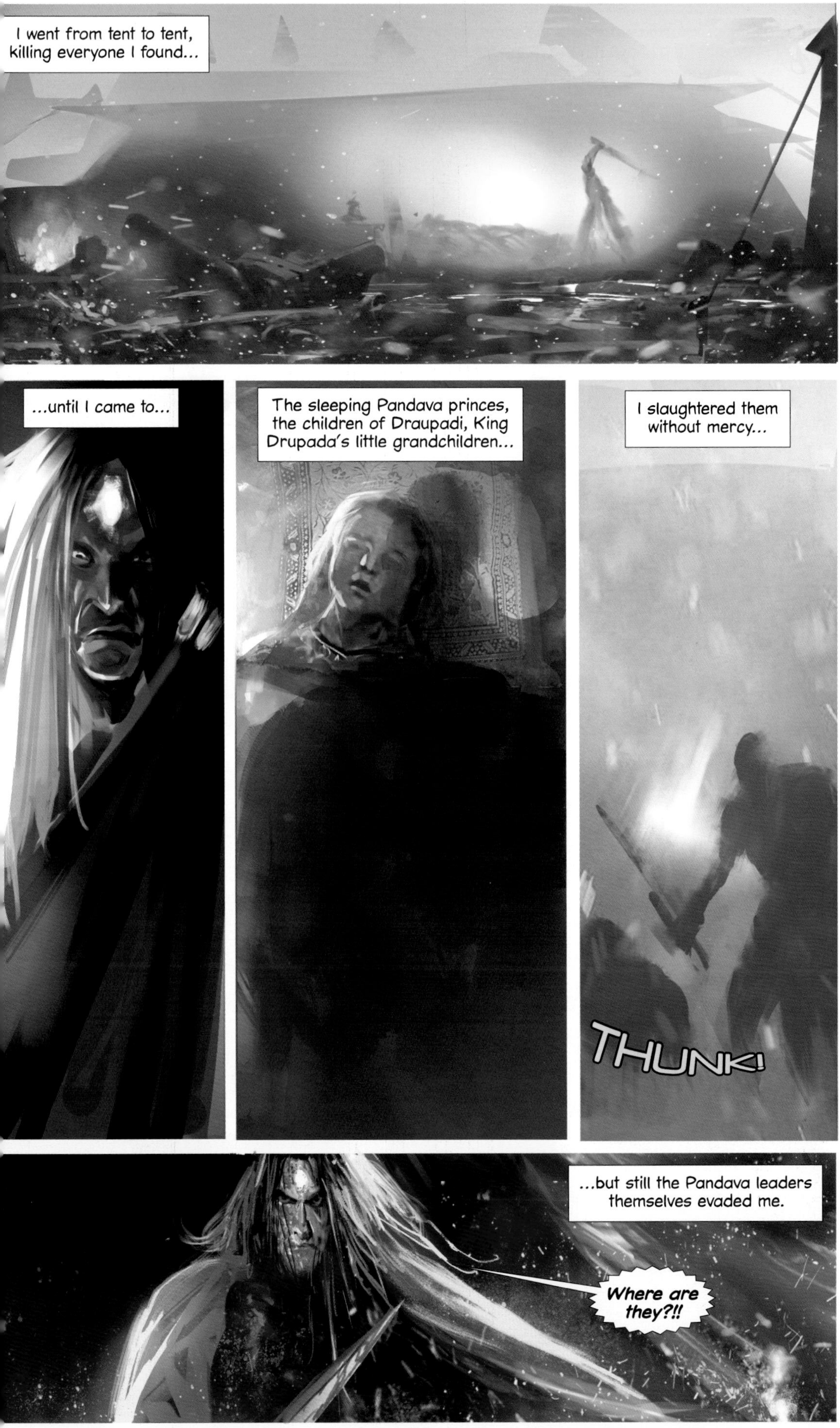
I went from tent to tent, killing everyone I found...
...until I came to...
The sleeping Pandava princes, the children of Draupadi, King Drupada's little grandchildren...
I slaughtered them without mercy...
THUNK!
...but still the Pandava leaders themselves evaded me.
Where are they?!!

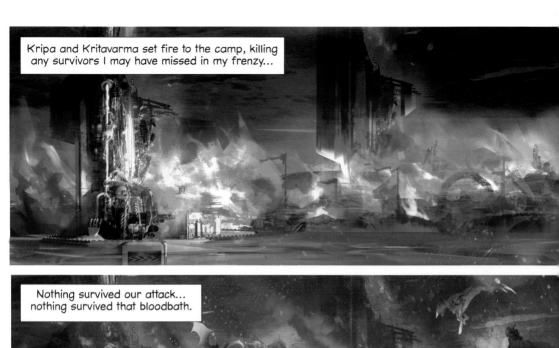

Kripa and Kritavarma set fire to the camp, killing any survivors I may have missed in my frenzy...

Nothing survived our attack... nothing survived that bloodbath.

What have we done?

We have done what no others could do. We have brought vengeance for all our dead.

We went our separate ways then, we three survivors of the *Great War*. They to seek sanctuary, I to await the final showdown...

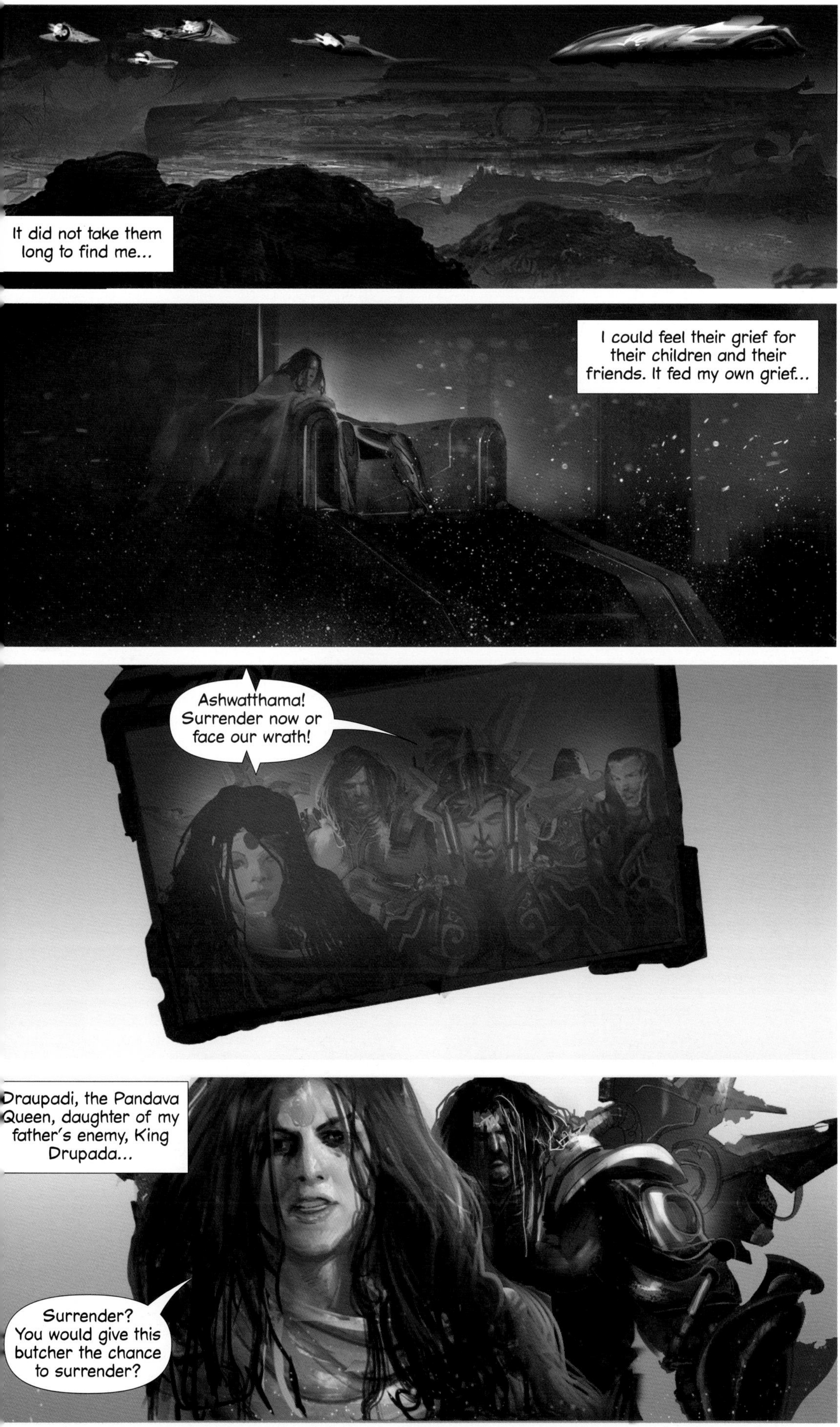
It did not take them long to find me...
I could feel their grief for their children and their friends. It fed my own grief...
Ashwatthama! Surrender now or face our wrath!
Draupadi, the Pandava Queen, daughter of my father's enemy, King Drupada...
Surrender? You would give this butcher the chance to surrender?

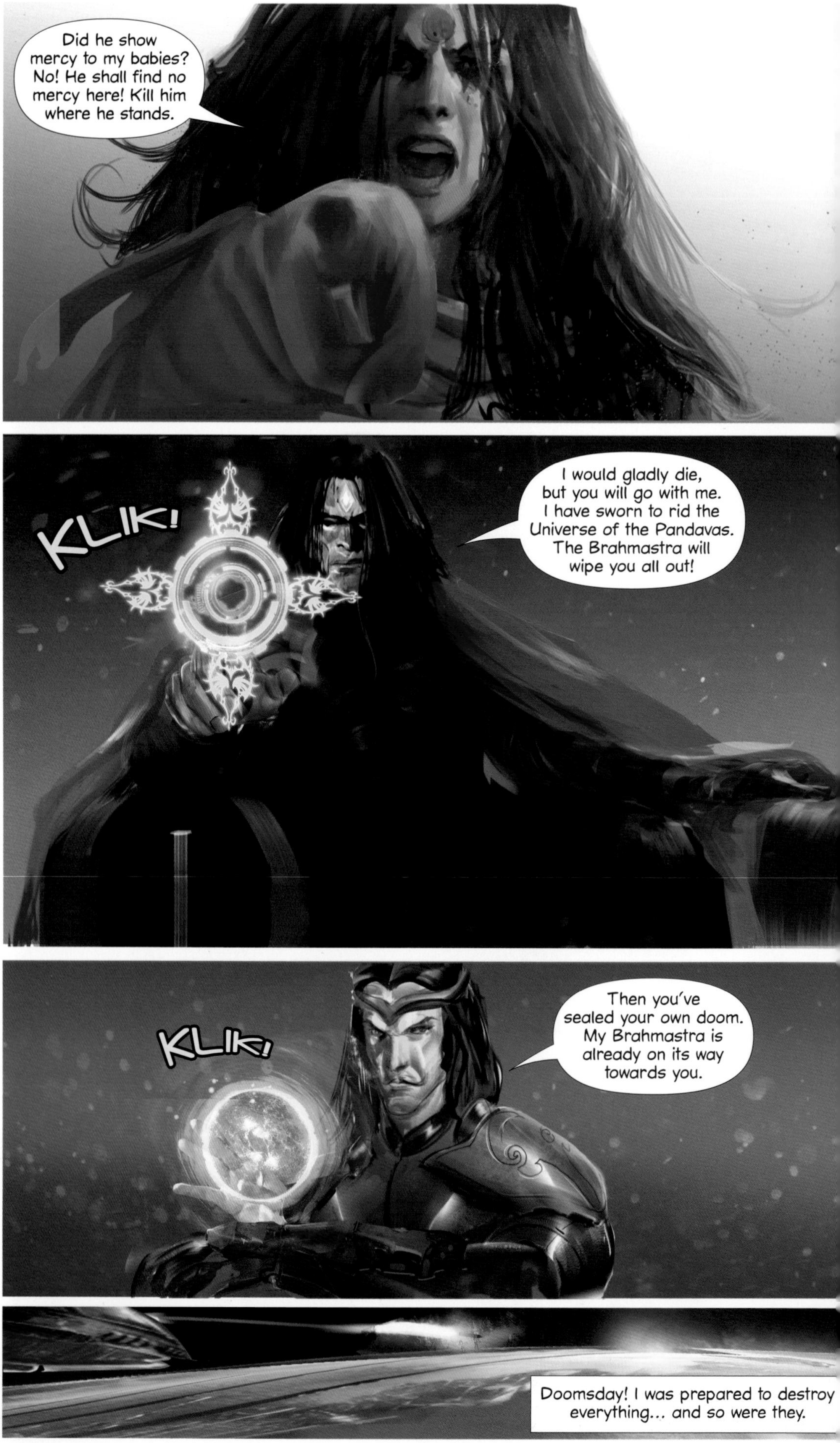
Did he show mercy to my babies? No! He shall find no mercy here! Kill him where he stands.
KLIK!
I would gladly die, but you will go with me. I have sworn to rid the Universe of the Pandavas. The Brahmastra will wipe you all out!
KLIK!
Then you've sealed your own doom. My Brahmastra is already on its way towards you.
Doomsday! I was prepared to destroy everything... and so were they.

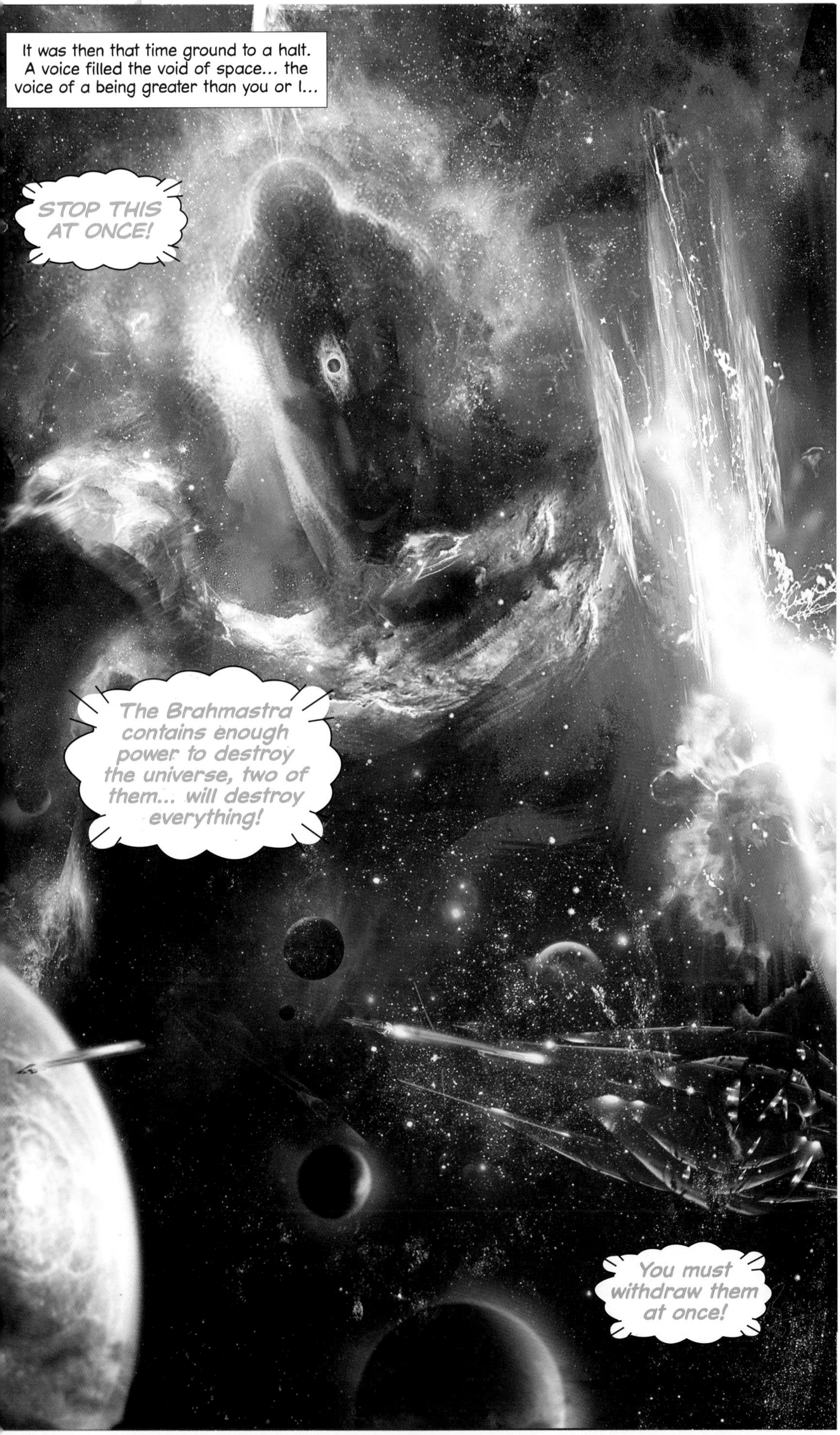
It was then that time ground to a halt. A voice filled the void of space... the voice of a being greater than you or I...
STOP THIS AT ONCE!
The Brahmastra contains enough power to destroy the universe, two of them... will destroy everything!
You must withdraw them at once!

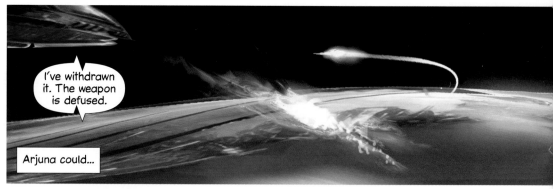

I've withdrawn it. The weapon is defused.

Arjuna could...

But I couldn't.

I can't withdraw it! I don't know how!

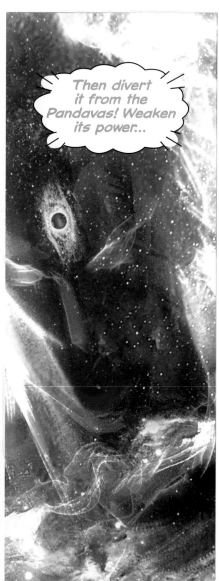

Then divert it from the Pandavas! Weaken its power...

I had unleashed the Brahmastra with the intention of wiping out the Pandavas. I could not withdraw it. The best I could do was divert it from them and still ensure the Pandava line would not continue...

I.... I... I can do this...

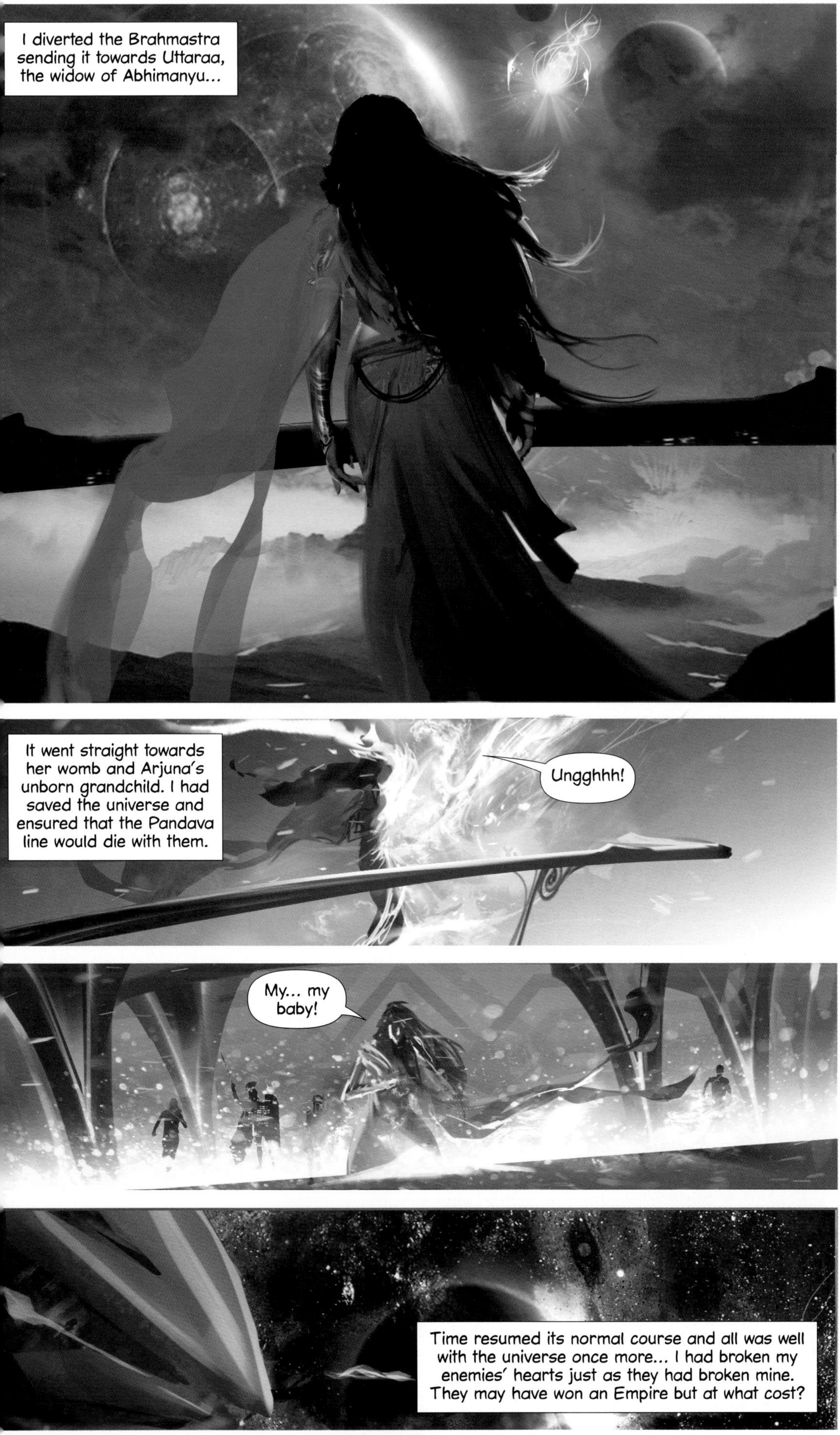
I diverted the Brahmastra sending it towards Uttaraa, the widow of Abhimanyu...
It went straight towards her womb and Arjuna's unborn grandchild. I had saved the universe and ensured that the Pandava line would die with them.
Ungghhh!
My... my baby!
Time resumed its normal course and all was well with the universe once more... I had broken my enemies' hearts just as they had broken mine. They may have won an Empire but at what cost?

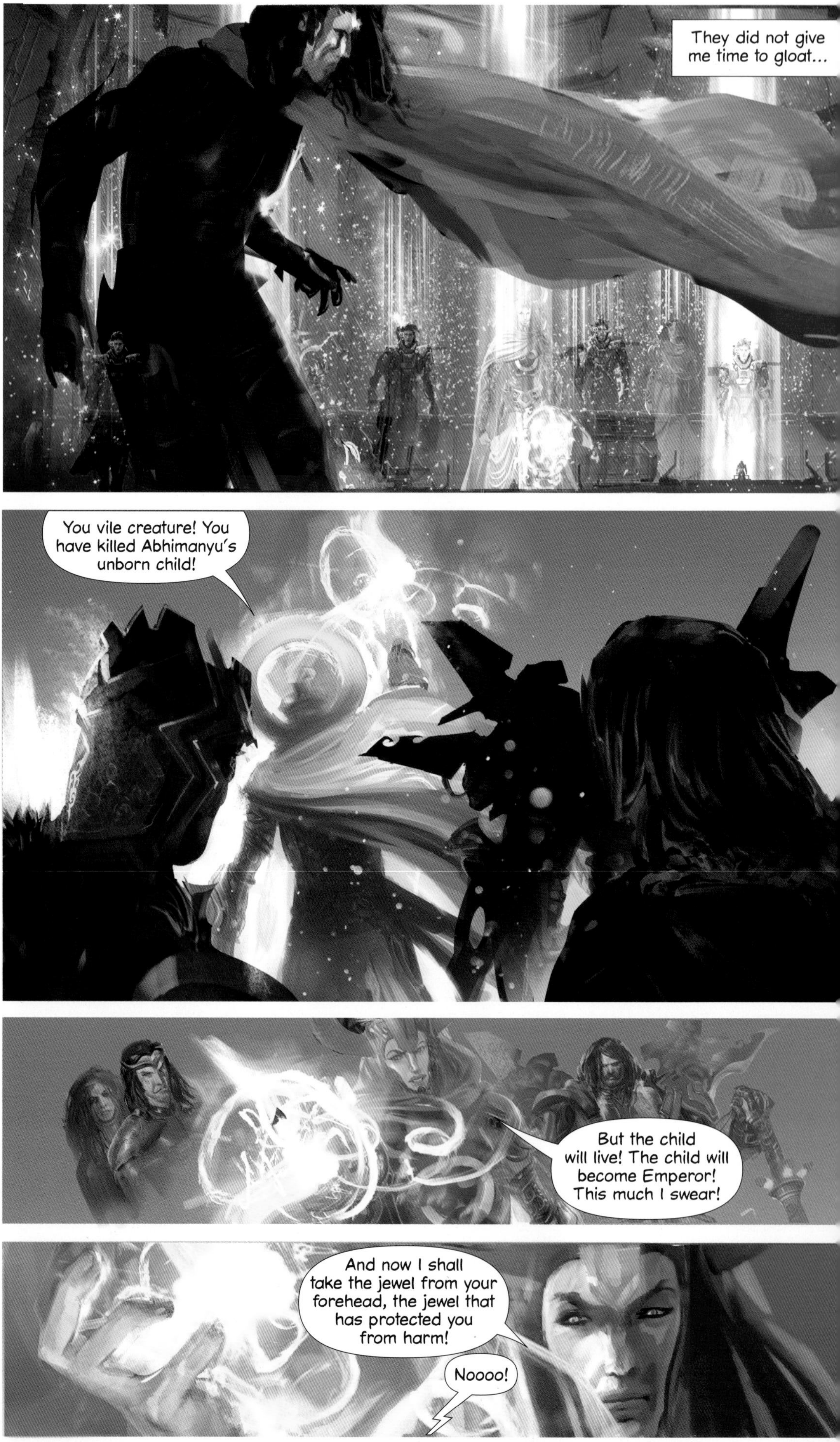
They did not give me time to gloat...
You vile creature! You have killed Abhimanyu's unborn child!
But the child will live! The child will become Emperor! This much I swear!
And now I shall take the jewel from your forehead, the jewel that has protected you from harm!
Noooo!

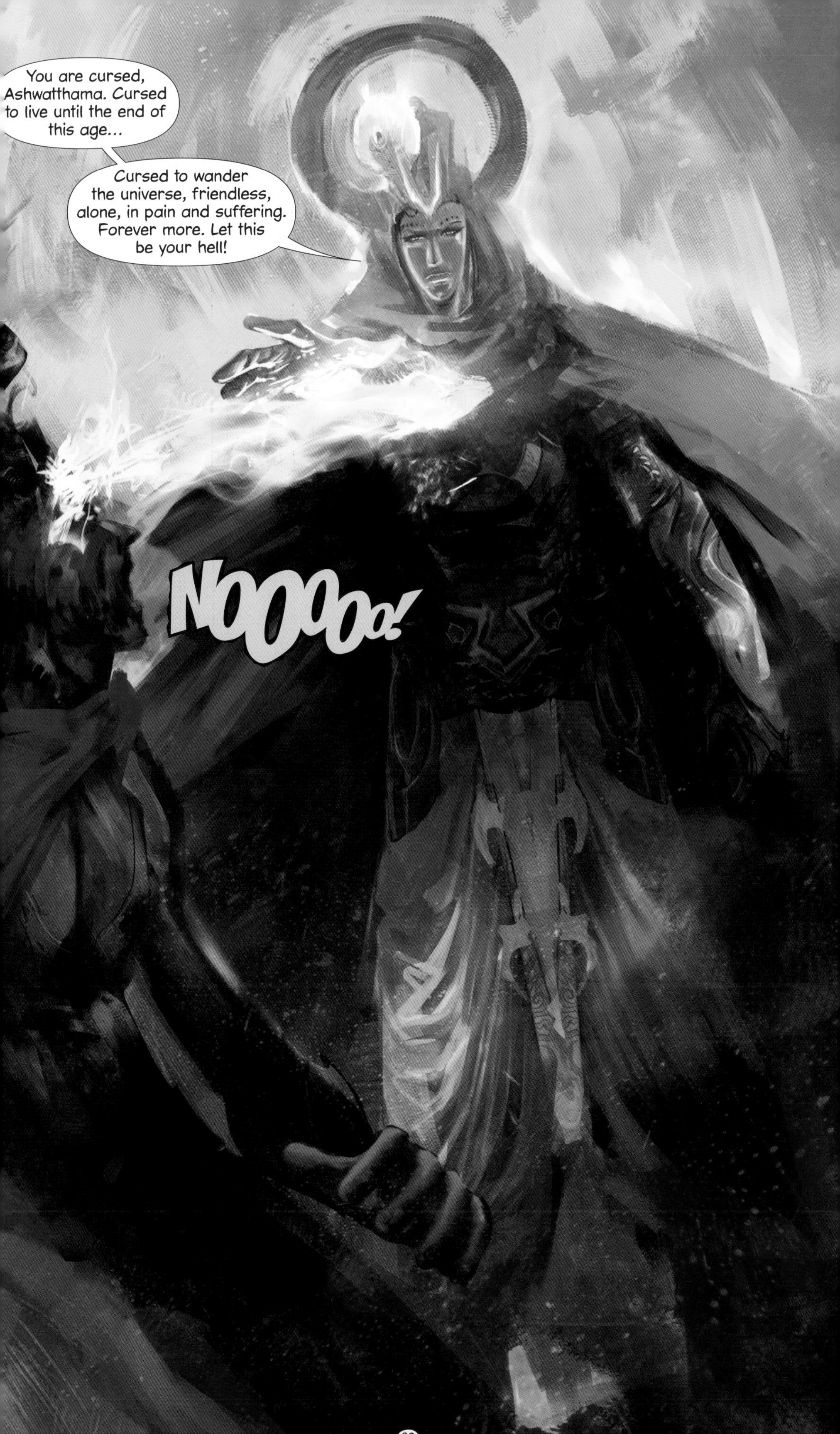
You are cursed, Ashwatthama. Cursed to live until the end of this age...
Cursed to wander the universe, friendless, alone, in pain and suffering. Forever more. Let this be your hell!
NOOOOO!

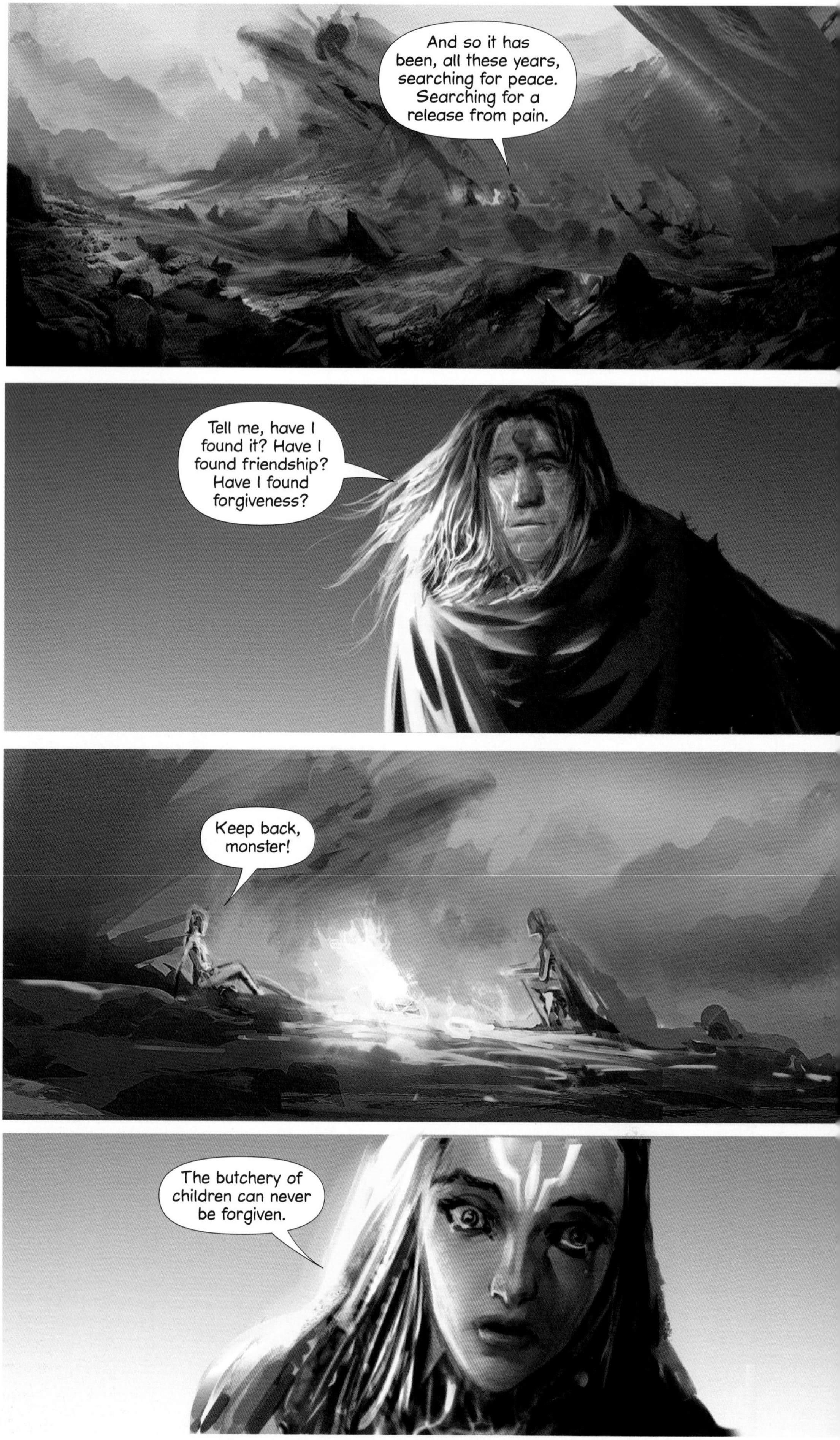
And so it has been, all these years, searching for peace. Searching for a release from pain.
Tell me, have I found it? Have I found friendship? Have I found forgiveness?
Keep back, monster!
The butchery of children can never be forgiven.

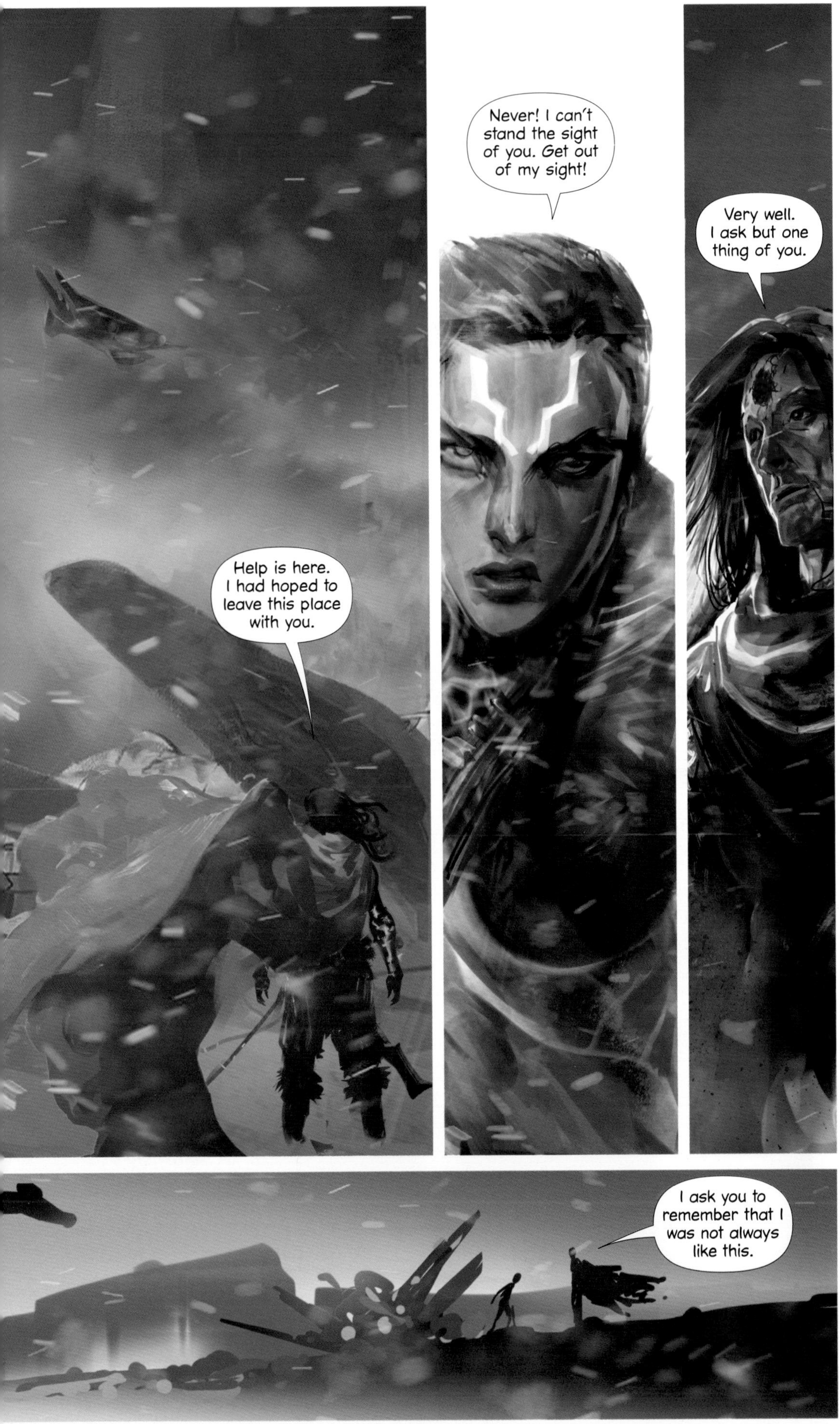
Help is here. I had hoped to leave this place with you.
Never! I can't stand the sight of you. Get out of my sight!
Very well. I ask but one thing of you.
I ask you to remember that I was not always like this.

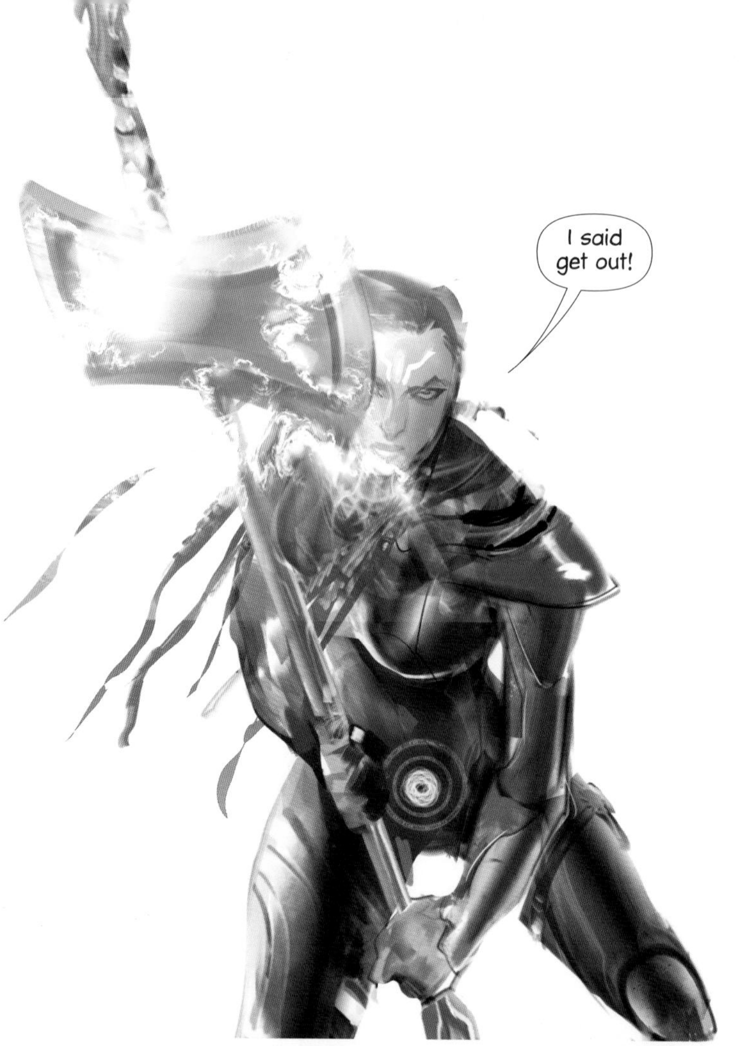
I said get out!

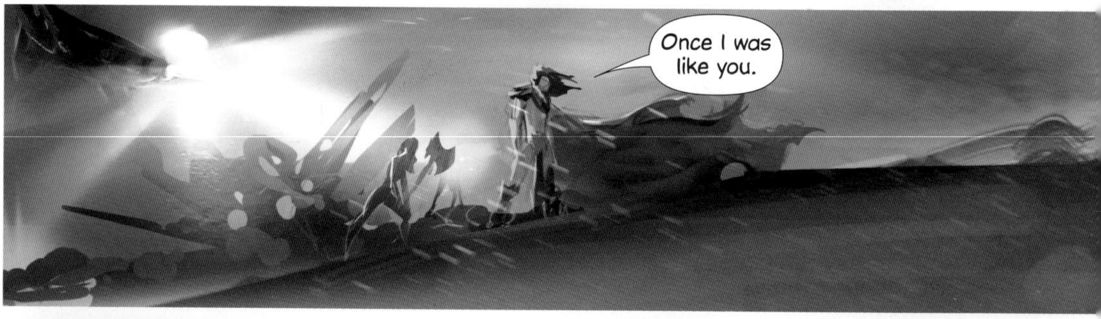
Once I was like you.

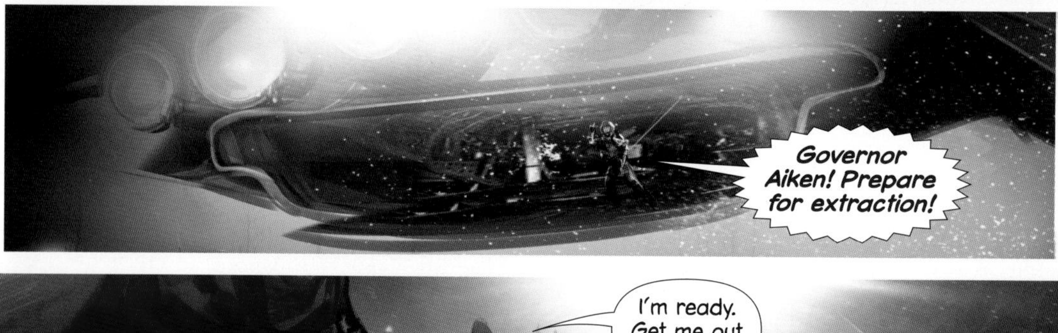
Governor Aiken! Prepare for extraction!

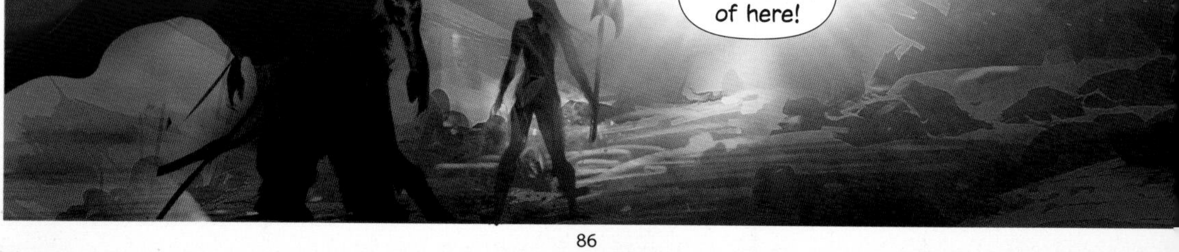
I'm ready. Get me out of here!

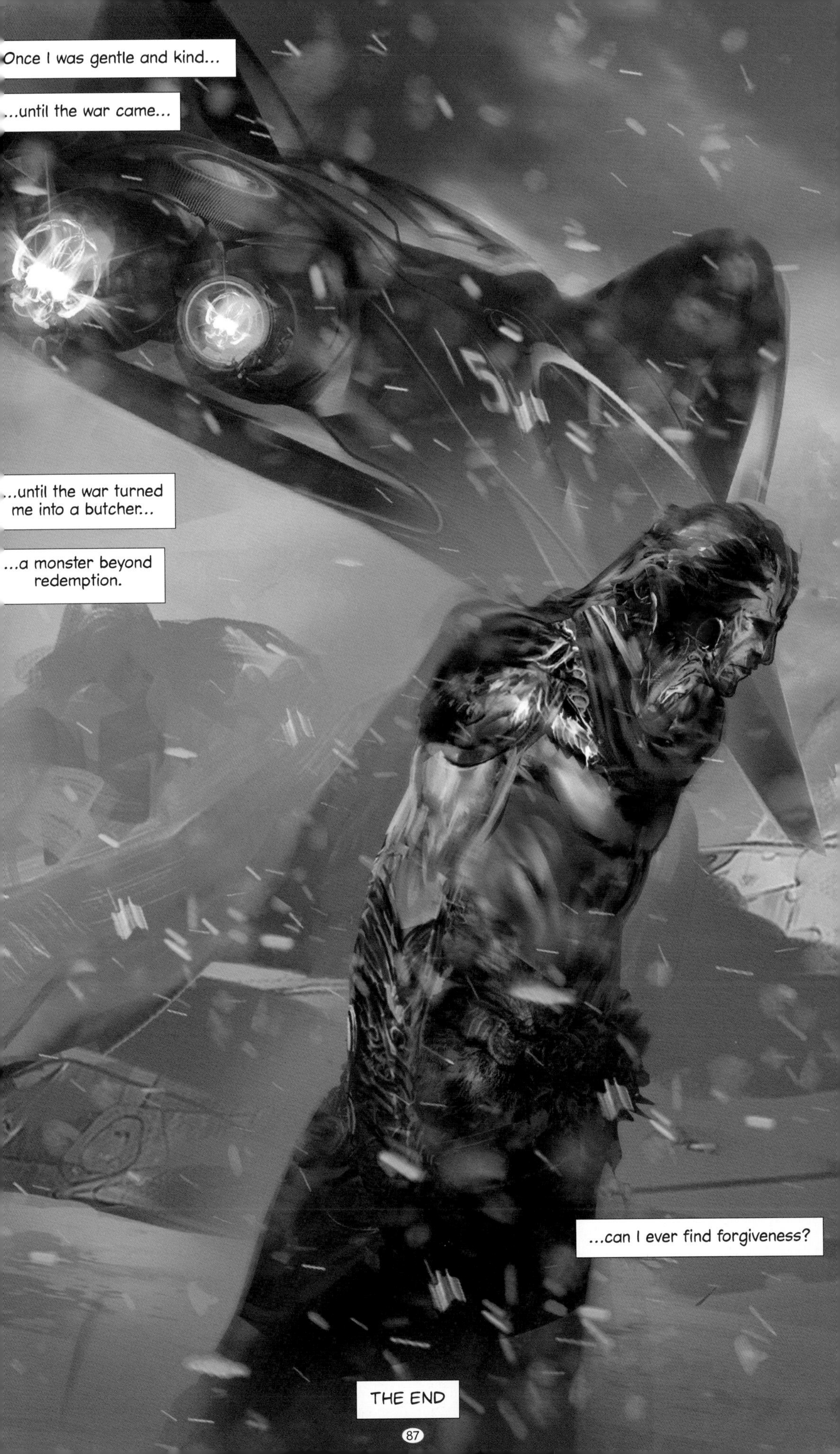
Once I was gentle and kind...
...until the war came...
...until the war turned me into a butcher...
...a monster beyond redemption.
...can I ever find forgiveness?
THE END

THE KAURAVA EMPIRE

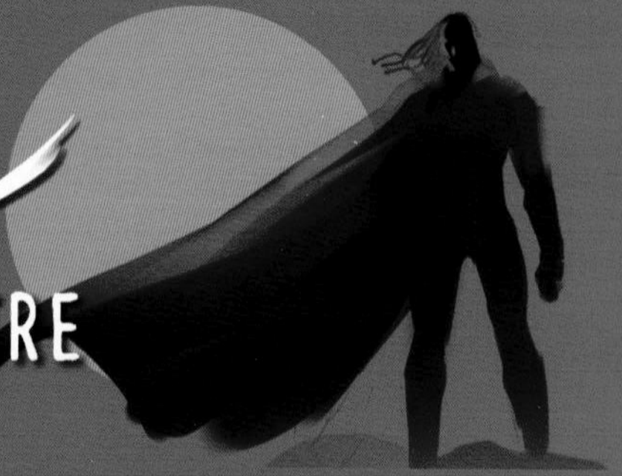

RE-IMAGINING THE GREATEST STORIES EVER TOLD

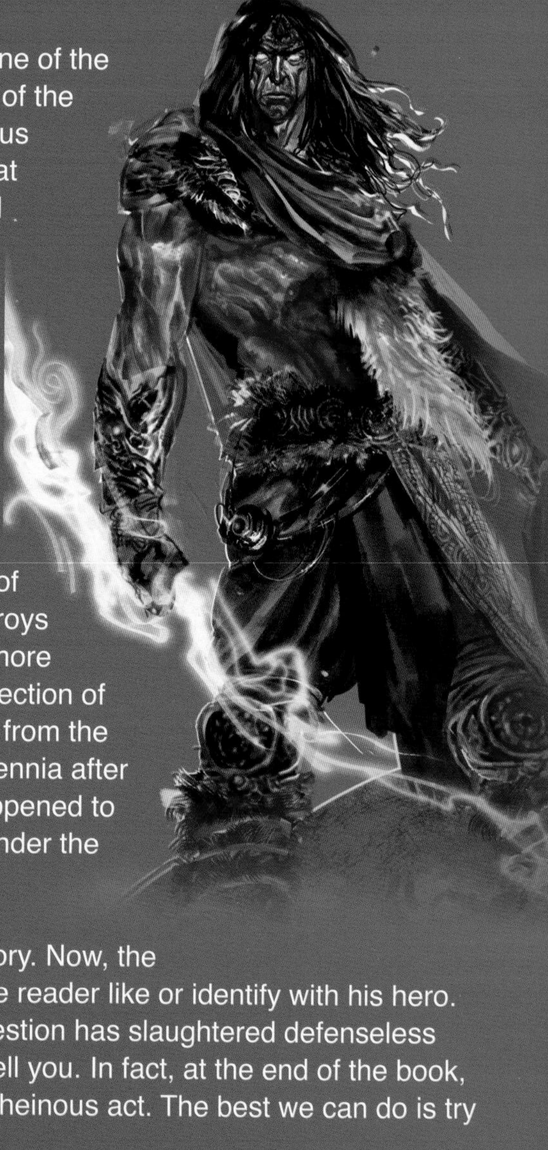

As always when working on this series, one of the most difficult problems is choosing which of the mammoth cast of the Mahabharata to focus on. I have so many favorite characters that it's almost impossible to choose. I wanted to pick one of the characters who often gets over-shadowed by the main stars of this epic. I wanted someone we could sympathize with. I wanted to make the reader love these characters just as much as I do. The choice in the end was simple, Ashwatthama.

Ashwatthama is a great character and the best thing about him is that he is one of the few survivors of the civil war that destroys the Kaurava Empire. Not only that, he is more or less immortal. In fact, for the opening section of this book, we don't even see anyone else from the Mahabharata. We begin centuries, or millennia after the war on Kurukshetra. We see what happened to him after he was cursed by Krishna to wander the universe for eternity.

Then we go back in time as he tells his story. Now, the important task for any writer is to make the reader like or identify with his hero. How can you do that when the hero in question has slaughtered defenseless children in their sleep? It's difficult, I can tell you. In fact, at the end of the book, Ashwatthama remains unforgiven for that heinous act. The best we can do is try to understand him.

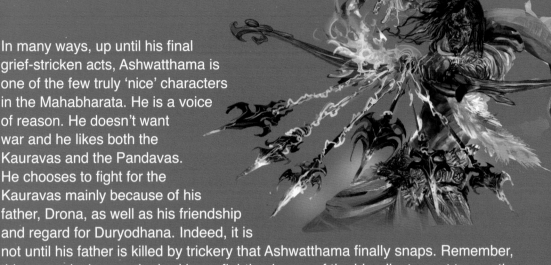

In many ways, up until his final grief-stricken acts, Ashwatthama is one of the few truly 'nice' characters in the Mahabharata. He is a voice of reason. He doesn't want war and he likes both the Kauravas and the Pandavas. He chooses to fight for the Kauravas mainly because of his father, Drona, as well as his friendship and regard for Duryodhana. Indeed, it is not until his father is killed by trickery that Ashwatthama finally snaps. Remember, this peace loving warrior had been fighting in one of the bloodiest, most traumatic wars the universe has ever known. Shell-shock? Battle Fatigue? Post Traumatic Stress? You can bet your life poor Ashwatthama was suffering from all those things.

When I finished work on the script for this I couldn't wait to see Sachin's work, to see how he would bring Ashwatthama to life. Whereas volume 1 dealt only with events during the battle of Kurukshetra, this story explores the childhood of our main protagonists right up until the end. The scope and the canvas is bigger and grander and Sachin has really stepped up to the plate on this one and delivered in spades. I love it. I love every page. In fact, I've got several of the pages from this book hanging on my wall.

I just hope you, the reader, will love this volume of *The Kaurava Empire*, as much as we do. Now, it's time for me to crack on with the script for the next volume. Be seeing you!

JASON QUINN
NEW DELHI 2014

EPIC TALES REVISITED, RETOLD

A GRAPHIC NOVEL
THE KAURAVA EMPIRE
VOL. 1
ABHIMANYU AND THE CONQUEST OF THE CHAKRAVYUHA
Sachin Nagar

Come with us to rediscover the Mahabharata as you have never seen before. The Mahabharata is unquestionably India's greatest epic. It is also timeless. We are proud to present to you tales from the Mahabharata, but with a twist. What if those tales of bravery, heroism, anguish and tragedy took place in a distant future, spanning not lands and kingdoms, but galaxies? What if the weapons used were not from the Iron Age, but from the Space Age? What if the soldiers rode not horses and chariots, but spaceships?

Also Available

THE KAURAVA EMPIRE

Vol.1

Abhimanyu and the Conquest of the Chakravyuha

In war there are no rules...

Civil war strikes at the heart of the greatest empire the universe has ever known; a civil war that tears families and nations apart, pitting cousin against cousin and friend against friend. Two teenage warriors find themselves on opposite sides of the conflict. For the Pandavas, we have Abhimanyu, son of the great Arjuna, and for the Kauravas we have Durmashana, son of Dusasana. Abhimanyu already has a fearsome reputation as a mighty warrior, and Durmashana is anxious to build a reputation of his own by slaying the Pandava Prince. When the Kauravas unleash the unstoppable Chakravyuha on their enemies, only Abhimanyu can save his family from total annihilation, but to do this he will have to make the ultimate sacrifice.

Are you sure about this? It smells like a trap... or suicide.
Don't worry. It's not suicide.

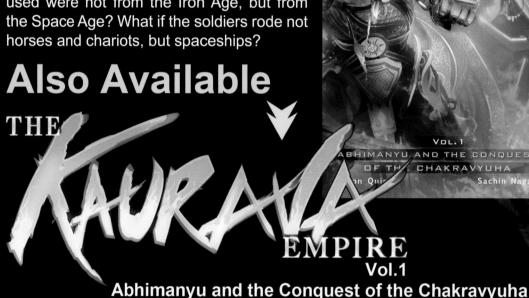

COMING SOON

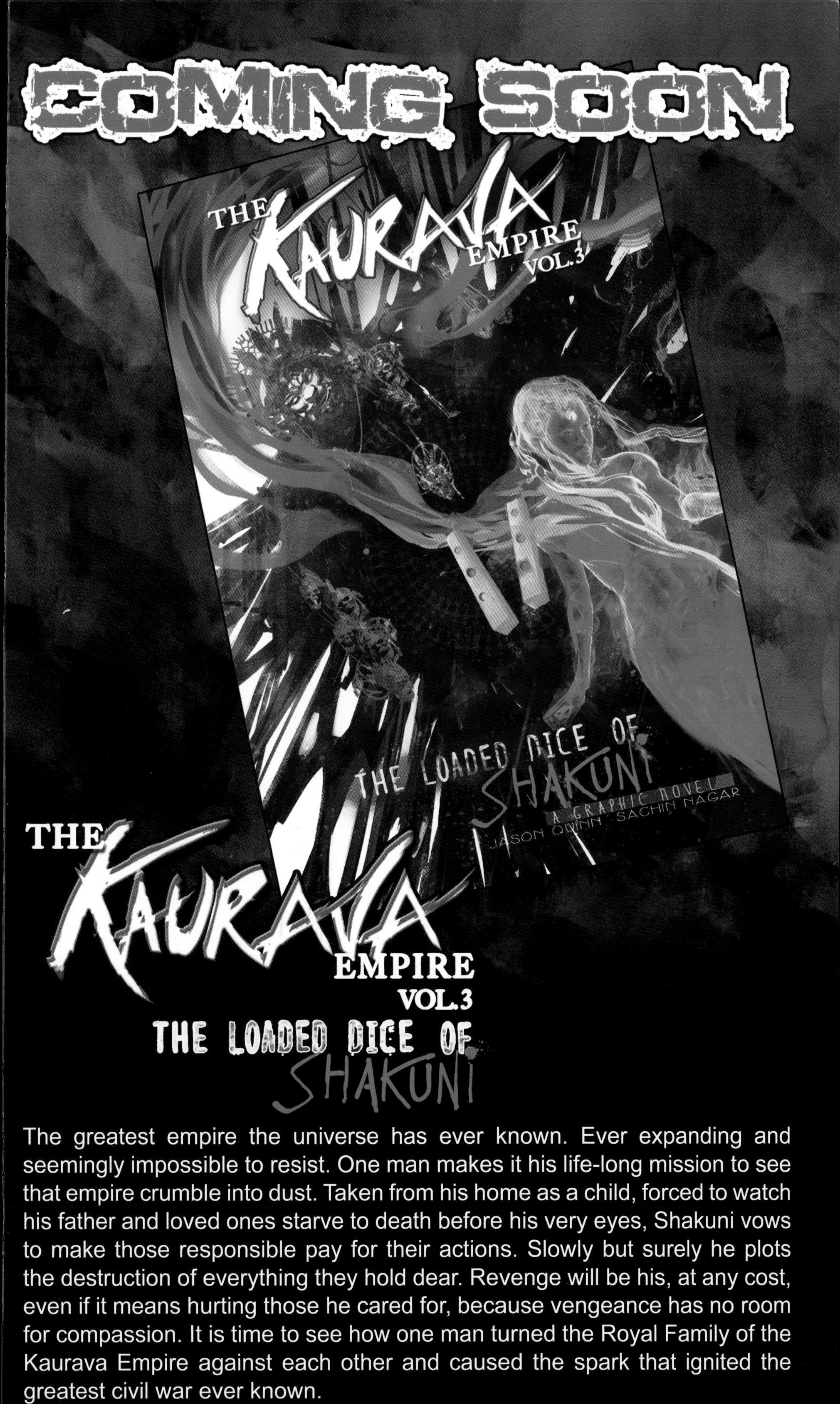

THE KAURAVA EMPIRE VOL.3
THE LOADED DICE OF SHAKUNI
A GRAPHIC NOVEL
JASON QUINN SACHIN NAGAR

THE KAURAVA EMPIRE VOL.3

THE LOADED DICE OF SHAKUNI

The greatest empire the universe has ever known. Ever expanding and seemingly impossible to resist. One man makes it his life-long mission to see that empire crumble into dust. Taken from his home as a child, forced to watch his father and loved ones starve to death before his very eyes, Shakuni vows to make those responsible pay for their actions. Slowly but surely he plots the destruction of everything they hold dear. Revenge will be his, at any cost, even if it means hurting those he cared for, because vengeance has no room for compassion. It is time to see how one man turned the Royal Family of the Kaurava Empire against each other and caused the spark that ignited the greatest civil war ever known.